FUR BEARERS

JOHN FORT

CALUMET EDITIONS

Chanhassen, Minnesota

SECOND EDITION DECEMBER 2022

This is a work of fiction. Names, characters, places and incidents either are the product of the author's imagination or are used fictitiously.

ISBN – 978-1-959770-68-8

10 9 8 7 6 5 4 3 2

Cover art and book design by Gary Lindberg

DEDICATION

To my wife ViAnn for her patience and support, and to our twelve
grandchildren who have always enjoyed a good story.

About the Author

John L. Fort was born in Ironton, Minnesota. From an early age, he knew that he wanted to be a Biology teacher. He attended St. Cloud University and majored in Biology and History. He received a Master's Degree in Biology from the University of Wisconsin.

John taught Biology, Anatomy & Physiology, Environmental Problems and A.P. Biology during his thirty-five years of teaching. He started teaching at Remer, Minnesota, in 1960, and later moved to Pine River, Cottage Grove and Woodbury Minnesota. John has always had a vivid imagination and began to write fiction several years before retiring.

Acknowledgements

During the journey to complete my novel, I have learned one thing—books are not written by individuals. Many people contributed to the writing and improving of my story.

My friends Nancy Blair, daughter-in-law Bonnie Fort and Jerry Walker did some of the early editing that helped focus my writing and remove many of the spelling and grammatical errors. Cameron Lepisto's criticism and words of wisdom helped improve my novel greatly.

Before publication of this edition of *Fur Bearers,* my new publisher and editor, Gary Lindberg, of Calumet Editions, contributed a great deal to the overall quality of my story. He showed a great deal of patience through his many editorial changes on the way to a finished product. He is a great teacher and helped me to learn much about the art of writing.

Above all—I must never forget the kernel of truth that is at the heart of any good novel—the art of telling a good story.

FUR BEARERS

CHAPTER 1
HOSPITALIZED

Death was in the air.

    Tear-shaped raindrops slammed down on the black pavement, shattering into miniature droplets. The gusting wind caught the micro-droplets and drove them horizontally. The unpredictable winds died, and the droplets fell on the street, fused into torrents of water swirling along the gutters. They pooled at the end of the block and disappeared down the storm drain.

Across the street, neon lights from Old Country Buffet, Applebee's, Barnes & Noble, a BP gas station, and MGM Liquors, reflected from the pavement in a kaleidoscope of colors. Angry, dark clouds rolled overhead, pushed westward by gusting winds.

Red lights flashed down Valley Creek Road, accompanied by the shrill sound of a siren. An approaching emergency vehicle sent a row of cars to the curb. It threw red lights out as if protesting the cold, wet evening. Two cars shot through the intersection as the stop light turned red. The ambulance swerved around the second car and continued north on Valley Creek Road toward Woodwinds Hospital. In the back of the ambulance, two paramedics worked to stop the flow of blood from two bullet holes in the chest of a brown-haired teenager. Five minutes later, the vehicle swerved down a ramp lined with bright lights. At the bottom was the emergency entrance to the hospital. The ambulance turned away from the dock, stopped, and then backed within eight feet of the waist-high ramp.. The driver jumped out, pushed his glasses up, and hurried to the back of the ambulance. He jerked open the rear doors while shielding his eyes from the pelting rain.

An overweight police officer stepped out, pulling his cap down over his eyes. He strolled to the back corner of the ambulance and frowned. "Is he still alive?" the officer asked.

"Barely," came the curt reply.

The paramedics pulled the gurney out of the ambulance and moved it toward the glass entrance doors.

The chubby police officer followed the paramedics into the ER. A doctor in a white lab coat, accompanied by a nurse and two orderlies, jogged down the hall toward them, taking control.

The doctor leaned over the unconscious patient and forced his eyelids open. He flashed a pen light across the eyes. "What happened here, fellas?"

One of the paramedics consulted a clipboard. "The patient is Butch Guhl. He tried to hold up a liquor store in Woodbury and the clerk put two bullets into him. We tried to stabilize him, without much success. Shows signs of internal bleeding."

The other paramedic said, "He's going downhill fast."

The doctor gave orders to his nurse. "Get a saline IV running. Type him for blood and get two units into him fast."

Turning to look at the paramedics, the doctor said, "What was his last blood pressure?"

The sandy-haired paramedic skipped a step to keep up and said, "89 over 54."

"Get me x-rays of the chest and abdominal area. Let's put him in…" The doctor looked at the nurse with a puzzled expression.

"OP 2 is open," the nurse finished.

"Okay, and prep him for surgery—fast."

"Yes, doctor," the nurse, said.

The doctor lifted the white, blood-spattered sheet covering Butch's chest. He noted the bright red circle of blood on the bandages. When he lifted the bandage, he saw red, frothy bubbles welling from the chest wound. Shaking his head he said, "His lung is penetrated. Jesus, we might lose this one. Let's move!"

The cop, panting from keeping up with the fast-moving gurney, shook his head and said, to nobody in particular, "It'll save the county a lot of money if the bastard dies." He raised his voice at the doctor and said, "His partner shot the liquor store clerk during the holdup. He'll go to prison if he lives."

CHAPTER 2
BLOOD CONVERSION

A dark-haired man with furrows around his eyes sat on an orange chair in the ER waiting room. Without thinking, he picked at a torn piece of vinyl on the seat. Rod Guhl thought of all the trouble his son had caused him over the past several years. With a shake of his head, he thought, *"...and now he's in the operating room fighting for his life."*

Rod was over six feet tall, with a narrow waist and broad shoulders. He had a runner's body. Exhaustion and worry distorted his normally handsome face. His wrinkled white t-shirt and sawdust-covered jeans suggested he had dropped everything when the call caught him working in his home workshop.

* * *

Doctor Roberts stepped into the waiting room and looked at the half-dozen people inside. He walked over to Rod. "Hi, I'm Dr. Roberts. Are you Mr. Guhl, Butch's father?"

Rod blinked and looked up with steely eyes and asked, "How's my son? Did the surgery go well?" His eyes were red.

The doctor's face sagged. "He made it through surgery. He suffered considerable internal damage, but we managed to stop most of the bleeding. He's stable for now. He lost part of the posterior lobe of his right lung. A bullet shattered two of his ribs and sent bone fragments slicing down through his intestines. The chance of peritoneal infection is high in these cases so we're pumping him full of antibiotics. That's all we can do for now."

A pain moved down Rod's left arm. It felt like someone had hit his funny bone. The pain fanned across his chest, leaving him short of breath. His stomach churned. Between two big breaths, Rod asked, "What are his chances?"

The surgeon shook his head. "Not good. He has a ten percent chance of surviving the next twenty-four hours. If he makes it that long, then I would say he has a fifty percent chance of pulling through."

Before Rod could respond, the doctor reached with a shaky hand and patted Rod's shoulder. "I'm sorry. We did our best. His fate is in God's hands now."

"Thank you doctor, but that's not good enough," Rod extended his hand and shook the doctor's, then walked toward the courtesy phone in the corner of the waiting room. He was going to make sure Butch survived.

* * *

The phone rang twice, followed by silence. Rod knew someone was listening on the other end.

With a shaky voice, Rod said, "Father, this is Rod. I'm at Woodwind Hospital."

"What's the problem?" Jerrold Guhl said in a stern, reserved voice.

"Butch was involved in a liquor store robbery tonight. The clerk shot him twice. He just got out of surgery and the prognosis is not good. I think he is going to die. Can you come?"

A long silence followed.

"For my grandson, I'll come."

"Thank you."

The phone went dead.

Rod walked back to his orange chair and sat down with a weary sigh. It had taken a lot of courage for Rod to call his father.

The last time he had spoken to his father had been ten years ago. A dark family secret had created the schism between them because Rod had refused to let his family take part in the Guhl family's activities. Breaking from his father had ostracized him and his family from the rest of the clan.

Rod walked to the coffee server in the corner of the room. He stood lost in a fog of concern. After a few moments, he shook his head, dispelling the thoughts of his past. He poured himself a cup of dark, stale coffee and made his way back to the orange chair. He plopped down to wait the arrival of his father.

He dreaded facing Jerrold Guhl, but it was the only way to save Butch's life. Asking his father to save Butch would force him to become involved in the Guhl family affairs again. Rod shrugged his shoulders. He would wait and see what demands his father would make. A tear welled up in his eye and slid down the edge of his nose. Was saving Butch's life worth the sacrifice he was about to make?

* * *

Twenty-five minutes later, Jerrold Guhl pushed through the glass doors of the emergency waiting room. He was still a very distinguished man. He was six feet four inches tall, with a broad chest and steel-gray eyes. He hadn't seemed to change in ten years. His hair was thick, gray, and curly. He wore a double-breasted gray suit with a wrinkle-free, white shirt, fronted by a dark blue tie.

Rod's father glanced around the room until his eyes fell on Rod. He walked with brisk steps and stopped before Rod.

Without a friendly greeting for his son, Jerrold Guhl asked, "Rod, what is Butch's condition now?" Jerrold sat down next to Rod. Jerrold straightened his suit jacket and flicked a piece of lint from his sleeve. Then his eyes locked on Rod's face.

Rod flinched, "It hasn't changed since I talked to you." Rod rung his hands. "They removed part of his right lung and stopped most of the bleeding. The second bullet shattered two of his ribs. Some of the pieces of bone tore up his intestines. The doctor said he was afraid the intestines may have leaked and spread infection into his abdominal cavity."

Rod stared at his father, whose eyes were unreadable. A feeling of dread spread through Rod.

Jerrold returned Rod's stare and asked, "You understand what it means if I save Butch's life?"

"Yes," Rod said, tearing his gaze from his father's hypnotic stare.

"You are still asking me to save him?" Jerrold asked.

"Yes," Rod said, holding his folded hands out toward his father, in a pose that looked as though he was begging or praying. "I have no other choice. I love my son."

Jerrold nodded. "Okay, bring the doctor to me." He leaned back in his chair, crossed his legs, and waited for Rod to carry out his command.

A red patch sprouted on Rod's throat. Ordered around as if he were a servant angered him. As usual, there was no discussion. It was his father's way or nothing.

Rod rose and stormed from the waiting room to carry out his father's wishes.

Jerrold moved his shoulders away from the back of the chair and straightened his back. He looked like a Bald Eagle preparing to dive on a rabbit. In this regal pose, Jerrold looked lean and feral. His predatory posture and stern look often instilled instant fear in other men.

Crow's feet at the corner of his eyes and bushy eyebrows were the focal points of his face. He exhibited an untamed intensity. A vibrant magnetism surrounded him with such strength that most people encountering him felt afraid and intimidated.

Across the waiting room, a middle-aged man sat next to his wife. The man was six feet tall with oversized hands. Muscles rippled in his shoulders, arms and back. He made the mistake of looking in Jerrold's direction with a smirk.

The man rose and headed towards of coffee machine. Jerrold's eyes followed him. As the man walked by Jerrold, their eyes locked. The man's legs buckled and his face paled. He pivoted on weak knees and retreated to his wife. With shaking fingers, he grabbed her hand and pulled her to her feet. She protested, but he led her out of the waiting room.

Jerrold smiled, squared his shoulders and sat up even straighter—he had won. His chair groaned with most of his weight on the front legs. He had intimidated the man. Jerrold was dangerous and enjoyed the fear he instilled in others.

Doctor Roberts was a thin, balding man who walked with small quick steps. He walked through the waiting room doors, accompanied by Rod. They hurried to where Jerrold sat.

"Doctor Roberts, this is my father," Rod said,

"Hello Mr. Guhl," the doctor offered his hand. "Rod tells me you want to talk to me regarding your grandson." The doctor looked at his watch. "What can I do for you?"

"I need absolute privacy with my grandson for an hour. I plan to pray for him and can't be disturbed," Jerrold said.

Rod tried to explain. "The head nurse said I would need your permission before my father could be alone with him."

The doctor just stared at Jerrold.

"He has my permission," Rod said, "but during the prayer session he must not be disturbed." His face flushed and he hoped the doctor did not notice. "Can you arrange for the necessary privacy, doctor?"

Jerrold sprung from his chair and stepped toward the doctor.

The doctor's eyes widened, as he lurched backwards.

Jerrold said, "No one must interrupt my prayers—do you understand, doctor?" It was a command, not a request.

The doctor swayed. "Well, the request is somewhat irregular, but prayer can't hurt anything as long as you're quiet." Doctor Roberts nodded. His Adam's apple bobbed up and down with small jerks. "I'll clear your request with the head nurse right away."

"Thank you, Dr. Roberts," Jerrold said. The corner of his lips curled upward.

Rod watched the exchange between his father and the doctor, afraid of what his father might do next. He sighed with relief when the doctor left the room.

Now he knew Butch would survive, but he was already worried about what would happen to his son after he recovered. He knew what his father was going to do. There was no doubt it would save Butch's life.

* * *

errold stood just inside Butch's hospital room door. He stared at his grandson for a few moments. He watched Butch's chest rise, followed by a slight wheezing sound. Jerrold walked to the bedside and studied his grandson's face. The skin around Butch's lips and neck was the color of bread dough. A wave of concern ran through Jerrold's mind. The last time he had seen his grandson's face was ten years ago. Butch had Jerrold's nose, eyes, and ears. Jerrold's face softened as he thought about the senselessness of those lost ten years.

He paced around the glass-enclosed room, pulling the drapes shut. He slid a green, fabric-covered chair from the wall up to Butch's bed.

Clear plastic tubes dripped blood, saline solution and antibiotics into his grandson's arm. Opening a drawer in the bedside cabinet, Jerrold found a length of rubber tubing and a packet of IV needles. He pulled two of the needles from the sterile package and attached one to each end of the rubber tubing.

Jerrold removed his jacket, flicked a couple of hairs from it, folded it neatly, and laid it on the foot of the bed. He rolled up the shirtsleeve on his left arm, tightened his fist, and watched the veins of his arm pop out.

With the touch of a professional, he inserted the needle from the tube into the puffed out vessel at the bend of his elbow. His blood filled the tube and squirted out the needle at the other end. He pinched the tube to stop the flow of blood and then stuck the needle into the IV tube leading from the blood and saline solution bag feeding Butch's arm. Jerrold mounted the chair and sat on the back of it, elevating himself over his grandson's body.

Jerrold's blood flowed down the IV tube to mingle with the antibiotics, saline solution and blood. The mixture flowed into Butch's arm.

Butch convulsed several times and then lay still. After a few minutes, Jerrold removed the needles from his arm and the IV tube. He pulled the needles from both ends of the tube, wrapped them in a tissue, and put them in his jacket pocket. Then he coiled the short rubber tube and put it in the same pocket.

An hour later, Doctor Roberts knocked lightly on the door of Butch's room. Receiving no response, he pushed his way into the room. A shocked expression spread across the doctor's face. "What the hell is going on?" the doctor stammered.

Butch was sitting up in bed, talking with his grandfather. Butch turned with a puzzled look and smiled at the bewildered doctor.

The doctor rushed to Butch's bedside. With shaking hands, he glanced at the bank of monitors. He put a hand on Butch's forehead, while his mouth continued to sputter incomplete words. His mind could not comprehend the fact that a patient, who he believed was going to die, was now sitting up in bed acting like a normal healthy person. "What the hell happened? What did you do? This cannot be . . ." the doctor sputtered.

Grandfather Jerrold laid his hand on the doctor's shoulder smiling. "Take it easy. We don't want you to have a heart attack."

The doctor ignored Jerrold as he removed the bandages covering Butch's chest. He became even more unsettled when he could not find the stitches or scars where he had cut open Butch's chest two hours ago. "This is impossible." The doctor looked at Jerrold. "Prayer can't do this, can it?" The strength went out of the doctor's legs and he dropped down on the green hospital chair next to the bed. He shook his head back and forth. "Tell me what you did." His arms flew in circles, as though he was trying to draw a picture of his confusion. "I do not accept this. I have never seen.... My God, this is a miracle."

Jerrold glanced at Butch. "It looks like we won't be allowed to finish our visit after all—not with all these interruptions." Jerrold grabbed his suit jacket, swung it over his shoulders and slipped his arms into the sleeves, all in one smooth motion. "Butch, I will see you tomorrow." He casually walked out of the room.

Jerrold walked down the corridor to the waiting room. Inside, he found Rod reclined on a vinyl sofa with his eyes closed. As Jerrold's shadow blocked the light, Rod opened his eyes and sat up, a look of concern etched on his face.

"Relax Rod. Everything is fine," Jerrold said, with a wink and a smile. Then a serious look stole across his face. "You do understand that you are now obligated to the family? I expect you and Butch to be at the next family gathering—for his sake. You do understand why?"

"Yes, I understand. We'll be there. Just let me know when." Sadness smothered Rob's heart. He knew he had lost his son to the family.

* * *

The next morning, two police detectives walked into Butch's hospital room. Butch looked up from his breakfast.

"Butch," one of the detectives said. "I'm Captain Walter Stevens from the Woodbury Police Department." He pointed to the other officer and said, "This is Detective Dale Smith. We'd like to ask you some questions."

"Do I have to talk with you?"

"At some point in time you will. We know you didn't shoot the clerk. We have a good idea who did, and he's the one we really want. If you cooperate with us, we'll see that you get a break. If you don't want to work with us, you have the right to have your attorney present before we ask you any questions. Is that what you want?

"No, an attorney isn't necessary."

"You realize that anything you say can be used against you in court?"

"Yes."

"You are willing to set aside your legal rights and talk with us?" Officer Smith said.

"Sure."

"Okay, explain your role in the robbery." Captain Stevens said.

"It's simple, I let myself get shamed into taking part," Butch said, as he pushed his tray table away from his bed.

"What do you mean *shamed?*"

"Ben called me a chicken. He said I didn't have the guts to help him rob a store. I couldn't lose face in front of my friends, so I said I'd do it. I guess that was stupid, huh?"

"That's too bad, because the clerk was seriously injured and that means you are just as responsible as Ben," Captain Stevens said.

"Is Ben's last name Johnson," Sergeant Smith asked, holding a pad up before his eyes with a pencil poised to take down Butch's answer.

"Yes. He lives in an apartment in Newport, just behind the Super America station."

"Do you know the address?"

I don't know the address. Look for a two-story building with yellow vinyl siding. There's a staircase on the side of the house leading upstairs to his apartment."

Captain Stevens sat back in his chair and said, "Thanks for being up front with us. You realize you're in a whole lot of trouble?"

"Yes, I know. I did try to stop Ben from shooting the clerk." Butch hung his head.

"Because you cooperated, we'll try to help you," Captain Stevens said.

Butch looked up, "I'm sorry that old man was hurt. No one was supposed to get shot."

"You should have considered that before getting involved."

"Yeah, I know that—*now!*"

Stevens raised an eyebrow and said, "By the way, how do you explain your miraculous recovery? According to Dr. Roberts, the bullets caused extensive damage. He expected you to die."

"I don't know," Butch said shaking his head. "All I know is that I woke up in my hospital bed with my grandfather in the room."

"What was he doing there?"

I—I don't know. Praying, I guess. All I remember is he was mumbling something like *blood would tell* and when I asked him what he meant, he said he would tell me later."

"Hmm." Detective Stevens pinched the point of his chin. "I wonder what he meant by *blood will tell*?" With a shake of his head he added, "Beats me."

"What's going to happen to me?" Butch asked.

Walter Stevens stood up, followed by Officer Smith. "I don't know, kid. It doesn't look good." From the doorway, he said, "Thanks for being honest. We'll see what the D. A. will do for you."

* * *

A short time later, Jerrold Guhl called the Woodbury Police Headquarters and asked for Captain Walter Stevens. The desk sergeant told him that Stevens was on special assignment and gave Jerrold Guhl a number to call. Jerrold tried the number.

"Good afternoon Mr. Guhl," Walter Stevens said. "What can I do for you?"

"I understand you interrogated my grandson at the hospital this morning. Is that correct?" Jerrold Guhl said firmly.

"It is. He admitted being involved in the robbery and the shooting of the clerk during the robbery, he was very cooperative."

"I don't want you or anyone else interrogating him without my attorney being present. Do you understand?"

"Don't give me that crap! Butch is an adult. He consented to answer our questions. He was read his rights and everything we did was legal," Stevens said.

A cold silence hung over the open phone line and then Jerrold Guhl said in very controlled, but choppy words, "I don't make idle threats Captain. If you don't follow my instructions regarding my grandson, you will find out just what I mean."

"Let me ask you a question, Mr. Guhl," Stevens said, not intimidated. "How is it your grandson survived two bullet wounds that should have killed him? What did blood have to do with his survival?"

That's when Jerrold Guhl hung up.

CHAPTER 3
FRUSTRATION AND CONFUSION

Rod leaned over the drafting table in his office and put the final touches on his design for a new twenty-eight story office building. A thick stack of blueprints and drawings highlighted the last of his recommended changes. After months of effort bringing the project to this point, he was now ready to move on to the construction phase. This project was his pride and joy.

He was apprehensive, thinking he was done, but feeling he had forgotten something important. He was experiencing the emotional high that always came when the designing phase was completed and the construction phase was ready to begin.

Next week he would make his presentation of the final design to his backers. If they approved, construction would begin within a month. He was confident approval was a mere formality. No other building like it existed in the United States. Once the building was completed, he was certain to receive national acclaim for his architectural wizardry.

The phone rang. Rod jumped. A chill ran down his spine. He had a bad feeling it was a call he didn't want to take. He hesitated to answer, dreading the message he knew was waiting on the other end of the line.

The phone rang again and then a third time. Rod just stared at the phone. After six rings, he picked up the phone. There was no way to postpone the inevitable.

After a few seconds, a voice broke the silence. "Hello Rod, this is your father."

He said without enthusiasm. "Yes, I thought it might be you."

"The family meeting is set for two weeks from this Friday. We'll meet at the hunting shack. Be there with Butch. Do you remember how to get there?"

"I remember. We'll both be there. Goodbye."

Rod hung up. His mind raced, trying to come up with some way to avoid the family meeting. Maybe we could leave the country. What could my father do then? Butch and I could go to Cancun—no—maybe Europe. What was going to happen to Butch would happen, whether he was at the shack or in Mexico or Europe. What Butch was going to experience required the presence of his grandfather and other members of the family. When Rod decided to involve his father, there was no stopping the inevitable. Rod's shoulders sagged. He knew it was useless. It would make no difference where they were.

* * *

On Wednesday morning, Rod, Butch, and his attorney met with the Washington County Attorney in Stillwater. The County Attorney agreed to petition for probation in exchange for Butch's testimony against Ben Johnson. Ben was a hardened criminal and the D. A. was anxious to put him in prison for good.

Butch felt guilty for testifying against Ben. His moral code said he should not rat on a friend, but then Ben was not really his friend. There was another reason for giving Ben up. He had lied to Butch. He'd promised no one would be shot. Ben's fingerprints were on the cash register, the glass counter top, and the shotgun found in Ben's apartment. The evidence proved Ben was the one who had shot the clerk. He was a liar and a jerk.

Butch gave his deposition to the County Attorney and received instructions about when to appear in court. The trial proceeded and Butch testified against Ben, who was a three-time loser. He received a prison sentence of twenty-five years to life. Butch felt no remorse. Something had happened to him in the hospital. Whatever it was changed the way he now thought about everything.

* * *

The night after the trial ended, Butch was getting ready to go to sleep. He sat on the edge of his bed trying to sort through everything that plagued him. His thoughts turned to the robbery and the role he had played in it. He wasn't proud of what he did. The shooting of the store clerk still bothered him. The biggest confusion came from trying to understand how he had survived. The doctor had expected him to die, but he didn't. The thought of dying scared him. What had happened to him in the hospital?

As much as he tried, his mind would not let him remember.

Butch couldn't accept his father's explanation that he had not been hurt as badly as the doctor had said. The doctor had shown him x-rays of his wounds, and they looked bad to him. What had happened to the scars that should have been present? The doctor had said the wounds and surgery would leave scars and couldn't explain how or why they had disappeared.

Butch knew he was different—a *changed* person. Before the robbery, he had been an ass, always negative, often depressed—a loudmouth, cocksure of himself. Those feelings were gone. Now he was quiet, thoughtful and reserved. He could hold his rebellious nature in check. The hostile feelings he exhibited toward his father had changed to appreciation and respect. He couldn't explain the change in his personality and that bothered him. No matter how hard he tried, most of what had happened after the robbery was a blank. Somehow, his grandfather was involved, but Butch could not put his finger on what role he had played.

Butch's drug-using, heavy-drinking friends no longer came around. What surprised him the most was that he did not even care. He no longer wanted to associate with them. In fact, after the first few phone calls from them, they gave up trying to pull him back into the gang. He sensed something was tugging him in a new direction, but again he could not explain what it was or where it was nudging him.

Butch also suspected his father was hiding something from him. It was as if his father was afraid *for* him. Butch was sure it had nothing to do with the robbery, but in some way involved his grandfather. Every time he asked his father what had happened to him in the hospital, he received a frightened stare, and then silence.

His parents were pleased with the change in him. Butch was surprised that he and his father could now have a calm, intelligent conversation without yelling and screaming at each other. Hell, Butch even listened to his father's ideas without becoming angry and running out of the house, as he used to do.

Butch sat on the edge of his bed trying to sort through everything that bewildered him. He looked out the window and saw the full moon. Suddenly, yellow bolts of lightning shot through his mind. His body started to shake as if he was experiencing a seizure. He fell backwards, unaware that his body was beginning to change in astonishing ways.

CHAPTER 4
NORTHWARD TO DESTINY

Butch woke the next morning wondering why he was lying on top of his bed with his clothes on. This was just one more thing he couldn't explain. There was so much happening to him he didn't understand. He got up, straightened the bed and put the latest problem out of his mind.

Today was Friday, the day he and his dad were heading north for the Guhl family gathering. Butch took two sleeping bags from his closet and threw them into the back of the Jeep Cherokee. Later, he added a box of candy, a bag of chips, and a six-pack of Pepsi.

Butch was excited to get on with the trip. The last time he attended one of the family gatherings was when he was nine years old. He remembered his uncles and aunts walking the woods with his grandpa, while he played with all of his cousins. He had fun playing games with them.

He remembered driving down a bumpy road for a long time before they arrived at a big brick building that looked like a castle tucked back in the woods. He smiled recalling the time he got so mad at his father for making him go to bed and missing the bonfire. With a sad note, he remembered that was the last time he saw any of his relatives.

He sensed his father was not thrilled they were going to the gathering. For the last two weeks, he complained that it was a three-hour trip 'up north', that he didn't have time to waste a weekend away from his project.

Many years ago, his Grandpa Jerrold bought six hundred and forty acres of wooded hunting land south of Crosby, Minnesota. He enclosed the entire area with a ten-foot high chain link fence topped with razor wire. The land around the enclosure was state and county tax-forfeited land used by a few grouse and deer hunters in the fall.

Butch heard the kitchen door open and his father walked into the garage carrying a cup of coffee and a sandwich.

Butch asked, "Did we forget anything?"

Rod shrugged his shoulders, "No, we got everything." He set his coffee cup in the holder on the dash and laid the sandwich next to it. Rod walked out of the garage to the deck, grabbed a black suitcase and carried it to the back of the Jeep. A frown creased his forehead as he slid the suitcase through the back window. He turned and said, "Butch, Crosby is just ten miles from the shack, if we need anything it'll give us an excuse to go to town." Then he added, "Unless your grandfather has changed, he'll have a spare of anything we need at the shack."

Elizabeth stuck her head through the window of the Jeep and gave Rod a peck on the cheek. Rod turned to her, gave her a kiss and said, "Are you sure you don't want to come with us?"

Butch chimed in, "Yeah, mom why don't you come?"

A pained look spread across her face. "No thanks, you know how I feel about your family. You do what you have to. I'll see both of you when you return."

Butch jumped into the front seat and Rod backed the Jeep out of the garage and into the street. Rod's thoughts were on the dreaded family gathering. With a shake of his head, he admitted to himself that it would be nice to see his siblings again. Ten years was a long time. Rod had five brothers, two sisters, eight nephews and eleven nieces. All of them would be at the shack this weekend. Only his wife, Elizabeth, would be missing.

The sun peeked out from behind a dark cloud. A smile broke across Rod's strained face. He told himself that somehow everything would be okay.

* * *

As they passed through Elk River, Butch turned to his dad with a puzzled expression. Questions raced through his mind. He still did not understand the reasons for the family pow-wow. He couldn't hold the questions back any longer.

"Dad, why are we doing this? We haven't gotten together for ten years."

Rod did not answer.

"Come on, Dad, the last time we did anything with the family I was nine years old. Why are we getting back with them now?" Butch watched his dad pucker his lips.

Rod finally said, "All I can tell you is my father and I talked the night he came to the hospital to see you. I made him a promise that if you lived, we would forget the past and take part in family activities again."

Butch stared at his father's face, searching for some clue to the hidden meaning of what he was not saying.

When Rod was a young boy, the family had been close-knit. When he'd reached the age of consent, he had chosen not to participate in any more of the family gatherings. He had not wanted that kind of life for his family. He believed, what the family did was wrong and he wanted no part of it.

"Dad what did grandpa do to me in the hospital?" Butch probed, studying the suspicious look on his father's face. "I know he did something! The doctors were shocked that I survived." Butch's voice took on a pleading tone. "I would like to know."

Rob shook his head. "I can't tell you son. Your grandfather must be the one to tell you what happened."

"Aha, then something did happen to me?"

Rod glanced over at Butch. "Wait until tonight, then all of your questions will be answered. I promise."

Butch could tell from the look on his father's face that he wouldn't get anything out of him. He shrugged his shoulders and said, "Okay, I'll wait, but I don't know what the big deal is."

Butch crawled over the front seat and plopped down on the back seat. He leaned over the back seat, grabbing a sleeping bag. He laid his head on the bag, punched it a few times until his head fit better, and relaxed.

As Butch lay there, he felt a tightening around his temples. He closed his eyes. Bright yellow lightning bolts flashed across his vision, blinding him. He scrunched his eyes tight, trying to make the flashes and pain go away. He brought his fists up to his eyes and pushed his knuckles into the sockets. The area around his temples throbbed.

Every time he experienced one of these headaches, weird thoughts spun through his mind. Often the thoughts were frightening. At other times, exhilarating. He kept his eyes closed and waited for the pain to subside. The headaches never lasted too long, but they were occurring more often.

In a few minutes, the pain relented and he fell asleep.

At Garrison, they turned west to connect with Highway 6, which would take them up to Deerwood. A half hour later, they followed the Deerwood shortcut west.

Rod reached into the back seat and shook Butch. "It's 8:30, time to wake up. We just left Deerwood. We'll be at the shack soon."

Butch grumbled and rolled over.

Rod said in a louder voice, "Butch, wake up!"

Butch stirred, stretched his arms over his head and pushed his hands against the roof of the jeep. "Ohhh, I could sleep for six more hours."

Rod said under his breath, "It wouldn't do you any good."

"Huh, what did you say?"

"Nothing, don't worry about it."

Gray clouds raced up from the south as if in a hurry to cover the setting sun. The sun's rays shimmered, trying to postpone their disappearance. Red rays shot upward around the edges of the clouds, forming a golden-red corona.

Rod turned on the headlights. When he came to County Road 112, he turned south, driving past the McMillan Truss Plant. The buildings at the plant housed machinery for converting logs into long strands. Then the strands were glued together to form roof trusses. Yellow light shined from the windows, like eyes watching them pass.

Two miles farther down the road Rod guided the Jeep east onto a bumpy, narrow gravel road. Another mile brought them to the forest road cutoff that took them through a thick growth of oak, aspen, and birch. The shack was not far away now.

Rod flipped on the 4-wheel drive as they entered the rut-filled cutoff. Fifty yards ahead, a metal gate stood open, inviting them in. Rod stared ahead into a dark foreboding tunnel of overhanging tree branches.

Thoughts of turning back tempted him, but then he remembered the promise he had made to his father. Rod steered the Jeep down the dark bleak tunnel.

Destiny awaited his son.

Darkness wrapped itself around the Jeep and propelled it forward. To go on was to bring his son closer to a legacy Rod had worked hard to avoid. What his father had done to Butch in the hospital meant all Rod's hard work was lost. There was no turning back.

Rod sighed and yielded to the overwhelming frustration at work in his life. "SHIT!" he said, pounding his fist on the steering wheel. He held his breath for a moment, and then let it out with a big sigh. "Well, we passed the point of no return, and I did give him my word."

Butch leaned forward and hung his arms over the front seat. "Dad, what did you mean by the point of no return?"

The corners of Rod's mouth drooped, "Nothing son."

Butch pulled his face into a scowl. "You also said something about no going back."

"I was just expressing my thoughts out loud. Forget it, son."

Through the trees ahead, Butch saw the lights from the shack shining from its hilltop perch. The Jeep turned up the hill. Off to the right side of the trail he saw a clearing.

The Jeep bounced over roots and potholes in the grassy trail. The headlights played on the hazel bushes. Butch imagined that he saw black shadowy monsters rise from the mix of light and shadows. The monsters wavered for a moment, and then disappeared back into the blackness. The Jeep's headlights created ever-changing monsters.

The clearing sloped down to a pond nestled among a grove of spruce trees. Butch's eyes grew wide. He remembered that trail leading from the shack down to the pond. He recalled walking on that path when he was nine.

Rod said, "Butch, do you see the pond down there?"

"Yes, I was just looking at it. The clearing and the pond with the moon shining on them sure make a pretty picture."

"I helped Dad build benches around the pond. I bet they're still there. Do you see the field off to the side of the pond? When I was a kid, we used to play softball there, and then at night, we would start a roaring bonfire and roast marshmallows and wieners. My brothers, sisters and I used to have a lot of fun playing together."

Butch smiled as he pictured the scene his dad painted.

A few moments later, Butch jumped. His heart pounded in his chest. A spooky reflection appeared next to the car window. He recognized the face—it belonged to his grandfather.

Butch glanced at the speedometer. The Jeep was traveling twelve miles per hour, and his grandfather was running alongside the vehicle with ease, a smile spread across his face.

"Hi Butch," grandfather's reflection said through the window.

Butch rolled the window down, "Hi Grandpa."

Rod parked the Jeep alongside a dozen other vehicles.

Jerrold stared at Butch inside the Jeep, "We've been waiting for you to arrive. The family is anxious to begin the festivities."

As an afterthought, Jerrold glanced at Rod and said, "Hi son. I'm glad to have you here with us again."

Butch noted the sour look on his dad's face.

Jerrold said, "Don't worry, everything will be okay."

Butch jumped out of the Jeep and gave his grandfather a hug. Rod walked around the Jeep and coolly shook his father's hand. Rod and Butch walked to the back of the Jeep, grabbed their gear, and followed Jerrold toward the shack.

Some shack. A four-story brick fortress with ten bedrooms stood before Butch. It looked more like a medieval castle.

Jerrold pulled Butch close in another hug. Together they stepped onto the wooden bridge, which took them over a small creek that meandered in front of the shack and then disappeared beneath overhanging branches of oak trees at the side of the yard.

Standing just inside the door of the shack, Butch saw two of his uncles, Richard and Bruce. Behind them stood three of his cousins.

Butch thought, gosh I haven't seen them since I was nine. They've sure grown.

Everyone started yelling greetings at the same time. The words merged into a blur of noise. Once Butch stepped inside, a feeling of belonging overwhelmed him. It was as though the shack in all its brightness was inviting him home. There was no doubt he had missed many years of being with his family, but there was still time to make up for it.

When everyone quieted down, Butch was able to move around the family room and greet everyone.

"Hey, Butch, I'm glad to see you," cousin Dean blurted out.

"I'm happy you could come," Uncle William said, waving at him from the bar.

Brad, another of Butch's cousins said, "I haven't seen you in years. About time you came back to the family." Ten years ago, Brad had been Butch's favorite cousin.

A sense of acceptance swept through Butch. Being part of an extended, caring family left him with a warm feeling. He had missed his relatives more than he had known.

Butch watched his dad greeting everyone. He looked happy to see his brothers and sisters.

Brad grabbed Butch's gear and threw the sleeping bag to Butch. "Come on," Brad said, "I'll help you get settled upstairs."

Brad led Butch into one of the bedrooms on the third floor. Together, they laid out his sleeping bag next to Brad's bag. Butch shoved his duffel bag into a corner. They both lay down on the sleeping bags.

Brad's face broke into a wide smile. "So, you're one of us, huh?" Brad said.

Butch gave a questioning scowl. "What do you mean one of us? I've always been a Guhl."

Brad looked at Butch with a sheepish gaze, alarm showing on his crimson face. "Oh, no—*you don't know?*" he blurted out.

Before Butch could pursue the mystery, someone downstairs yelled. "Come and get it."

Brad jumped up and raced for the stairs. Butch lurched to his feet and followed him down, two steps at a time. Spread on the kitchen table was a late supper of hamburgers, hot dogs, chips, pickles, potato salad, and liters of pop.

Butch heaped a paper plate full of food and followed Brad out to the porch. The rest of the teenagers soon joined them. Some sat around a long table while others seated themselves on patio chairs or sat on the floor. Everyone stuffed food into their mouths and listened as Brad brought Butch up to date on family gossip.

After they finished eating, the teenagers ran out of the shack, across the bridge, and followed a gravel path toward a bonfire that flashed in the distant clearing. They crossed an open field and followed the path around the pond.

Butch's vision was excellent in the moonlight. He saw details like belt loops and patterns in the clothes others were wearing. He followed his noisy cousins as they galloped through the field around him.

The whooping teenagers burst into the second clearing where the bonfire blazed high in the night air. Butch recognized two of his cousins, Jake and George standing next to a brick fire ring filled with burning logs. He slid to a stop in the circle of light and greeted them.

After the usual arguments about the existence of ghosts and goblins, Cherrie suggested they play a game of Hooper Rye. The cousins selected Butch as the first catcher and then they fled into the surrounding woods, while Butch counted to the traditional one hundred.

When he'd finished counting, Butch walked away from the fire to alleviate the night blindness he was suddenly experiencing. It took a few moments for his vision to adjust to the dark. He walked along the edge of the field away from the bonfire and stared into the trees.

The flickering light from the bonfire painted tree trunks and illuminated leafy plants. The firelight cast shadows, which made it hard to distinguish what Butch was looking at. He squinted and strained to see beyond the shadows, looking for one of his cousins lying on the ground or hiding behind a tree. He felt his cousins watching him from the darkness, waiting for him to venture after them into the woods.

Butch slipped in among the dark tree trunks and shadows. He crawled fifty feet from the edge of the clearing, until he was well beyond the lighted area. He rose to a crouch next to an oak tree. He cocked his head and listened for any movement coming from the surrounding bushes.

Butch looked up at the full moon hanging in a cloudless sky. The stars twinkled with bright flashes around the yellow moon. He followed moonbeams down through the leafy canopy, where the light splattered across the forest floor, creating wavering shadows among the shrubs.

Butch's head turned in the direction of a noise. It was like cloth scraping on a bush. In a moment, his eye caught a movement.

His eyesight sharpened and he recognized the silhouette of Brad next to an oak tree with rough, scaled bark. Butch remained motionless. Brad moved with slow steps towards Butch. He stopped a few feet from Butch.

Butch waited, controlling his breathing and movement. Butch bunched his muscles and launched his body through the air. His knees hit Brad and slipped around his cousin's waist. His arms draped around Brad's shoulders. Brad screamed. Their tangled bodies flew through the air, arms and feet flailing around each other. The two boys landed in a heap among the ferns and grass.

Butch laughed at the thrashing bundle he held in his arms. "At least you can't say I didn't catch you," Butch said, as Brad continued to struggle.

Brad relaxed and said, "Jesus, you scared the shit out of me." He shrugged off Butch's arms.

"Come on, you have to help me catch the others." Butch said, as he stood up and pulled Brad to his feet.

"I'll let the others know I caught you," Butch said, as he cupped his mouth and yelled, "HOOPER RYE—BRAD IS CAUGHT."

Butch and Brad huddled together, discussing their strategy for going after the others. They agreed to split up and walk parallel to each other, staying fifty feet apart. That way one might flush someone hiding toward the other person.

As Butch moved through the trees, he heard Brad stepping on twigs and sliding his feet through the leaves. *With all the noise Brad is making, he's sure easy to keep tabs on,* Butch thought. He closed his eyes and formed a mental picture of Brad stumbling along in the dark. The picture he created was so clear it surprised him.

Butch could feel that something was changing within him. He had never before seen pictures that clearly in his mind, or heard noises so far away. He was amazed how well he could see in the dark. It wasn't normal.

Butch's skin tingled. He felt so alive. He was experiencing things he had never noticed before. All of his senses were more acute. He focused his hearing and was able to detect the rustle of grass from the movement of a mouse beneath an oak tree twenty feet away. He even saw the mouse. The blades of grass stood out individually, but in an off-green color.

Butch sniffed, and then turned his head into the gentle breeze, which blew from the northwest. The wind brought the scent of a new victim to him. He sniffed the air again, detecting a weak skunk-like odor. Then it dawned on him. The smell came from the body odor of his cousin, Carey. He had smelled that same mixture of Right Guard and sweat earlier tonight when Carey had hugged him.

Butch dropped to his knees and crawled toward the scent. His unsuspecting victim would not know what hit him. Five feet in front of Butch, a shadow separated from the trunk of a tree and moved in his direction. Butch froze and adjusted his vision until he was able to see Carey's outline clearly against the backdrop of dark vegetation.

Butch covered his mouth and suppressed a giggle that tried to escape from his throat. He could not prevent a low growl from escaping. *I will scare the shit out of him.*

He watched Carey's head rivet back and forth, trying to pinpoint where the growl had come from.

Carey whispered, "Hey, you guys, we are not supposed to do that, not until grandpa starts the ceremony."

"GRRRRRRSSSSsss," Butch growled, in a louder voice this time. The growl echoed from the trees. Butch covered his mouth to stop from laughing.

"If you do that again, I'm going to change and come after you," Carey threatened.

Butch thought, *Change—what did he mean? Change what?*

He decided to capture Carey before he lost track of him, or before he *changed.* Butch crawled closer to Carey, and then rose up into a crouch. He launched himself through the air. Butch's clothing brushed against some branches. Carey started to turn, but was too late. Butch slammed into Carey's chest. The two boys staggered and tumbled into a stand of ironwood saplings. The boys crashed to the ground.

"Ohhh," Carey moaned, grabbing the back of his head.

As he fell, a sharp stick poked into Butch's shoulder. He sat up in the dark massaging his right shoulder. He felt something wet and sticky.

Carey turned toward Butch with a snarl, "Christ, Butch, all you needed to do was tag me, not kill me." Air hissed out of his lungs as he relaxed, still rubbing his head.

"Sorry, I guess I got carried away with the game." Butch turned to face Carey's silhouette, resting his chin on his arms. "Say, what did you mean with that talk of changing?"

"What do you mean?" Carey said, his voice shaking. He stood and brushed debris from his shirt and pants.

"You know, when I growled at you, you said you would change and come after me. What did you mean?"

"Oh, I can't tell you. You'll have to wait until grandpa explains that to you tonight during the ceremony." Carey walked away from Butch into the shadows.

CHAPTER 5
INITIATION

Around midnight, members of the Guhl family gathered around the bonfire, joined by the kids.

Cirrus clouds moved across the full moon, which was poised just above the feathery top branches of the surrounding trees. Moonbeams penetrated into the surrounding forest, splashing everything with a blue-white light.

A gentle breeze produced shadows that moved among the trees, giving life to the darkness. The odor of pine and cherry blossoms filled the field.

Jerrold Guhl glided up to stand in front of the bonfire. He gazed out over the gathered family members. Butch heard a rumbling growl come from deep within his grandfather's chest and a quiet fell over the family. Butch sat next to his father on a log, just behind Uncle Richard and Brad.

Jerrold raised both of his arms with palms extended toward the moon. He said in a low haunting voice, "Tonight we welcome back Rod, and especially Butch, who is the newest member of our pack."

Butch stared at his grandfather and then jerked back on the log when he saw that the man's eyes glowed bright red. A trickle of fear shot through him. Goose bumps rose on the back of his arms and neck.

Butch tried to explain away what he had just seen. It must have been the reflection of the red flames from the bonfire. In his heart, though, he knew he was lying to himself.

Jerrold lowered his arms and looked at Butch. "Butch, when I came to you in the hospital you were dying. I saved you by giving you a transfusion of my blood. Now you will become one with the pack."

Butch straightened his back, leaned against his father and whispered, "Dad, what does he mean?"

"Shh, Butch," Rod said. "Just listen. Everything will be explained to you soon enough."

Jerrold put up a hand to still Butch and said, "Look at the moon. Does the light hurt your eyes?"

Butch stared at the full moon. The bright light held his eyes even as tears filled them and spilled down his cheeks. Butch moaned, "Oh yes, it hurts." His breath came in short gasps. His muscles contracted and relaxed like squirming worms. His mind swirled with prehistoric scenes of animals running from him in horror. With an effort, Butch tore his eyes from the moon.

He grabbed his father's arm and said, "Dad, what's happening to me? I feel funny. Weird thoughts are shooting through my mind."

"Butch," Jerrold said, "You are experiencing the *change*. Do not fight it. As a pack member, you will have to learn to control the change."

"Yes, yes, we control the change," echoed from several of the family members around the campfire.

Jerrold said, "No one is allowed to hunt alone."

A chorus sounded, "We hunt as a pack."

Jerrold raised his arms toward the moon. "If any pack member hunts without permission of the pack, they are an enemy of the pack, no longer part of the family, and will be hunted down and killed. The pack must be protected and never exposed."

The chorus replied, "We must protect the pack."

Butch stared at the moving shadows outlined by the flames of the bonfire. His mouth dropped open when he caught glimpses of several hairy animals moving among the family members. His mind screamed, *God, they look like wolves—no, like werewolves!*

Butch started to shake. Cold shivers ran down his spine. He tried to convince himself grandfather was just telling a scary story, but he knew better.

Butch knew werewolves were fictitious beings, a figment of someone's imagination. There is no way a human could change into a wolf.

He turned to stare at the shadows and listen to his family members chanting in unison, "The pack must be protected. We control the change."

Butch was no longer sure that werewolves did not exist. How else could he explain the furry beasts moving around him?

Chapter 6
Welcome to the Pack

Butch wondered if he was going crazy. He couldn't comprehend what he was seeing. Frightened, he grabbed onto his father's arm.

Thick clouds rolled over the moon, thrusting the grassy area around the bonfire into semi-darkness. Something slammed into Butch and he lost his grip on his father's arm. Butch's eyes dilated. His head jerked around trying to locate his father. Shaggy, fur-covered creatures swirled around him. He could not recognize anyone. All he could see was moving shadows. Large, hairy creatures bumped into him.

He tried to move to the outside of the swirling group. As he did, he kept tripping over something. He bent down and tried to see what it was—it was discarded pieces of clothing.

One of the hairy creatures bumped into Butch, knocking him down. He looked up and heard growls and snarls. Fear gripped him.

Someone threw more logs on the fire, sending flames and sparks shooting into the air. Yellow light reflected down from the treetops. Butch's eyes flared wide as he recognized Uncle Richard standing before him in the form of a large werewolf. To the left of Richard were Uncle Thomas and Cousin Brad, both of them now fur covered beasts.

Butch's heart slammed against his chest. He jumped up and tried to back away, but his legs wouldn't move. Yellow bolts of lightning flashed across his vision. He sagged to his knees moaning, "Oh, God."

He closed his eyes, hoping the wolf-beings that were prancing around him would be gone when he opened them again. But when he opened his eyes, the beasts were still there. Some of the creatures sat on their rear haunches, staring at him. Others stood upright on two padded feet. Shaggy fur covered their bodies.

The clouds drifted away and moonbeams brightened the scene around him. "My God," Butch screamed, "You're all werewolves!"

He swayed, and twisted around, looking for his father. He wanted to run—to escape this madness—but they were all around him. There was nowhere to go.

When his vision cleared, Butch rose to his feet and backed away from the encircling werewolves. They were not paying any attention to him. He thought he was free, and was about to make a run for it, when two of the creatures grabbed his arms. Butch looked at the two beasts holding him. He screamed. Carey, in his werewolf form, held Butch's left arm. Brad held his right arm and growled at him when he tried to pull free.

His fur-bearing cousins held him with grips of iron. Butch glanced at Carey, who growled in his face. He stared into Carey's deep yellow eyes and felt his soul shriveling. Butch thrashed and squirmed, but could not free himself.

"No—no—," Butch screamed. "You can't do this to me. Let me go. You're all crazy. Dad—help me!" He struggled to break loose. "Dad, they're going to kill me."

Rod pushed through the circle of hulking creatures. He reached his son's side and threw his arms around him. Tears rolled down his face. He stepped back and shook Butch by the shoulders. "Son, listen to me, decisions were made and now there's no turning back. You're one of them. The change is already in your blood."

Through tear-filled eyes, Butch looked at his father. "No—no—I'm not one of those things."

Rod sobbed and shook Butch again. "Listen to me. I had to make a decision. You would have died in the hospital if I had not asked my father to save you. He transfused his blood into you, and that saved your life, but it also made you one of them."

Butch collapsed, sobbing in Rod's arms. "No—no—," he moaned.

Rod held Butch. "I'm sorry, it was selfish of me, but I loved you too much to let you die."

Jerrold pranced forward on pawed hind feet, and shouldered Rod out of the way.

Butch looked into his grandfather's blood-red eyes and knew everything his father had said was true. Jerrold stood in front of him, a big, red-haired werewolf, with elongated snout and long, sharp fangs. His grandfather placed his furry arms on Butch's shoulder and then raised his head to the moon and let out a blood-curdling howl.

Butch convulsed as electric shocks rocked through his body.

Jerrold gave Butch a shake and then said in a soothing voice, "Butch, you must not fight the change. You cannot. The change will come over you no matter what you do." He moved his hair-covered paws up both sides of Butch's head and squeezed. "The pack is here to help you. You are one with the pack, and we will let no harm come to you. Now listen to me and be calm—calm— calm," he chanted.

The words filled Butch's head with a ringing echo. Calmness settled over him, soothing frayed nerves. The calmness flooded through his body. He opened his eyes and stared into Grandfather Jerrold's red eyes. Something in those evil-looking eyes brought comfort to him.

He glanced over his grandfather's shoulder and noticed the milling group of werewolves. They were growling and snapping at the moon—completely possessed. Peace descended over him. It no longer bothered Butch. It felt natural that they should be here. Jerrold dropped his hairy paws and turned to the others.

Butch shook his head, as though he was waking up from a bad dream. A turbulent whirlpool of new and violent feelings boiled through his mind, rising toward the surface of his consciousness. Butch shook his head trying to blot out the wicked thoughts. He overpowered the thoughts and pushed them into a hidden corner of his mind. Relief surged through him, until he turned his head upward.

Moonlight flooded his eyes, blinding him. Wicked thoughts resurfaced. He closed his eyes and screamed in pain. The moonlight penetrated though his eyelids and the pain increased.

He felt like he was looking into the sun. Flashes of light exploded on the back of his retinas, sending fireworks bursting out along neural pathways to all parts of his brain. Madness spiraled upward, growing and flooding his consciousness. An uncontrollable rage was set free within him. He wanted to kill something. *Anything.*

Butch struggled to break free from those holding him. An overpowering urge to run and kill grew stronger within him and brought on a frantic attempt to escape. When he found he could not pull loose, a small amount of rationality returned. He looked to see what was holding him back and saw Brad and Carey holding his arms. He screamed, "Let me go!"

His two cousins were much larger and stronger than Butch. Again, the madness welled up in him. He whipped his arms back and forth until he tore free. Brad and Carey glanced at each other, shocked that Butch was able to break their grip.

Butch could no longer contain the inner primitive forces. The juices of change flowed without restriction. A scream of primordial ferocity exploded from Butch's lungs. He released a howl from his contorted mouth, into the clearing. "NOOOOoooooo. ARRRRoooooo." His body raced through its transformation. No longer restrained by his werewolf cousins, he ripped off his clothing and dropped to his hands and knees. Coarse, reddish-brown hair grew from his follicles, covering his entire body with a dense mat of fur. The shape of his bones altered, shifting and remolding into new shapes.

His face caved in and then elongated. His nose protruded from his face, pointed fangs jutting from both upper and lower jaws. Butch's feet became round paws. Curved claws replaced toenails and fingernails. Butch no longer resembled a human nor a wolf, but something in-between. His front shoulders stood higher than his hindquarters, so that his body sloped backwards.

Rabid thoughts flashed through Butch's mind. It was impossible to stop the madness that welled up inside of him. He wanted to kill—to rip flesh with his claws. Insatiable cravings for human blood and flesh blotted out all other thoughts.

The gathered werewolves received Butch's telepathic thoughts and experienced his heightened wildness. The group absorbed Butch's ungovernable rage. Fear and anger emanated from Butch in distorted waves.

The other werewolves gasped and trembled, as they drank in those waves, which carried them to a higher level of excitement. Experiencing Butch's strong emotional eruption encouraged an urgent need in them to kill.

The strength of Butch's *sending* shocked Jerrold. A frown creased his hairy brow and his lips peeled back in a snarl. He had never witnessed another werewolf elicit such total empathy in others. Jerrold concentrated on Butch's mental emanations and felt the animal side of his change smash into his mind with unleashed fury. He had never experienced such savagery before. Jerrold flinched when he saw how Butch's fury affected the others.

Jerrold grew concerned. He needed to do something before Butch grew too strong. He couldn't afford to lose control of the pack. Visions of his pack on an uncontrolled killing spree flooded his mind. Exposure of the pack would result from any unplanned killing of humans. He could not allow that to happen. He was the pack leader, and responsible for keeping the pack from getting out of control. Jerrold jumped to the center of the swirling pack, knocking several werewolves aside. He released a loud howl. "AAARRRROOOOOOOOOOO."

Members of the pack pushed and jostled one another. Heads swiveled toward the pack leader. The leader always led the hunt and they were more than ready to follow. Jerrold smiled at the ease with which he regained control.

Then he noticed a disturbance at the edge of the pack. Thomas was circling away from the pack in an agitated, stiff-legged gait. "Oh, no," Jerrold said to himself, "He's out of control." Hard knots twisted and turned in Jerrold's stomach. A wave of nausea passed through his body as he rushed toward Thomas.

Thomas ran among the fringe of gathered werewolves, nipping at their necks, trying to entice them to follow him on a killing spree. Two of the younger werewolves turned and followed Thomas.

Jerrold overtook Thomas in two powerful leaps and rammed his shoulder into his side, sending him flying. Thomas rolled over several times and came to rest against the legs of his brother, Steve. Stunned by the blow, Thomas blinked his eyes several times. He didn't remember what had happened or how he had ended up on the ground. Thomas's lips peeled back with fear at the rapid approach of the angry pack leader.

Jerrold leaped through the air and landed with his front legs on Thomas's stomach. The air whooshed from Thomas's lungs, like the air from a blown tire. Jerrold's muzzle flashed towards Thomas's exposed throat and clamped down on fur and skin.

Overshadowed by the fear of imminent death, his earlier desire to race off and kill humans melted away. His madness evaporated. Thomas realized that one bite separated him from death. Thomas whimpered and offered no further resistance.

In a moment, Jerrold relaxed. Thomas whined as he regained sanity.

Jerrold growled and backed away from Thomas. He turned toward the rest of the pack and said, "Don't let the wild side control you."

The strength of those words sent electric shocks through Butch's whole body and he dropped to the ground on all four legs like the others. He waited for the pack leader to issue instructions. Even though the pack needed to hunt and kill, intelligence regained dominance over the wild animal instincts. They were a unified pack once again.

Thomas stood and shook dust and leaf litter from his fur. Embarrassed by his loss of control, he lowered his head submissively before the others.

Jerrold shook his head in relief and thought; I am getting too old for this. I need to step down. I averted a breakout this time, but will I be able to stop it next time?

Butch walked on shaky feet to Jerrold. Still aroused and impatient to make his first kill, he whined.

Jerrold's red eyes locked on Butch. He spoke in a low voice, "Butch, you no longer have control of your own destiny. It lies with the pack. You must never allow the animal part of you to gain the upper hand. If you cross too far to that side, getting back to the human side is difficult. If you can't control yourself, you will put the pack in great danger. Do you realize what would happen if one of us were seen as a werewolf by the humans? They would hunt us down. All of us would perish. You must remember the safety of the pack always comes first—never forget this."

Butch said, "Yes, Grandfather. I hear you."

"Good." Jerrold turned and stood erect on his hind legs. He released a menacing growl. "Now—all of you listen to me."

The entire pack grew silent.

"Our hunt tonight will be for deer. Do not kill any other animals. No human will be harmed." Jerrold peered at Butch through red-slotted eyes. "Butch, as the newest member of our pack, you will have the honor of making your first kill with me."

Jerrold swept his gaze over the rest of the pack and said, "The rest of you control your hunt and keep your howling to a minimum. We don't want the surrounding humans to get alarmed and call the sheriff. Remember, kill one deer per team."

He looked at Butch, a proud smile on his muzzle, then turned to the rest of the pack. "Everyone should return to the bonfire in three hours. Do you all understand?"

The pack members growled their understanding. Small groups of werewolves broke away from the campfire and loped into the surrounding forest to begin their hunt.

Butch followed his grandfather around the edge of the pond, loping with awkward jumps, not yet used to running on four legs. He was clumsy for a few minutes, but soon adjusted and caught up to Jerrold. They followed the edge of a swamp, which took them towards Ward Lake, two miles away. Butch was amazed how easy it was to run through the woods. The trees, highlighted in an eerie bluish color, flashed by the edge of his vision.

"Grandfather, I must be running fifteen miles an hour and I'm not even breathing hard," Butch said.

"We're traveling faster than that," Jerrold corrected. "Your physiological make-up has been altered quite a bit from what you are used to in human form. Werewolves can run at this speed for hours without tiring."

Butch felt giddy. He leaped with abandon over a fallen log without breaking stride, and with a feeling of joy and true freedom. The desire to kill made him feel more alive than he had ever felt before. Butch bunched his muscles and sprang high into the air, celebrating his newfound freedom. He blinked his eyes, which were still sensitive to the light from the full moon. His vision was more acute in the moonlight than it was in human form on a cloudy day.

An exhilarating feeling permeated his body and mind. It was as if the physical exertion from each step pumped euphoric compounds through his body. He had never felt this free or so in tune with his surroundings. Butch could not contain the pent-up feelings any longer, and let slip from his muzzle a howl of intoxication. "AAARRRROOOOOOOOO."

Jerrold glanced at Butch from ten feet away and uttered a snarl of understanding.

Butch's mind snapped to attention, as the smell of deer musk entered his nostrils. A picture of a doe flashed into his mind. The deer was just ahead of them, standing at the base of a fir tree, poised to run away. The deer's nose wrinkled as it sniffed the air. Butch marveled at his ability to know what the deer was experiencing.

The deer was not physically aware of any danger, but in its simple mind, a twinge of anxiety about something it could not see was troubling it.

Butch was amazed. The deer felt the presence of a predator, even though it could not see or smell him. Butch tasted the fear emanating from the deer and felt his excitement grow. He found it hard to concentrate on what he was doing

Butch sensed his grandfather veer to the left.

Again, he was amazed, because he did not see Jerrold make the move. It was more a feeling of awareness that his grandfather had veered off. Butch reacted by jumping off the trail to his right. He wondered how he knew that this was what he was supposed to do. Apparently, instinct came into play and he just automatically reacted.

The desire to kill grew in his mind, driving him faster and faster toward the deer, his first kill.

Jerrold came in toward the deer from the left side. When Jerrold was fifty feet from the deer, he made a slight noise. The deer swiveled its head toward him. Butch was less than twenty feet from the deer, coming in from the right side. The deer bunched its muscles in preparation to flee.

By the time the deer made its second jump, a large, fur-covered beast flew through the air over its back. The deer blinked when it saw the wolf-being coming at it from the left. The deer, sure it was escaping from Jerrold, bunched its massive muscles for another jump. It never happened.

Butch reached down as though in slow motion and raked the claws of his right front paw across the deer's throat. Razor sharp claws passed through the carotid artery and trachea. Blood squirted into the night air. The stream of blood looked black in the moonlight. The deer jumped into the air before dropping to the ground.

Butch hit the ground ten feet beyond the deer. He sprang back toward the deer and landed near the carcass. The deer's hind legs gave a final reflexive kick and its eyes dimmed.

Butch stood with four legs spread on both side of the deer. He reached down with his muzzle and used his canine teeth to rip a strip of flesh from the deer's throat. He threw his head back, flipping the slab of quivering meat into the air. He reared up on his hind feet and caught the descending flesh in his mouth. Warm juices and blood flowed down his throat, causing him to squirm with ecstasy.

Not able to control his emotions, Butch reared back and let a howl of victory spring from his throat, "AAARRRROOOOOO."

Butch's lips curled back with deep satisfaction when he heard the answering cries of the pack acknowledge his first kill.

Jerrold approached the kill and stopped a few feet away. Butch looked up from the bloody throat of the deer and said, "Grandfather, why are you just standing there?"

Jerrold's lips curled, "Custom dictates one needs an invitation to feed by the one who makes the kill."

Butch stepped back in deference to the leader of the pack, the Alpha male. "You are my grandfather," he said. "Come and feed, I can't eat this whole deer by myself."

Jerrold was happy to see Butch demonstrate the proper respect. Butch and Jerrold ripped fur and flesh from the deer's front and hindquarters, gulping down chunks of venison. In short order, the choice pieces of venison disappeared from the carcass as the two werewolves gorged on the deer. When they finished feeding, they stepped back and used their long tongues to lick the blood from each other's face.

Jerrold looked at Butch with a satisfied expression. "Well done, Butch. You made an efficient kill." Jerrold looked at the skyline. "We should return to the bonfire."

Jerrold took the lead as the two ran in the direction of the shack. Butch was full and happy.

Butch broke out of the woods in the field near the pond. The glowing coals from the bonfire mesmerized him. He stopped well back in the shadows to check things out before continuing to move out into the opening.

A few family members who were not werewolves sat on logs around the fire.

Butch saw his father slumped against a log near the fire. A wave of disappointment swept over him. He wondered why his father couldn't stay awake to see how everything went for him on his first hunt.

Jerrold changed back to his human form with apparent ease. He approached the fire, where he gathered up his clothes and dressed. Butch watched him throw logs on the dying embers, sending sparks twirling skyward. The area around the fire brightened and pushed back the gray of pre-dawn. Butch settled down on his rear haunches in front of the rekindled fire to await the return of the rest of the pack.

It wasn't long before the other teams began to return. Each member approached the fire circle, walked up to Butch and licked his muzzle, congratulating him for his first successful kill. His chest pushed out, as he accepted the accolades from the pack. He realized this was just the beginning of his adventures as a werewolf.

* * *

Rod awoke and pulled himself up from the log. He watched the pack congratulating Butch. Seeing the look of excitement on Butch's muzzle brought a feeling of heaviness to Rod's heart. He knew there was nothing he could do to reverse what happened tonight. He had lost his son to the pack.

Butch watched his father walk toward him. He studied his father's eyes trying to read his thoughts.

Butch stood on his hind legs and said, "Dad, I made my first kill tonight."

"I know, son," Rod said, with a sad expression. "You are a member of the pack now, and even though you have turned into what I feared you would, I am still happy you are alive."

Butch was disappointed. He wondered why his father didn't show more support and excitement for him. *The hell with it*, he thought. He remembered how all of the werewolves accepted him, and his dejected feeling lifted.

Suddenly, a buzzing raced through his nerves. Butch dropped to the grass and curled up like a sleeping dog. The buzzing increased. Bolts of electricity exploded in his muscles. Feelings ran through his mind alternating between agitation and elation—agitated because he felt something unpleasant was going to happen to him, and yet elated because of what he had accomplished.

The buzzing grew stronger and his body started to jerk and spasm. He staggered to his feet and moved farther into the trees where he collapsed.

He moaned, "What's happening to me?"

Like echoes, he heard the crunching and cracking of his bones. He was changing. Pain coursed through his muscles. Fright welled in his mind. He realized he was changing back to his human form.

He whimpered. The transition took him from the height of pain, down into a valley of fear and back again. His body convulsed as the changes continued. Bones melted and then reformed into their human shapes. The pain diminished as the change reached completion. Perspiration soaked his body. He lay exhausted on the grass and leaves, relieved that the buzzing and pain were gone.

Cold seeped into his body as perspiration evaporated from his bare skin. Images of the night's activities played in his mind. The chase and the kill brought forth exhilarating feelings. Other emotions he experienced pushed their way to the forefront of his mind. When he realized all that really happened, his heart thumped and banged in his chest. The deer was there once again and he experienced the elation of flying over its back poised for the kill.

Experiencing the feelings brought on an intoxicating euphoria. He wondered if killing a human being would be more exciting than killing a deer. A twinge of guilt shot through him, but the pleasurable memory of killing the deer washed away the guilt. He could barely wait for the next hunt.

Jerrold stood behind some shrubs and watched Butch go through the change, then approached him.

The hair at the base of Butch's head sprang erect as he sensed grandfather's presence. Butch rolled over and his eyes riveted on his grandfather's eyes.

Jerrold was surprised that Butch had become aware of his presence so fast. Jerrold had never seen another werewolf react that quickly. He realized Butch was on his way to becoming an exceptional werewolf. A big smile widened across Jerrold's face at Butch's nakedness. He removed his jacket, draped it over Butch's shoulder and smiled again when Butch blushed.

"I didn't realize I was naked," Butch said, "Where are my clothes?" He tried to cover his genitals by sliding the jacket down around his waist and tying the arms together.

"You shredded them when you changed," Jerrold said. "You will learn to remove your clothing before making the change. Then you will have them when you change back. Don't worry, you can get dressed when we get back to the shack."

Jerrold put his arm around Butch's shoulder and guided him toward a bench overlooking the pond. Grandfather sat down, leaned back, extended his feet in front of him, and crossed them at his ankles. With a contented look, Jerrold gazed out over the pond, watching the cattails sway in a light breeze. Lily pads, yellow-blue in the gray of predawn, danced at the pleasure of miniature waves. Jerrold patted the spot next to him. Butch sat on the edge of the bench.

Jerrold stared at Butch for a moment and then said, "Butch, I know a lot has happened to you in a short time. I am sure you have a lot of questions you'd like answered."

Butch leaned forward and his mouth opened to speak.

Jerrold raised a hand. "Let me finish talking and then I will answer any questions you have. Right now, I need to make sure you understand some important things that come with being a part of a werewolf pack. What I'm going to say should answer most of your questions."

Butch nodded toward Jerrold. "Okay."

Jerrold uncrossed his legs and sat up straight. "Among humans, there exist many superstitions about werewolves."

Butch shook his head, but said nothing.

"You've perhaps heard that vampires and werewolves can be killed by silver bullets," Jerrold said. "That's a bunch of nonsense. Any bullet can kill us. The truth is any weapon can kill us just as they kill any other being. The reason humans think we cannot be killed is because we heal so much faster than humans do. Our tissues possess special properties that repair damaged cells and flesh within seconds. So it takes a lot of damage to kill us."

"Another misunderstanding that has been around for hundreds of years is the idea that werewolves must change every time a full moon lights the sky. That is pure hogwash," Jerrold said. "We have full control over the change, when and where the change takes place. We do need to eat human flesh but can go without it for as long as five years. If we wait longer than that, we start to lose control of our change. When that happens, we can be lost to the wild side. Self-preservation, protection of the pack, and the need for human flesh are by far the three biggest factors influencing our transformation."

Butch could not hold back any longer. "Tonight, as soon as I looked at the moon, the light hurt my eyes and I started to change," Butch, blurted out.

Jerrold smiled, "Remember, this was your first time. When you are not prepared, or are in a weakened condition, the full moon can be influential in causing a change. If you are in control, you will not change unless you choose to. Moonlight does have an effect on us, it still excites me after all these years, but it is a minor factor in bringing on the change."

Jerrold reached over and grabbed Butch by the shoulder. In a serious voice, he said, "But the main thing I want to emphasize is the importance of maintaining a tight rein on your control. Once you lose control of the change, the madness makes you careless and you can end up doing something crazy. For example, you may kill a human in front of witnesses." A shudder vibrated through the bench as Jerrold shivered. His voice grew louder. "Under no circumstances can you ever be seen in your werewolf form. If humans learn we exist, they'll hunt us down and exterminate us."

Butch absorbed the fear permeating from the Alpha and turned toward him, a concerned look on his face. "Grandpa, I didn't control my change tonight, it just happened. How do I learn to control it?"

"Don't worry Butch," Jerrold said in a comforting tone. "We'll guide you until you have full control of your change. Once you gain control, you can exist in either form."

"So I'll be able to control my change once I gain experience?"

"Yes, you will." The safety of the pack must be your first consideration." Jerrold cleared his throat. "To avoid anyone hunting on their own, the family plans a controlled human hunt as the individual need arises. An elder accompanies and assists the one who needs to make the kill. Everyone gets his or her turn within the five-year cycle. This has worked well for us. No one has gone over to the wild side since I became pack leader."

"But, Thomas lost control tonight," Butch reminded him.

"Yes, he did. These breakouts occur from time to time. That is why we never hunt alone. His lapse was due to his need to kill a human. His time must be close," Jerrold lowered his head and continued, "I stopped Thomas from going all the way over. If I couldn't have snapped him out of his wildness, I would have been forced to kill him." Jerrold looked up into Butch's eyes. "Do you know what sent him over the edge?"

Butch shrugged his shoulders and said, "No."

Jerrold said, "Last night you gave off many strong waves of excitement."

"Me?"

"Yes you! When you were going through your change, your emotions were unchecked. Those emotions transmitted to all of the pack. Thomas didn't hold his emotions in check and toppled over the edge. I hope you see how important maintaining self-control is."

Butch gulped before responding, "I didn't know. I'll make sure I control myself in the future."

"I know you will."

Curious, Butch asked, "Has anyone ever gone all the way over to the wild side?"

Jerrold hesitated and then said, "Yes, before my father became a werewolf, a whole pack lost control and stayed on the wild side. He and the townsmen hunted the werewolves down and killed them. It was at this time my father became infected by the Alpha."

"That must have happened when you were very young," Butch said.

"Yes, it did. There was one other instance of someone going over to the wild side." Jerrold shook his head remembering the incident. "When I was a young man, I was involved in tracking him down. It was a very sad time for my family. He was my uncle. My father and I hunted him for two days. We caught up to him in an isolated rural area and killed him." Jerrold choked back a sob, then said, "We ripped him to shreds."

Butch asked, "That is what would happen to me if I lost control?" He hoped grandfather might say he would be an exception.

"Yes, the pack would hunt you down and kill you," Jerrold said. "Remember, once you are lost to the wild side, getting back is next to impossible."

Butch shivered as he pictured his own pack ripping him apart. "Don't worry, I won't ever forget." Butch leaned forward on the park bench, his eyes widened. "Are all of my relatives werewolves?"

"No, your parents aren't. Rod decided not to become a werewolf, and you wouldn't have been one either, except he called on me to save your life."

"But, I don't understand. Why isn't Dad one?"

"All family members have a choice of becoming a werewolf. They need the blood of the Alpha to become a werewolf. Some chose not to, but they still serve the family in other ways. With Rod back in the fold, only your mother refuses to work with the family. The rest of the non-werewolf members are involved in family hunts and activities. The fact that I saved your life obligated your dad to become involved in the packs activities again."

"Why didn't dad want to be part of the pack?" Butch asked, trying to understand.

"He was ashamed of us. He wanted nothing to do with the pack from the time he was a child. He preferred to isolate himself and his own family from us."

"He rejected your way of life," Butch said.

"Right, but when he asked me to save your life, he knew what it would cost. Only an active pack member can ask a favor of the Alpha. When he asked me to save your life, he knew you would become one of us."

A lump grew in Butch's throat. He reached over, picked up his grandfather's hand, and held it tenderly. "I'm glad you saved me. I've never felt as alive as I did tonight when we were hunting. I'm glad Dad is a part of the pack again. He'll be here when I need him."

Jerrold gazed over the pond and watched a pink bubble grow on the horizon. "Listen to what I'm going to tell you," Jerrold said, as he gazed into

Butch's eyes. "To kill a human is a privilege requiring permission from the pack leader. Every member must preserve the secrecy of the pack. If humans learn of our existence, they will hunt us down and destroy us. The extinction of the pack is my greatest fear."

Butch pulled his hand free from his grandfather's hand. "I know, Grandpa, you already told me that. Don't treat me like a child."

Jerrold noted the irritation in Butch and said, "Well, here's something you don't know. You'll live much longer than a human."

Butch looked puzzled, "How much longer?"

"At least four hundred years."

"What? You mean I won't die when I'm seventy or eighty?"

"Not unless someone kills you."

Butch slapped his leg. "Hell, that's wonderful."

"Yes, but it will also create some problems for you."

Butch's eyebrows furrowed. He could not think of any disadvantages of living four hundred years. "How can living that long be a bad thing?"

"For instance, do you plan on ever getting married?" Jerrold said.

"Well, sure I do."

"What happens when your wife grows old and dies long before you do?"

Butch thought of losing someone he loved, and understood what his grandfather was trying to tell him.

Jerrold hesitated and then said, "Of course, you could always make her a werewolf."

Butch's face brightened, as the problem appeared solved. "Yeah, I could do that."

"I have married three times," Jerrold said. "Each time my wife chose to remain a human. I have outlived each of these women I loved." Grandfather looked down.

Butch watched sadness sweep over Grandpa Jerrold's face.

"It hurts to lose someone you've loved for forty years or longer."

"I see what you mean."

"The sun will be up soon," Jerrold said. "Let's get back to the shack and get you some clothes and a few hours' sleep."

Butch extended his hand and stopped Jerrold from getting up. "I'm still worried about how to control the change. I have no idea how I did it last night."

"You need not worry."

"What if the change happens when I don't want it to?"

Jerrold chuckled and patted Butch's hand. "Don't worry. To change takes effort on your part. Like learning anything new, you'll find a way that works best for you and then perfect it. Some of us use anger to work the change. Others recall previous experiences or feelings to bring on the change."

Butch's eyes grew bigger. "You mean, like when I saw that all of you were werewolves, the fear I felt caused me to change?"

Jerrold nodded. "It may not be the way you do it in the future. Just make sure you find a method you can control." Jerrold pinched his lips into a pout and then continued. "Anger isn't the best way to bring on the change. Most of us can't control our anger well enough. It often results in things getting out of hand. With anger, you might find yourself changing too fast. If that happens, you have to regain control of your thoughts and slow down the process."

"But how do I control my thoughts?"

"With a steel will—balance is the key," Jerrold said. "Remember, as a werewolf, you still retain your intelligence. You have to learn at what point to stop the transition. If you let it go too far, you will cross to the animal side. Then it is just a matter of bringing yourself back until you are in balance with the two forms—human and werewolf."

Butch said, "How far did Uncle Thomas go?"

Jerrold felt goose bumps as he remembered that earlier incident. "He was through his change, and a little bit too far toward the animal side. He was losing control. If I hadn't stopped him, he would've continued on."

"And then what?"

"When you get far enough to the wild side, only human flesh will satisfy the madness. Thomas would have run off in search of the nearest humans and killed them." Jerrold grabbed Butch's arm. "Can you see what that would have done to the rest of us? We could have been exposed by his madness. I would have killed him tonight rather than let that happen to the pack."

Butch stared at the ground and then looked up and changed the subject. "You know, Grandfather, it scares me to think of killing another human being. I don't know if I can do it." A pained expression covered Butch's face. "What if I can't?"

Jerrold smiled. "That should be the least of your concerns. Take my word for it. You will be ready and able to kill a human when the time comes. The desire for human flesh will increase in you until your entire mind can think of nothing else. You will have to kill and eat human flesh to drive the incessant wild thoughts from your mind."

Butch did not understand everything his grandfather had told him. "Why is human flesh so special? I was satisfied after killing and eating the deer."

Jerrold said, "You became a werewolf for the first time last night. The need for human flesh has not developed in you yet, but it will. We do not know what makes human flesh able to satisfy our craving, but it does. There may be some chemical present in human flesh that helps us keep the animal side in submission."

Jerrold rubbed his shoulder. "Maybe the frenzy that goes along with killing a human satisfies the need to kill again, or maybe it's the excitement of the hunt—the chase and the kill. Hunting and killing deer is nothing compared to hunting and killing humans." Grandfather shook his head. "Whatever the reason, all I know is that every five years I have to kill and eat human flesh or risk the slide into madness."

Butch gave serious thought to what Grandfather shared with him. He nodded, "I hope I'm ready when the time comes. You know, I enjoyed hunting and killing that deer tonight, but killing a human will take some getting used to."

Jerrold faded from Butch's view, as thoughts of the night's hunt raced through his mind. His heart started thumping. The mental picture of the deer brought back the wonderful feelings he had experienced during the chase. He wondered if maybe he could use those thoughts to start his change.

He blinked and saw that Jerrold was still standing before him.

"I know what you're saying Butch, but when the time comes, you will kill humans and enjoy doing it."

Butch gave Grandfather's words some more thought. He was shocked that his subconscious had already accepted the idea of killing humans, of eating another human being. The growing excitement in his mind was euphoric. The desire to taste human flesh welled up in his mind. He shook his buzzing head and realized that when the time came to kill a human, he would not hesitate. His human side tried to tell him it was wrong to kill another human, but the stronger animal side rationalized the necessity for doing it.

Butch asked, "When will I be able to hunt humans?"

"It will be very soon. We waste so much time killing humans one at a time, so I've decided to do a mass killing instead of spreading them out over five years."

"Isn't that going to draw a lot of attention to our pack?"

"Not if we do everything according to my plan. I've scheduled a special hunt for this coming October. We'll do it the night of the harvest moon."

Butch straightened his shoulders. "Should I feel guilty for wanting to kill a human?"

"No, my son, we are what we are. Being a werewolf is what we are. We don't have to apologize for what we have inherited. We have no more control over our needs than any of our other drives, such as thirst, hunger, or survival."

Jerrold put his arms around Butch and hugged him

The sunshine of a new dawn broke over the treetops signaling the beginning of not just a new day, but also a new era.

CHAPTER 7
LET'S PLAN THE FEAST

The first Saturday in August started out as a cold, dreary day. Black cumulonimbus clouds rolled overhead threatening the peace and tranquility of what was to be a memorable day for the Guhl family. Accompanying the menacing weather was a cold north wind. Raindrops splattered against the basement window. The rat-tat-tat noise of pellets hitting the window caught Butch's attention.

Butch poked Brad and pointed to the windows. Brad made a face, hit Carey on the arm, and pointed to the ice crystals on the window.

Carey pounded the arm of the couch. "Shit, that's all we need is an ice storm in August."

The entire Guhl pack gathered in the basement of Jerrold's mansion. The meeting room was more than adequate to hold all the family members. They waited for Jerrold to start the meeting. Older family members sat around a large oblong mahogany table occupying the center of the room. Many of the non-werewolf members made up the second circle, sitting on chairs and sofas.

The walls of the meeting room were ten feet high. Ornate decorations and expensive family portraits covered the walls. The house served as the headquarters for the Guhl werewolf pack. Who would expect a werewolf to live in the prestigious and expensive Wedgewood development in Woodbury, Minnesota?

The back of the mansion faced an eighteen-hole golf course. Large homes occupied the land around Colby Lake and surrounded the golf course to the south and east.

Logs blazed in the massive brick fireplace at the end of the room, creating a cozy atmosphere for an unusual meeting on a cold day. Brad complained that the basement felt like a sauna. Avoiding the heat was one of the reasons Butch, Carey, and Brad sat on the floor against the wall where it was cooler.

This was a very important meeting. The Guhl pack was here to plan for their human hunt in October, when each of the twenty-four members of the pack would make a kill.

Butch jumped when Jerrold banged his hands on the table. "Okay everyone. Let's get down to business. As each of you know we're changing the way we make our kills. For too long we have made our kill one werewolf at a time, spread out over the five-year cycle. But that takes up too much time and energy of the pack. So from now on we will make all of our kills in one attack."

Butch pushed Carey over and sat up with a determined look on his face. He did not want to miss anything to do with his first hunt.

Jerrold turned the slide projector on. An enlarged map of Minnesota flashed on a beady, white screen, suspended over the fireplace.

"The summer is coming to an end and we need to begin preparations for our Autumn Hunt. I sent a number of you out to search for a suitable target. Let's hear what you've found," Jerrold said, as he panned the room waiting for a response.

Brad started to whisper something to Butch.

"Brad, be quiet," Butch said. "I don't want to miss anything."

Brad leaned back against the wall with a sullen look on his face.

Bruce, Jerrold's second son, with jet-black hair and smooth olive skin, pushed his chair back from the table and stood up. "Yes, Father, I've found one. I scouted the town of McGregor. It's located on Highway 210."

Jerrold slapped a pointer on the screen and looked quizzically at Bruce, waiting for additional directions.

"It's farther to the right."

The pointer moved across the screen.

"East of Aitkin," Bruce said. "Yes, right there. The town has a population of 450 people."

Jerrold studied the spot on the map and the surrounding area for a minute and then said, "Okay, any comments?"

Thomas, Jerrold's fifth oldest son, raised his hand like a student.

Jerrold smiled. "Thomas, go ahead."

"I think I've found the perfect spot. This town is smaller than McGregor. The population is two hundred and forty people. It's located in the western part of the state, just east of Fergus Falls."

Jerrold moved the pointer to the western boundary of Minnesota.

"Right there is Ottertail lake. The city of Ottertail is next to the lake." Thomas waited until his father moved the pointer to the right spot before continuing. "Ottertail is a quiet farming community located on Highway 108. We would have to block traffic on the east and west sides of town. There are three possible escape routes—one being across the lake, another through farm land, and the third on one of three other roads leading out of town."

Jerrold studied Thomas' selection and then turned back to the group. "Good job, boys," Jerrold said, "both spots have potential."

Butch watched Jerrold, suspecting he did not like either of the spots mentioned.

Jerrold looked around the room before saying, "Has anyone else found a good target?"

Butch watched Uncle Steve lean back, studying the map, with furrowed brow.

"I don't like McGregor," Steve said, more to himself but loud enough for everyone to hear. "The population is too large for our family to handle without losing control of the situation. With that many people, the chance that someone would escape and summon help is too great. We can't afford exposure, or the chance of not being able to make a safe withdrawal. I think we would have a problem interrupting traffic on Highway 210, because of the large amount of traffic it carries. All that heavy traffic might get in the way of our project and lead to someone seeing something they shouldn't."

"Good point Steve," chimed in Barbara, Jerrold's oldest daughter. She flipped the bottom of her curls and then, without being aware of it, wrapped hair around her fingers. "I was thinking the same thing, regarding both Mc-Gregor and Ottertail." She banged her pencil twice on the table to emphasize her point and then added, "Ottertail has too many roads. For me, the risks with both of these places are too great."

Diana interrupted Barbra in a high-pitched, excited voice. "Well, if you don't like those two targets, let me tell you the perfect town for this year's feeding."

Even though Diana, who was Jerrold's youngest daughter, was not a were-wolf member of the family, she was still involved in pack activities.

"Charles, the kids and I spent a week in June vacationing near a small town called Longville, which is located in North Central Minnesota."

Jerrold moved the pointer across the map and looked at her for directions.

"Further to the right, Dad—no, east of Walker on Highway 200," she directed. "Now, go south on Highway 84—there, you got it. The population is under 200. We would have to block Highway 84, both north and south of town. Two smaller highways come into town. Highway 5 from the west and Highway 7 from the east. They don't carry much traffic and shouldn't be a problem. We can use either of them as escape routes if needed. If we can't use the roads, then the surrounding wooded areas offer many escape routes. For example, Land-O-Lakes State Forest is just southeast of Longville. This whole area is a wilderness where we could disappear without a trace. Swamp land to the east of town would make a nice place to dispose of the kills."

Butch smiled when Diana sucked in a big volume of air and continued talking, "I believe Longville is a better town than the one we attacked seven or eight years ago. What was the name of it?" She pumped her hand in the air trying to remember the name of it and looked around the table for some help. "C'mon, you remember when six of the pack needed to make a kill and we couldn't wait to do them one at a time. We didn't do any planning and a couple of humans saw us. We fled town leaving three of the bodies unburied. What was the name of that town?"

"It was—uh—Littlefork," Francis said. He was Jerrold's youngest son, the only blond child in the Guhl family.

"Yeah, that's right," Diana said, shaking her head. "Well, Dad, how does Longville look to you?"

Jerrold studied the map, looking back and forth between the three suggested sites. A few heads began to nod. Smiles broke out on faces of several of the older pack members seated around the table.

Butch felt a rise of excitement in the room. He suspected his first hunt with the pack for humans would take place in Longville.

Grandfather looked around the room and noted the nodding heads, "Okay, it looks like we've picked the target. Let's get down to our assignments." He clicked to the next slide and a list of names and assignments popped onto the screen.

Coordination of project—Jerrold, Richard, Diana and Butch

Street and house attack assignments—Richard, Amy, and
   Aerial

Road isolation—Bruce, Barbara, George, Butch and Dean

Communications disruption—Francis, Steve, Xianth, Fred and
   Aerial

Escape routes and safe houses—Thomas, Brad, Jake, Elliot and
   Carey

Community scouts—Diana, Charles, William, Coreen and
   Cherrie

Jerrold gave everyone ample time to study the list and then said, "The rest of you will volunteer for the committee you would like to serve on. If you have any objections to your assignments and would like to be on a different committee, talk to me."

Thomas scratched his head. "How many hideouts should we plan for?"

Richard turned toward his younger brother, "I'd suggest at least two." He looked at his father. "This looks good to me. Do you think we need more than two?"

"You'd better plan on two for now. Once we are further along in the planning we may want to add another one. Just make sure to cover every possible contingency."

"Money is no problem," Richard said. "Just make sure you turn in expense vouchers for everything."

Butch caught Grandfather looking at him and flinched at the intensity of his gaze.

Jerrold looked around the room and said, "The full moon occurs on the third Wednesday in October. I've set our attack for that night. The pack will meet in one month. That should give everyone time to work out the details of their assignments and arrange vacation time to visit Longville. Report any useful information to the Coordinating Committee. When you complete your assignments, we'll add your information to our database."

Remember, we kill one human for each werewolf. If we carefully dispose of the remains in the swamps around Longville, there shouldn't be too big a big stink over the missing people. All plans must be completed a week before the full moon or we'll postpone the attack until November."

"Okay, remember—we need to do it right, so we don't put ourselves at risk for another five years. If anything goes wrong during the attack and we don't complete our quota, we'll finish the necessary kills individually sometime in November or December. The worst thing that could possibly happen is for us to be exposed."

Butch felt the excitement emanating from others in the room. Like an aphrodisiac, a growing excitement pulsed through his body. The remembrance of his deer kill earlier in the summer rolled like a film through his mind. For him, the deer kill was a memorable time, where he lived on the edge. It was hard to imagine that killing humans could be that much better than killing a deer. He understood there was much more at stake in an operation involving so many werewolves and the killing of twenty-four humans.

Fear shot through his mind when he considered that humans would hunt them down if they screwed up. He saw the value of planning each step carefully, as they were doing.

He returned to the moment and heard Grandfather say, "If there are no other comments or concerns, let's go to work. Happy hunting."

* * *

The next day, Diana called Woman Lake Lodge and arranged to stay there again. She asked for the same cabin her family had occupied in June and was surprised when the owner said it was available. Charles and Diana talked to Walter Jacobson, their dry cleaning business manager and arranged for him to take over the shop for the rest of August and September. The following Monday they left on an extended vacation.

As second in command, Richard insisted that before the pack carried out the invasion of Longville, everyone must become familiar with the town. It was important they see the houses they were going to attack, and the places where they would dispose of their kills. Once the safe sites had been set up, each pack member would travel the various escape routes. Charles worked out a schedule of when each of the pack members would visit the Longville area and stay with Diana and Charles on Woman Lake. This would be the pack's base of operations until the Longville attack.

Butch, Carey, and Brad started referring to the expedition in October as 'Moonlight Madness'. Soon everyone was using the title.

Bruce, Barbara, and Thomas drove up to Longville two days after Diana and Charles had settled in at the resort. They met with an agent from the Cass Real Estate agency. They let the realtor know they were looking for two parcels of land along Highway 84. The real estate agent showed them two twenty-acre sites, one on the north side and the other south of town. The cost of the wooded parcels was inflated, but they did not haggle over a few dollars and purchased both.

Water covered part of both pieces of property near Highway 84. Culverts under the highway would drain the wet spots and a road into the property would make the parcels acceptable to build on. Putting in culverts was the perfect reason for digging up Highway 84 and stopping traffic the night of the attack.

Thomas, Jake, and Elliot hired a four-passenger Cessna to fly them to Longville during the second week of August. The reason given was to scout out a good deer hunting spot for November's hunting season. They spent the whole week flying over the area. Using aerial maps, they located three different trails leading to safe sites. One site was at a resort on Inguadona Lake. The team rented six cabins for the last two weeks in October. They told the owners they were going to have a family reunion. The second site was for backup. It was isolated in the Land-O-Lakes State Forest where a group of rustic cabins the Forest Service rented out for a nominal fee. This location was quite a hike, but not for a pack of werewolves.

They entertained the pilot in the evenings by hitting all of the local dance spots and bars. Jake, being fourteen, stayed with Charles and Diana at the resort on Woman's Lake.

Brad and Carey arrived in Longville toward the end of the second week of August and grumbled as they hiked the trails. The mosquitoes and black flies were tenacious, especially when hiking in human form through the swamps. They confirmed the usability of the swamp trail leading to Inguadona Lodge. A number of the spouses, who were not werewolves, would occupy the cabins and have everything set up for the family reunion. Butch's parents, Rod and Elizabeth volunteered to prepare the Land-O-Lakes site, in case the alternate site was needed.

Dean, George and Butch drove to Walker, the county seat of Cass County. At the courthouse, they arranged for the necessary permits needed to dig up Highway 84. After getting the go ahead, they hired an excavation company from Walker to install the culverts under Highway 84, at sites north and south of Longville. They arranged for the digging to take place on the day of the attack—Wednesday.

When Francis and Xianth visited Woman Lake Lodge the last week in August, they spent time locating telephone, electrical relay stations and cell phone towers. It took them several days to select the best spots to disrupt communications to the town. By the time their vacation ended, they had mapped the best approach to the structures and how they would be destroyed.

* * *

Three days later, Fred, Arial and Steve joined Francis and Xianth in Longville. They spent a few days water skiing and fishing on Woman Lake. In the evenings, they enjoyed the nightclubs in the area. They used the last two days before returning to the Twin Cities to locate the exact address of every ham operator with battery backup in Longville. Finding the ham operators was easy. Their antennas were visible. It took more effort to determine which ones possessed battery backup. Those operators would be the first people to die in Longville.

* * *

September arrived. School reopened and everything was proceeding as planned toward 'Moonlight Madness'. Every few days, information poured in from the various teams. When Butch was in the Twin Cities, he helped load the information into the Alpha's computers. The files were full of valuable information, including each member's name and assignment, a timeline of when pack members would journey to Longville and with whom, what they were to accomplish, and once the job was completed, a write-up of their findings.

Jerrold insisted the plan be established in such detail that he would know where every pack member was at any given minute during the actual attack.

October started out as a dry, warm month. Jerrold sat in the library studying the computer screen. Closing the Venetian blinds made it easier to see the computer screens. Jerrold stared at the information on the screen, reading the material over for the third time. He smiled with pride at the efficiency of his children and grandchildren. He was confident the details of the plan to attack Longville were fine-tuned. There should be no problems. But in the back of his mind he thought, *when you don't anticipate difficulty, that's when it pops up.*

Sitting on the other side of the library from Grandfather, Butch sat in a leather recliner analyzing printouts from the accumulated information coming in. He read page after page, running a red pen through changes and writing suggestions in the margin detailing how he would modify the plan.

Butch's eyes watered and itched from staring so long at the computer printouts. He pushed his knuckles against his eyelids and moved them back and forth, trying to relieve the strain. He looked up and stared at his grandfather.

Since Butch began working on the Longville raid, his every thought focused on the plan. Being involved made him feel needed. He wasn't sure if it was all the detailed work he did on the plan, or if it was the prize at the end of all the planning, that made him feel excited and alive.

Butch's thoughts flashed back several months, to his former life, as a stupid, lost kid. That life was a long time ago—ancient history now. He understood why his father had been so disappointed in him. He had been a liar, a cheat, and high on drugs most of the time.

In his new life, everything had changed; he was responsible, needed, and committed. Others depended on him to do his job and he worked hard to do it to the best of his ability. He felt like he belonged to the family. There was no way he was going to let them down.

Butch's imagination took him off into one of his daydreams. He told himself, *Someday I will lead the pack.* He understood that in order for him to do that, he would have to challenge his grandfather for leadership of the pack. He would have to fight him and force him to step down. He pictured the two of them standing nose-to-nose, ready to do battle. After he was victorious, he would change some of the ways things operated in the pack. He saw himself speaking to the pack at a future planning session. He would be the one that everyone looked to for leadership.

Butch also envisioned a new scene. He saw himself breaking down the front door of a home, attacking and killing the people inside. The scene was real in his mind. His heart started to bang in his chest. He moaned at the realism of the daydream. He could almost taste the human flesh. The vision looked so real, saliva squirted into his mouth at the thought of eating human flesh. His stomach growled in protest—it wanted the real thing. Sweat beaded on his forehead and ran down his face. A loud buzzing grew in his mind. He moaned aloud, losing his daydream.

His heart still slammed against his ribs. He gasped for breath. His hands tingled. He held them up to his face and recoiled. A dense mass of tangled fur covered the misshapen bony structure of his former hands. Fingernails curled into claws. With a frightened inhalation, he brushed his face with his hand and felt a knobby, elongated jawbone. He moved his hand down the length of the jaw and felt the sharp fangs protruding from his mouth. He knew he was changing, and had to stop it.

The springs of Jerrold's chair squeaked as he turned and watched Butch fight the transformation.

Butch wasn't aware of Jerrold or the squeaking chair. He said, "Shit." He trembled and slipped to the edge of his chair. *I won't lose control. I can't,* he thought, then he bit down on his tongue. Pain shot through his brain. Blood leaked from the edge of his mouth.

Anxiety and fear over the change caused it to accelerate. His spine cracked, reshaping itself to better accommodate the contour of the werewolf form. Butch was afraid that if he did not stop the emotional high he was experiencing, he would lose control and end up locked on the wild side.

Butch took in a deep breath of air and let it out with a hiss. He forced himself to visualize white, cottony clouds, floating in a bright, blue sky. He focused on relaxing his muscles as he floated on one of the soft clouds. Butch crunched his eyes closed and saw yellow stars exploding on a black background. He pictured his racing heart, and then clamped down on that thought as he tried to slow it down. After a few anxious seconds, his pulse slowed.

He felt there might be a chance to regain control of his runaway emotions. He breathed in and then let the air escape from his lungs. He concentrated on calm thoughts and pictured himself in human form. In seconds, the crunching of bones stopped. The room was quiet for what felt like an eternity, and then Butch felt his bones begin to bend and melt, as the reversal began. The change back to his human form picked up speed.

With fear racing through his mind, Butch opened his eyes and glanced at his hands. A wave of relief swept through his stomach. His hands were human again. He sighed with relief, but his body continued to shake. He was surprised to see the legs of his jeans and the sleeves of his shirt were tattered and torn.

"Well done, my boy."

Butch jumped when he heard his grandfather's voice. He turned with a snarl and saw Jerrold examining him from across the room.

Grandfather stood next to his computer, a big smile on his face. "I have never seen another werewolf reverse the change as fast or as easily as you did, Butch."

"Easy," Butch cried. "I had a hard time stopping the change. I was so frightened. I didn't even know the change had started until it was already happening."

Jerrold tapped the computer table with his knuckle emphasizing each word he said. "Well, you've learned something, haven't you?"

Butch breathed a sigh of relief. "Yeah, I learned that it is easy to change, and that I've got to keep better control of my thoughts."

Jerrold shook his head in agreement. "Butch, you will be a leader of the pack someday. Work hard and learn all you can. Remember, being stronger than others is only one requirement of being a leader. You must also be intelligent and able to see the big picture. You just proved you have exceptional self-control. No one in the pack could have stopped the change as fast as you did."

Butch's face broke out into a wide smile. He was happy for the praise his grandfather bestowed on him. He now knew where his destiny lay—as leader of the pack.

CHAPTER 8
REGRETS AND ACCEPTANCE

Butch switched on the lamp on his father's desk. It was not late, but the clouds outside made the room darker. Butch plopped down in Rod's padded swivel chair and threw his feet up on the desk. He squinted as he sat back and peeled a banana.

Rod walked into his office and saw Butch sitting in his chair. He changed direction and sat on the stuffed leather sofa. "Son, I need to talk with you."

"Sure, Dad, what's up?"

"I knew there was no turning back once you received the tainted blood from my father," Rod said, exhibiting a degree of nervousness.

"Hey, Pops, I don't consider my blood tainted."

Rod nodded. "Okay, that's a matter of opinion," Rod countered, and then continued before Butch could mount his defense. "Your grandfather told me you experienced an unexpected change yesterday and that you were able to easily regain control."

"Boy did I ever have a problem. I wouldn't say it was easy to handle," Butch said. He looked at his father and a frown crept across his forehead. "Don't worry. I handled it. I just let my thoughts get away from me. It won't happen again."

"Good," Rod said with a smile and then his face grew serious. "Butch, I'd like you to make me a promise."

"Yeah," Butch said gazing at his dad with a suspicious look.

"For my sake, will you promise not to kill more humans than the one you have to kill every five years?"

A puzzled expression grew across Butch's face, "Grandfather says we can't kill at any other time."

Rod bounced his hands on his knees and said, "What he says isn't necessarily what happens. There are a number of humans killed by werewolves that father is never aware of. Some don't tell him everything they do."

Butch stood up with a surprised look on his face, "I find that hard to believe."

"Some of your relatives don't always control their changes. Some kill humans without the Alpha knowing. A few enjoy killing too much. They don't wait for their regularly scheduled feeding time. They are not out of control, but kill just for the thrill. A few indulge their desires as the opportunity presents itself. I believe they actually get enjoyment from violating the Alpha's orders. I think father suspects it is happening, but doesn't know how to stop it."

Butch stepped closer to his father and interrupted him. "But—but—Grandfather said he would hunt down and kill anyone that goes off and kills on their own."

"The ones doing the killings are not out of control. They are very careful. Your grandfather would discipline them if he knew who was doing it. The kills are made on homeless people who are seldom missed or reported to the authorities."

Ashen-faced, Butch stumbled back to the desk chair and sat down. "Jesus, I can't believe it."

"Believe it! I have researched the killings and know it's happening. I just don't know who is doing it."

"Okay, I believe you, but I don't know if I can promise not to kill more than one human. It depends upon the circumstances. I don't know enough about my needs. I don't want to lie to you Dad, but if I can control this force that has me, I'll do what you ask."

"Thank you for that much. I guess that's all I can hope for."

Butch sat up and looked into his father's eyes. "Dad, is that why you never became a werewolf, because you'd have to kill a human?"

"That's the main reason." Rod's eyes drooped. "When I was very young . . . seven or eight, I witnessed the killing of a human child by Richard. It sickened me. I could not condone killing innocent children. After that, I wanted nothing to do with being a werewolf." Rod looked at Butch. "Do you understand, son?"

"Yeah, Dad, I do. Remember, there was no choice for me. I don't blame you, but for me getting the werewolf blood was the best thing that could have happened to me. The way my life was heading, I would have ended up in prison, or killed in some holdup. As much as you detest the werewolf way. I owe my life to it."

Rod sat up straight and slapped his knees with open hands. "You're right."

Butch's eyes dilated in surprise. He didn't expect his father to agree with him. "You know, Dad, today I learned two things. I learned how easy it is to lose control and that I need to clamp down on my emotions. And I realize that if I can gain that control, someday I'll be the pack leader."

Rod's eyebrows rose.

Butch read his father's skepticism in his face. "I mean it, Dad. I've found something that really interests me, something that I can devote all of my energy to."

Rod lifted his hands palms-up. "I hope you can fulfill your dream. And yet, at the same time, I'm filled with sadness for humanity."

"Dad, I understand where you're coming from, but the world will have to take care of itself, just like I'm going to take care of myself."

CHAPTER 9
THE NIGHT OF THE HARVEST MOON

quaking aspen trees stood like sentinels around Colby Lake. The crisp autumn air had turned the leaves yellow. In a gentle breeze, the leaves trembled, weakening their hold on the branches.

Along the west shore of the lake, a cluster of Red pine trees huddled, preparing for the colder days that lay ahead. Wind whistled through the needles, breaking free the dead, reddish-brown ones, which floated to the ground to form a spongy cushion. October marked the end of the growing season.

Butch trembled, as though he was empathizing with the shaking leaves. Philosophically, he thought all things must look forward to the same fate—death. He sat on a park bench looking out over Colby Lake and listened to the wind whistle through the pines.

The smell of decaying leaves and fresh mown grass came to him on the wind. In front of him, several milkweed plants, with pods open and dry, glistened in the sun. The wind picked up a few of the remaining silken parachutes from the pods and carried them away, spreading hope for the next generation.

Butch felt agitated, because the job of planning for 'Moonlight Madness' was completed and now all he could do was wait impatiently for the event to arrive. He was anxious for the human hunt to take place. The entire pack was showing signs of anxiety. It was becoming difficult to control his feelings. He had to force himself to complete his daily mundane tasks. He needed to feed.

To lay his anxiety aside, he busied himself with several projects at once, hoping the increased workload would divert his thoughts from the promise of ultimate ecstasy. He thought that by working hard, the date for 'Moonlight Madness' would arrive that much faster. He was not sure if any of these tactics would work, but he knew that the killing of his first human lay just ahead. As far as he was concerned, all the preparations for the invasion of Longville were in place, waiting implementation. He was more than ready.

The non-werewolf members, Sharrie, Eleanor, Marsha, Nicole, and several others had left on Sunday to join the rest of the pack already at the resort on Inguadona Lake. The family reunion would be held at the resort with everyone in attendance. Rod and Elizabeth would open up the cabins in the woods near Land-O-Lakes State Forest. This second site would be available if necessary.

On Monday, the Isolation Committee left for Longville. All of the necessary County and State permits had been approved two weeks ago. The committees' primary task was to check on the road excavation crews to make sure everything took place on schedule. There could be no delays. The road equipment must begin digging Wednesday morning—no sooner, no later.

According to the plan, the excavation crew would close Highway 84 Wednesday and begin digging. Late in the afternoon, the culverts would be set. Thursday morning the workers would fill the ditches and the highway patched with new tarmac. By the end of the day, the highway would be back to normal and open to traffic.

Grandfather, Richard, Amy and Arial planned to arrive in Longville Monday afternoon. They would stay with Diana and Charles's family at Woman Lake Resort.

* * *

Late Wednesday morning the digging started on Highway 84 on both sides of town. The backhoe tore up the tarmac just south of where Hardy lane intersected the highway north of town. On the south end, a bulldozer dug up Highway 84 where it intersected School Lane. Backed-up traffic was diverted onto a temporary gravel road.

The group planning to disrupt communications arrived at the resort on Inguadona Lake Wednesday afternoon. After settling into the cabins, they drove to Longville and ate a late lunch. They would stay in town until it was time to take the necessary steps to shut down phone lines, cell phone towers, and electrical lines.

By 6:00 p. m., Highway 84 north and south of Longville were no longer passable. Townspeople left their cars at the excavation site and walked around the deep trench and piles of gravel to get home. It was either walk, or drive miles out of their way to come into town.

At 7:00 p.m., the phone service went dead. At 7:30, all of the lights in Longville went out. At 7:45, cell phone towers ceased to function. The Ham operators with battery backup were the only link to the outside world, and only until the batteries died. The feeding frenzy would begin soon.

The harvest moon, large and pale gold, rose above the eastern horizon an hour before sunset. Butch watched the sun disappear over the western horizon, as the moon rose higher in the east. Moonlight reached his eyes like burning flames, incapacitating any mercy that remained within him. In spite of what Grandfather had said about moonlight not being a strong factor in bringing on the change, it affected Butch a great deal.

This being his first hunt, he was to accompany Grandfather and Charles. For efficiency and safety, other members of the Guhl family hunted in groups of two or three. Before the night was over, twenty-four Longville residents would die and disappear, if everything went according to plan.

Jerrold stood with Charles and Butch behind a screen of trees in the forest near their first target. When it was dark, the long awaited feeding would begin.

Butch paced, glancing skyward each time he turned. As darkness increased, the moon became bright gold. It appeared suspended in the sky by a spider web of fine branches from a dozen trees. Moonbeams appeared to wrap around the branches and tether the moon in place. The moon looked like an alien spotlight, poised to witness the horror that would begin very soon.

Twenty-four werewolves were in their assigned positions. Butch and Charles stirred restlessly in the bushes nearby. Jerrold looked at the pair and said, "Time to change."

Fear shot through Butch's body—but he was ready. The waiting was over. What he had looked forward to all summer was finally here. He hunched his shoulders and concentrated on images of his first kill, the deer. He felt the change begin. Butch's head turned back and his eyes became glued on the moon. "The light's so bright," he cried out. He rubbed his eyes with hair-covered hands. "I can't see."

"Shh, it will pass," Jerrold said.

Butch twisted in pain as bones crunched. Growth hormones poured forth from his endocrine glands, stimulating the flow of calcium deposits from bones into his blood stream, and then back into the bone cells again. Bones reformed into their new shapes. Muscle elongated to accommodate the modified bones. Butch grimaced with pain as a new series of changes swept over him.

He welcomed the pain for what it promised—the pleasures to come. The pain intensified and he squirmed. Muscles bulged and hair shot out from his skin. A craving for human flesh multiplied with each breath and fueled the growing desire to kill and rip apart a human with his fangs. Gastric juices flooded into his growling stomach.

Careful, Butch thought, *I can't let the animal side overpower me and gain control.*

The warning did nothing to slow his change. If anything, it raced through him faster than ever. Primitive animal thoughts erupted in his mind. *I have to maintain control, I must,* he moaned. His body twisted as he reacted to the internal fight—a fight he was losing.

The intense feelings bursting from his neurons were pushing him beyond reason. The animal side surged to the forefront, becoming dominant, suppressing rational thought and any semblance of control.

Jerrold watched Butch battle for control. Jerrold raced through his own change and launched himself through the air at Butch, crashing into him.

Butch rolled against a tree trunk and lay stunned for a few moments. Uncontrollable anger flooded his brain like a glowing red ball. Then the red ball exploded. Butch growled and jumped back to his feet.

Grandfather bared his fangs and snarled a warning. "Listen to me, Butch."

Butch heard the warning, but his thoughts were unfocused. The warning echoed through an empty, unreceptive chamber.

"Maintain self-control," Jerrold said, walking stiff-legged toward Butch.

Slobber ran from the corners of Butch's mouth. Madness ruled. He stared at his grandfather without recognition. In his mind, he saw an enemy, a creature on the attack.

Butch pranced away from the attacker. The beast in him wanted to feed.

Jerrold recognized the signs. He feared Butch was ready to bolt. If he ran, Jerrold was not sure he could catch him. "Control yourself or I will have to hurt you." Jerrold said, lowering his body. He mentally projected as loudly as possible, "I am the pack leader. You must obey me." His body coiled.

Butch roared a challenge. His rational side had given way to animal desires. Hostile, evil thoughts flipped through his mind, relegating the clear message Grandfather sent him to some hidden recess in the back of his mind.

"I don't have to listen to you," Butch said, directing his rage back at Jerrold. "I don't have to obey anyone."

Butch's muscles bunched in preparation to attack. Before he could spring, Jerrold uncoiled like a spring and slammed into Butch's chest, bowling him over again. Jerrold's right paw slashed Butch across the neck, the claws biting deep.

The pain tore through Butch's growing wildness and fear exploded in his mind. The fear returned a bit of reason. Jerrold stood growling over Butch, fangs just inches from his exposed throat, ready to execute the killing bite, if necessary.

With a submissive yip, Butch relaxed and worked his way to a four-legged stance, his tail curled between his legs. He hung his head, embarrassed at having lost control. "Thank you," Butch said. "I didn't know I'd lost control. It won't happen again." Butch was repentant. He dropped to his belly and crawled forward until he lay exposed under the Alpha's bared fangs. Blood flowed from the wound on his neck and shoulder, matting his fur. Butch ignored the wounds, even as the damaged tissues began to close and the bleeding stopped.

Jerrold relaxed. He was glad to have his grandson under control again. He knew how easy it was to lose the battle. The important thing was that he had averted another calamity. "I warned you to control the wild side," Jerrold said. "If it happens again, I won't be so lenient. Now get up."

Butch raised his muzzle and licked the Alpha's face.

Charles, who had watched the conflict, remained mesmerized. He was still shaking as he stepped toward Butch. "Shit, Butch, you scared the hell out of me."

"Not half as scared as I'm feeling now," Butch said. He looked at the ground, not able to meet his uncle's eyes.

"Finish your change, Charles," Jerrold said. "We've got work to do."

Their target was one of the three ham operators on the list. It was essential that they eliminate those with battery backup. This was the most critical assignment. If they did not put the ham radios out of commission, calls for help could flood the airwaves and bring police from surrounding towns. The ham operators were now the only link between Longville and the outside world.

Jerrold led Charles and Butch toward a house with a tall aluminum antenna. Quiet rumblings emanated from their chests, like idling motors. The three werewolves walked erect with a rocking motion. Their hind legs consisted of muscular thighs tapered to narrow lower limbs with padded and clawed feet. Standing, Jerrold was over seven feet tall. Charles and Butch were slightly shorter.

Jerrold peered through a darkened window. Charles and Butch stepped to the other side of the window and gazed through the glass.

Butch saw three humans sitting around a kitchen table. They were talking to each other, unaware of what stood outside their window. A candle's flame illuminated their concerned faces.

The parents were attempting to comfort the boy, who was frightened and talking in a loud, irritated voice. The boy couldn't understand why the lights weren't working. Through the walls, Butch felt fear exude from the boy. The fear excited him and he trembled. He inhaled, trying to take in more of the fear, but it did not work that way.

Jerrold dropped to the ground and twirled on all fours. He ran back a few steps and then turned and raced toward the house. He launched himself into the air and smashed through the window.

Shards of glass flew into the kitchen, screams erupted from inside. Jerrold landed on the broken glass and slid against the wall before stopping.

The air around Butch reverberated with screams. Fear radiated from the house sending euphoric pulses racing through Butch's mind.

Jerrold struggled to right himself, but kept slipping on pieces of broken glass. Finally getting control, he walked on four feet toward the darker shadows highlighted by candlelight. He released a deep growl, which set the people screaming again.

Butch grew light-headed from the pleasurable waves of human fear filling his mind. He leaned against the side of the house.

Another chorus of screams erupted, as the humans recognized the terrifying wolf-like animal standing just outside the ring of candlelight.

Butch broke free from his stupor and jumped through the broken window. Charles followed him. They landed a few feet from Jerrold. The humans were frightened. Their eyes bulged in disbelief.

The father made sweeping motions with his hands and yelled, "Shoo, get out of here. Go on, get—you damn dogs."

The mother rose and grabbed a broom. Apparently, her maternal instincts had prompted her to defend her family. "Gill, do something," she screamed.

Jerrold growled and launched himself through the air. His front legs hit Gill's chest. The man's arms flailed, as he flew through the air. His back hit the refrigerator and he slumped to the floor. Jerrold dropped over him and thrust his fangs forward, grabbing the man's throat. He bit down, crushing the windpipe and severing the carotid arteries on both sides of the neck. He snarled and jerked his head to the side, ripping a mouthful of flesh from Gill's throat.

In the candlelight, blood squirted from severed arteries, flying several feet through the air to splash against the kitchen wall. The man convulsed, arms and legs tapping the floor. His eyes clouded over, but his feet kept jerking.

As he leaped to the top of the table, Butch's growl sounded gleeful. He was in a total state of frenzy. He whirled around and curled his body toward the boy. He slashed out with his right paw and then froze. His nose wrinkled as he sniffed. A smell of urine permeated the air. He shook his head in disgust as his nose pointed toward the boy. A dark stain ran down the boy's leg.

Butch's bloodshot eyes locked onto the boy's glistening, frantic eyes. The boy kicked back as he tried to get away from the creature. His chair slid across the floor and banged into the wall behind him.

Butch leaped to the boy's lap, clamping his fangs around the top of his head. Sharp, white, glistening teeth pierced the boy's skull a fraction of an inch.

The boy stiffened, rocking his chair to the side until it tipped over. The boy reached up, grabbed Butch's lower jaw and tore the teeth from his head. The upper fangs scraped across his skull pulling part of his scalp free. He screamed, scrambled to his feet and ran for the kitchen door.

Butch pounced on the boy's back, driving him to the floor. The boy spun around, grabbed the thick fur on both sides of Butch's neck, and pushed his muzzle back from his face. Butch yelped as his skin separated from the underlying muscles. He released his grip and pulled free from the boy's hands. Butch whirled and bit the boy just above the knee. He clamped down hard and felt the separation of the femur from the knee joint.

The boy's fear came in pulses, with such whirlpool intensity that Butch started to wobble. A feeling of weakness spread through his muscles. Butch's jaw released its hold on the boy's leg. The boy shuffled across the kitchen floor on his butt, screaming.

Afraid the boy might escape, Butch shook the dizziness from his head and leaped toward the squirming body. Angry with himself for his mental lapse, Butch clamped his fangs over the boy's head again. The boy shrieked. The fear from the boy coursed through Butch's mind like an orgasm. Butch whipped his head back and forth in time with the waves of pleasure assaulting him. The boy flopped through the air like a rag doll. Butch heard the skull crack and reduced his jaw pressure. He wanted to delay killing the boy in order to milk as much fear as possible from him. He wanted the exhilaration to continue forever.

Jerrold stood to the side of the kitchen, watching, "Butch, end it. We've got to get moving."

Butch growled defiantly, but relented when he saw Jerrold's fangs glisten in the candlelight. He shut down the ecstasy he was experiencing, bringing his upper and lower fangs together. They met in the middle of the boy's cerebrum.

The boy stiffened, convulsed once, and grew limp. Butch released the dead body, which no longer provided him any pleasure.

Butch looked around quickly for another victim. He lowered his head and swiveled it back and forth. His nerves were at their breaking point. He was coming down from his high and wanted more of the exhilarating feelings. He realized that he needed the fear and panic that came from frightened, dying humans to fuel his emotional high.

He saw Charles still toying with the mother. Butch's euphoria was subsiding, but the promise of more waited for him in the woman. Butch stood and moved toward her.

"No Butch!" the voice reverberated in his mind. "I said you were finished. You've already killed one. This is Charles's victim. Now consume yours so we can go."

Butch growled with frustration, but stopped moving in the woman's direction.

The woman swung the old, worn broom at Charles. Butch shuddered, experiencing the ecstasy of her fear. The mother had witnessed the savage killing her husband and son. Her mind was overcome with terror.

A chuckle slipped from Charles's throat, as he pranced toward her.

Jerrold stood over the body of the husband, feeding. With a mouthful of flesh, he said, "Charles, be done. "We have to go." He ripped another piece of flesh from the body in front of him.

Butch turned away from Charles and the mother. He began to feed on the boy.

Charles growled and swept aside the broom with one paw, and swung the other one, ripping open the woman's stomach. Like giant worms, her intestines snaked to the floor in front of her eyes. The broom dropped from her lifeless hands as she stared at the squirming mass on the floor. She was not aware when Charles's fangs ripped into her stomach cavity to reach upward and rip out her heart.

Charles chewed on the still pulsing organ with a sigh of satisfaction.

Butch glanced out the broken kitchen window and flinched. The golden moon was watching him. He recalled earlier thoughts of the moon rising to watch and record his actions. He shrugged his shaggy shoulders and turned back to feed on the cooling body.

After the three had finished feeding, Jerrold said, "Charles, bag the remains and dispose of them in the swamp. Make sure they will not be found."

* * *

On the other side of town, Gretchen Fletcher was walking home from the grocery store. She had lived in Longville all her life. She had married her high school sweetheart, and after ten years, the marriage had gone sour. Her husband was an alcoholic, seldom worked, and didn't contribute to the family's coffers. A constant check from the county kept food on the table and a roof over their heads.

She was upset. She had not yet finished shopping before the lights had gone out. Peter Henrick, the store's owner had told her to take the groceries and pay for them tomorrow. He could not open the cash register anyway. It was after nine o'clock and pitch dark.

Everyone in town considered Gretchen a pain in the ass. She wore a dark wool coat that reached down to her ankles. A purple scarf with swirling red lines covered her head. Without streetlights, she blended with the darkness, except when the moonlight reflected from her shiny scarf.

Just because the electricity was out and the streets were dark, Gretchen was not scared. She had walked to the store and back home many times over the past ten years. She could do it in the dark, and tonight she had her chance.

She grumbled, still angry with her oldest son, Arnie, for not getting home in time to run to the store for her. She carried a grocery bag filled with a half-gallon of milk, a loaf of bread, five pounds of potatoes, and a six-pack of Coke. She hurried homeward, with the grocery bag in her right arm. She swung her left arm in cadence with her rapid pace.

She felt guilty because she had left her one-year-old baby home alone. He had been sleeping in the crib when she left, so he'd be okay. She didn't want to wake him and take him to the store with her. He would have been so grouchy.

"Damn that Arnie," she said aloud. "I'll whip his ass for sure."

She followed Bell Street. Some of the sidewalk cement slabs were crooked from years of frost heaves and neglect. She moved forward shuffling her feet in the dark, until she tripped on a jutting edge of cement. She caught herself, then stepped over the uneven slab and shuffled on her way again.

She came to Highway 84 and crossed the bridge, following the edge of the road southward. She felt some comfort hearing the click-click of her shoes echoing back from the dark buildings.

The rundown Fletcher house was just beyond a grove of black spruce trees. She started into the tunnel of spruce, which towered over the highway from both sides. She sighed—the groceries were getting heavy—but her home was not far away.

Gretchen heard a soft growl in front of her. She turned her head from side to side, like a bat using radar to locate an insect. She couldn't pinpoint exactly where the noise had come from.

"Damn dogs," she said under her breath. "Why don't the stupid dog lovers keep them tied up?" She stooped and picked up a broken branch. She shifted the grocery bag to her left arm and held the stick with her right hand. Feeling more confident with a weapon, she shuffled ahead once more, seeing the moonlit roof of her home just down the road.

When she approached the spot where she thought the sound had come from, she heard another growl further ahead. Yet another one came from across the road. "Damn you, dogs," she shouted. "Come out here and I'll beat your growling asses."

Gretchen stopped and wet her lips. She took a few more steps but froze when she heard a shuffling noise behind her. She whirled around, raising the branch over her head. She squinted, finding it hard to decipher the shape at the edge of the spruce trees.

All she could make out was a dark shadow but had no idea what it was. She knew it wasn't a dog—it was just too big.

"Shit, it looks like a bear." She walked backwards a few steps, trying to distance herself from the animal.

She stuck the branch under her arm and rifled through the grocery bag thinking she might throw it a few slices of bread to distract it.

Suddenly, terror welled up in her breast. Her knees sagged. A couple dogs were one thing, but a bear was something else. The thought of screaming for help did not even enter her mind.

With shaking hands, she ripped open the package of Wonder Bread and pulled out several slices. She threw them toward the animal, then turned and hurried down the lane, back toward town. She wanted to get out of the darkened area and into the moonlight as fast as she could.

Thomas in 'were-form' jumped onto the road and advanced toward Gretchen who turned her head to look. Thomas was three feet behind her. All Gretchen could see was something that looked like a man wearing a shaggy, fur coat.

Another beast appeared at her side, advancing. Turning to face the third beast, she saw two hair-covered breasts protruding from her chest.

Taking small side steps, Gretchen moved away from the female creature. She still carried the stick and held it out in front of her, as if trying to ward off the animal. "Go on, get," she screamed. "Leave me alone."

Xianth advanced. Saliva drooled from the corners of her mouth. She kept pace with Gretchen, closing the distance between them. Xianth thrust her arms high into the air and emitted a blood-curdling scream. "AAiiiiiiiieeeOOOOOOOO."

Now Gretchen knew for sure the creature wasn't human. No human could scream like that, and neither could a bear. She squinted, watching the 'thing'. It surprised her when Xianth, the werewolf, leaped high into the air, somersaulted over Gretchen's head, and landed behind her.

She spun around to face the beast. Town buildings and moonlit streets were no longer open for her escape. The beast moved toward her, forcing her to move back, deeper into the darkness of the spruce trees. Step for step, Xianth followed, until Gretchen backed into the darkest region.

Over the growls of the 'thing' in front of her, Gretchen heard another snarl behind her. She started to swing her head, but before she could turn, she felt an excruciating pain in her neck. Thomas had driven his fangs through her cervical vertebrae severing Gretchen's head from her body.

The raking claws of Thomas ripped open her chest and exposed her quivering heart. Xianth leaned over the headless body, extended her muzzle into the opened cavity, and grabbed Gretchen's throbbing heart in her fangs. She twisted her head, tearing the heart from her chest as Thomas and William watched. Blood sprayed through the air, landing several feet from the body.

* * *

Gruesome attacks occurred on other streets and in homes throughout the besieged town. Barking dogs mixed their voices with the howls of the Guhl werewolves, which carried far beyond the town limits.

From the forests surrounding Longville, howls from three Timber wolf packs answered. The wolves were moving toward town to investigate the strange intruders who had invaded their territory.

* * *

Jerrold and Butch left the ham operator's house and moved along the street toward town center to check on their other teams. Suddenly, gunshots reverberated, and brought them to a halt. They sniffed the air, smelling 'were-danger'. A forced hush had drifted over the city. Butch looked toward the center of town. He knew where the shots had come from.

Jerrold listened for another moment and then said, with a trembling voice. "Come on." He ran down the street. "Hurry, members of our pack are in trouble."

Butch followed Jerrold across Randall Street, running at fifty miles per hour. As they approached the main street, two more shots filled the night air from a block ahead.

Butch swerved to the right side of the street, while Jerrold continued running down the middle. They covered the block in a few seconds.

As they approached the corner of Randall and Main Street, Butch saw a flash, and then heard a shotgun blast. A stream of fire reflected in the window of a white building on the corner. Butch saw a werewolf crumple to the ground in front of a building that housed a gift shop. He stopped behind a big oak tree and looked at the wounded werewolf. It was Fred. He lay a short distance from a white fence. Fred's father, Steve, huddled behind an oak tree avoiding the gunfire that sprayed from the building.

Using the same tree as a shield, Jerrold ran up behind Steve, who gave his father a mournful glance.

"What happened?" Jerrold asked.

"Be careful, Dad. The people in the building are good shots." Steve sobbed, "Fred is dead."

Jerrold said, "Steve, I'm sorry. What happened?"

"Steve calmed down, "We attacked three humans inside the white building. They must have been expecting us. We killed one of them, and then more men came into the room shooting. There are still two humans inside the house. They've killed Fred and wounded Barbara."

"Where is she?"

"She's around the corner of that gray building on the corner. Francis is with her," Steve said.

Jerrold glanced at the building just as Francis stuck his head around the corner.

Jerrold shouted, "Francis, stay with Barbara,"

"Yes, father."

Jerrold clapped Steve on the shoulder. "Stay here."

Jerrold peeked around the tree and then raced toward the white building. He was thirty feet from the Gift Shop when a shotgun blast from the first floor window hit him in his left shoulder.

Butch watched Jerrold's left front leg collapse, sending him tumbling to the ground. Jerrold howled more from frustration than pain.

The Alpha was down and the hunt was falling apart.

Flashes of blinding light burned across Butch's eyes. Without thinking, he ripped coarse bark from the trunk of the tree as he hurled himself toward the white house. He moved so fast, he was just a blur to the two men inside the building. He reached the Gift Shop and leaped through the window where the shotgun blast originated. He burst through the remaining splinters of glass and sent them showering in all directions. As he flew through the window, Butch sensed a man crouched to his left.

With lightning speed, Butch thrust out his left paw and sliced through the man's throat. Butch hit the floor and slid into a shelf loaded with trinkets.

As the man fell to the floor, he jerked the trigger of his twelve-gauge shotgun. The blast tore through the top frame of the window. Dying, the man squeezed the trigger again, sending a blast into a glass-enclosed counter of souvenirs. He thrashed on the floor choking on his own blood. His eyes glazed over and he stopped moving.

Butch rolled to his feet. With muscles contracting at super-speed, he bounced off a counter into a second room. A shotgun blast sizzled above his back, shattering a shelf of gifts.

Butch was operating on animal instinct alone. He used the wall to change direction and landed at the feet of the second man. Flickering light from a Coleman lantern illuminated this second room. Butch appeared before the man as if by magic, crouching before him. The man saw him, and his mouth dropped open.

Butch shoved his head forward. A muzzle full of fangs and grinding teeth clamped onto the man's testicles. Butch jerked his head to the side, ripping fabric and testicles from their sacks. The man dropped his gun and let out a pitiful squeak. On tiptoe, the man began a delicate dance as he pounded on Butch's forehead with both of his hands.

Butch released his hold and sat back on his rear haunches, enjoying the fear from his victim. The man grabbed his bleeding groin and sagged to his knees. With a vicious swipe of his right paw, Butch ripped the man's head from his body. With a second swing, he opened the man's chest and with snapping fangs, ripped out his heart.

Butch's attention shifted from the dead man when Jerrold's telepathic scream forced him to sag.

Jerrold broadcast to all the werewolves, **"COME TO ME!"**

Butch could not believe the intensity of the call. There was no way he or any of the others could not obey the demanding cry of their pack leader.

Butch backtracked through the Gift Shop and jumped out the broken window. He ran across the street and joined the other family members around the pack leader. He felt panicky. He didn't know what to do.

The Alpha stood over the dead body of Fred. Whimpering sounds escaped from his nostrils. Jerrold dropped down on his rear haunches and with tender movements lifted Fred with his forepaws. In spite of his wounded arm, Jerrold cradled Fred in his hairy legs and rocked him back and forth. He lifted his head to the sky. Heart-wrenching howls floated from his muzzle, "AHH-HOOOooo—AHHHOOOooo— AHHHHHOOoooooo."

The loud cries reverberated back and forth between the surrounding hills, sending a mournful lament to the skies and the all-seeing harvest moon. His cry expressed his loss, "We have lost one of our own."

Three wild wolf packs nearing town howled in reply, "ARRRRROoooo—ARRRROoooo—AAARRRROOOOOooo."

Butch understood what these howls meant. We understand. We've also lost many of our kind to the humans, but that is no reason for you to invade our territory.

Jerrold released Fred and stood up on three legs, favoring his wounded leg. He turned to the pack. "Steve, take your son's body and leave. Thomas, you and Jake help Barbara get away. We'll join you at the cabins on Lake Inguadona. The rest of you listen! I want revenge. I want you to wipe out this town. Go! Seek out any humans you can find. Kill them all. Do it now and be quick about it. Spare no one. We leave town in thirty minutes."

In twos and threes, the werewolves scattered in all directions.

In spite of the havoc, most townsfolk were not aware of the slaughter that was taking place. Several families had heard the gunshots, come out of their homes and moved toward the shooting.

Five werewolves descended upon three people standing in the middle of Randall Street, a block from Main Street. The werewolves charged through the group at top speed, slashing and tearing. Not one of the humans saw the werewolves.

As each person toppled over, none realized what caused them to fall. Not a single scream of fear escaped their lips until the shock of their wounds had worn off. Then, the fear and pain was so great, they trembled in sheer terror.

The werewolves went orgasmic from the peals of fear radiating from the dying humans. They stood frozen in an ecstatic stupor. Those that had not fed did so. The others left looking for more humans to kill.

On the north edge of town, Walt Peterson, old and cancerous, lay in shock. His left arm had been severed and was pumping blood out the main brachial artery. He turned his head until his eyes locked with Butch's red-rimmed eyes. "Are you the devil?" he asked. "Are you here to punish me for raping my daughter?"

Butch ripped open his throat.

Suddenly, the promise Butch had made to his father popped into his mind, the promise: I would not to kill more humans than I needed to. He thought, *Shit, dad doesn't understand what being a werewolf entails. There's no way I can resist the command of my Alpha.*

A single trickle of madness resurfaced. He was following orders. Well, maybe that was oversimplifying the situation, but Butch knew that without killing and eating human flesh, he would have been lost to the wild side. Butch's mouth pulled back into a smile as he bent to pull Walt's heart free. He swallowed the quivering organ in two bites.

* * *

Other werewolf teams hunted down and killed another twelve citizens of Longville. The werewolves traveled so fast, people did not see what hit them.

Four citizens of Longville saw the specters of death and lived. Traumatized by their encounters, two of them escaped into their own minds to never find their way out. Another became a babbling idiot.

The fourth was a five-year-old child, who hid beneath the front porch of his home. From his vantage point, he witnessed two werewolves kill his mother and sister on the front lawn, only yards from where he hid.

* * *

TO ME," Jerrold telepathically broadcast. "WE LEAVE-NOW."

Butch and Charles gulped one last piece of flesh and then raced toward the stand of trees on the east edge of town. Within a few minutes, the rest of the pack had joined them.

Jerrold limped among the returning pack members. "Is there anyone that hasn't satisfied their need to kill?"

All of the gathered werewolves answered in the affirmative. Each werewolf fed and would not need to feed again for another five years.

"Did everyone dispose of the remains?"

Butch and a few others said they had not had time to get rid of their last kills. They turned to take care of the task.

Jerrold said excitedly, "Stop, there is no time. We have to leave now. Butch, lead out."

Butch shrugged his shoulders and headed for the swamp. The Alpha limped behind him. Butch noticed the scabbed-over wound on Jerrold's left leg.

Butch entered the swamp grass followed by the rest of the pack, then loped off at a fast trot. He led the group through a stand of small aspen trees at the edge of the swamp and then followed a meandering trail through a stand of birch trees. Soon they were sheltered by the main swamp. Butch followed a deer trail through the swamp grass.

After a half hour, the deer trail came up out of the swamp onto a birch-covered ridge. In another mile, the trail ended at Lake Inguadona Lodge, where their 'safe cabins' were located.

The owners of the resort knew the family was having a reunion and that others would be arriving late into the night. Several non-werewolf members had arrived three days ago to set up for the family reunion.

The pack would be in the Twin Cities by early next week, once again safely hidden among thousands of people.

CHAPTER 10
THE WHOLE WORLD KNOWS

Minnesota radio and TV broadcast the first reports of the 'Longville Massacre' Thursday morning. By Thursday afternoon, the massacre had made the front pages of every national newspaper. The news media moved with amazing quickness. Personal interviews with residents of Longville were in the evening newspaper, and on radio and TV.

NBC News reported on the six o'clock news. "Fifty-four residents from a small city in north central Minnesota are missing or dead. The carnage and wanton destruction of human life was unprecedented. The preliminary reports suggest that on Wednesday evening, at least two packs of wolves entered Longville and may be responsible for the deaths of its citizens. Authorities found the slaughtered bodies of twenty men, women and children scattered around town. Thirty-four other residents are missing and presumed dead. At this time, no one knows what happened to them.

"Only in wartime has something this gruesome occurred. Authorities have found hundreds of wolf prints entering and leaving Longville. The experts say it is highly unlikely that wolves could have done all the killing. It is unusual for wolves to attack humans, but apparently, times are changing.

Longville is a small resort community located between Grand Rapids and Walker."

* * *

Butch got up from the sofa, worried. He walked to the table and leaned over, supporting himself on closed fists.

Bruce moaned from the other side of the sofa. "That's the third national TV network to broadcast information about the attack."

"Let's face it," Richard said, "We were supposed to kill only twenty-four people. We screwed up and killed many more than we needed to."

Dean sat on a rocking chair near the fireplace. He turned to Richard and said, "Killing that many humans was bound to draw unwanted attention. We brought national attention down upon ourselves."

Thomas jumped up from the sofa, "You darn right we screwed up. We killed more than two humans for every werewolf, and then to top it off, we didn't properly dispose of the remains. We left bodies all over town. What the hell happened to our plan?"

"I don't know. How did we let things get so far out of hand?" Richard asked, looking at his father. "One human would have satisfied our individual needs."

Butch looked accusingly at Jerrold. "Grandfather ordered us to go back and kill everyone."

Angry, Jerrold rose from his leather recliner and walked to the fireplace. He leaned against the mantle with the arm that had been injured, wincing The wound was scabbed over and nearly healed, but it still bothered him. He leaned forward, veins popping out on his forehead. "What were we supposed to do? Don't forget they killed one of my pack members and injured two more."

Richard saw his father's anger and replied carefully. "But, father, we didn't follow our plan. We weren't supposed to kill that many humans."

"We were a pack out of control," Butch said.

Jerrold slammed his fist down on the fireplace mantle. "My pack was not out of control!" he screamed. "You were doing what I ordered you to do." He stepped forward, his breath coming in gasps. "What difference does it make? Whether we killed twenty-four or fifty-four, the publicity and panic would have been the same?"

"I don't think so," Brad questioned, in a meek voice. "Would a wild wolf pack have slaughtered that many people?"

"No, they wouldn't have," Jerrold spit out, "but don't jump to conclusions. They've found only twenty bodies, which means the pack did dispose of many of the bodies." He threatened Brad with a sideways glance, but then relaxed. A big smile grew across his face. "Just remember, no one has blamed were-wolves for the attack." He returned to the mantle and said, "When they come knocking at our door, that's the time to panic."

Butch's anger exploded. He couldn't believe Jerrold was that unconcerned over the wanton killing of so many humans. He said loudly, "Grandfather, that's not right. We screwed up by killing that many humans. I admit that I'm to blame for six of those deaths, and responsible for putting the pack at risk. I'm sorry now that I followed your orders, but the time to correct that mistake has passed. We sure as hell shouldn't wait until the authorities come after us to be concerned and take precautions. We have to make sure something like this will never happen again."

Thomas felt a confrontation coming on and tried to diffuse the situation. "Butch, the pack leader has the job of controlling the hunt. You surely don't believe Father wanted things to get out of hand, do you?"

"By sending us back to kill everyone, it sure looks to me like he didn't care," Butch said. "Only the ones who needed to feed should have gone back to kill. What happened should have been anticipated and a plan worked out to prevent panic," Butch said, turning from the table to face Thomas.

Jerrold turned from the fireplace with a growl and dropped into a crouch. "I didn't panic! Are you challenging my leadership, Butch?" Jerrold didn't even wait for an answer. Hair sprouted from his face, as he started his change.

Thomas blanched. He knew Butch had pushed the Alpha too hard. "Father, Butch didn't mean it. It's just talk."

Butch felt the hair on the back of his neck stand erect as he, too, began to change.

Richard stumbled to the center of the room between the two glaring com-batants and extended his hands toward Jerrold. "Dad, you're right." Richard shrugged, hoping he could head off this one-sided challenge. "So far, were-wolves have not been blamed."

Jerrold was satisfied with Richard's comment. Seeing no challenge from Butch, he reversed his change.

Butch also stopped his change, but turned away, still angry over Jerrold's poor leadership. But he was glad he didn't have to fight his grandfather.

Diana stood in the kitchen with hands planted on her hips. "I think it was in poor taste for the TV stations to show pictures of the human victims. They even showed some of the bodies with chunks of flesh missing and their necks ripped open," Diana sputtered as she added. "They even showed bodies with arms, heads and legs missing. That sucks."

Butch smiled at the irony of Diana's comment. "Are you listening to what you're saying? We can kill humans, but the media shouldn't show the dead bodies on TV?"

Richard defended Diana. "I guess that's what she means."

"All three of you are out to lunch and not facing reality," Butch said.

Bruce pushed his chair back a few inches and raised his hand in the air, like a school kid. When no one paid any attention to him, he blurted out, "The media is getting closer to what really happened in Longville. CBS News said it was hard to believe unintelligent animals like wolves could have carried off a coordinated mass slaughter."

"I hope no one agrees with them," Richard sighed, "or we might be in the spotlight sooner than we'd like."

Jerrold turned white. "We can't let that happen."

Now he's concerned, Butch thought. He should admit he screwed up in Longville.

Chapter II
Public Speculation

Friday morning, Butch and Carey volunteered to go into the neighboring town of Remer to buy groceries and see what kind of talk was going around town. People there would know what stories were coming out of Longville.

Carey grabbed the Ford Explorer keys from the table. "Come on Butch, I get to drive," he said, shaking the keys in front of Butch's face.

Amy, their sixteen-year-old cousin, came out of the bathroom with toothpaste on the corner of her mouth. "Hey guys, can I go with you?"

Carey frowned and a pout grew on Amy's lips.

Butch smiled and said, "Sure Amy, you can come along."

Carey gave Butch a dirty look, but nodded his okay. The three headed out the door of the two-story chalet.

Amy stumbled on the bottom step of the Explorer.

Butch reached out and grabbed her arm. "Careful girl," he chided, "we can't afford to have you get injured."

Carey jumped behind the wheel of the Explorer, started it up and accelerated down the gravel road. Reaching the end of the half-mile driveway, he spun the wheel at the tar road and turned east. The road curved through a hilly, deciduous forest toward Highway 6 and Big Rice Lake. When they reached Highway 6, they turned north and headed for Remer.

Butch sat with his head halfway out the open window. He stared with watery eyes at Big Rice Lake on his right. A ring of golden-leafed aspen trees surrounded the lake. Close to shore, thick patches of wild rice stems hung broken from the recent harvest.

Butch eyed a flock of mallards splashing in the water a short distance from shore. A feral growl escaped his lips.

Carey slowed to the speed limit as they approached the outskirts of Remer.

Butch turned in his seat and slapped Carey on the shoulder as he said, "When we get into town, you and Amy pick up the groceries. Diana sent a list of things we need at the cabin." He dug in his shirt pocket, pulled out a quarter sheet of paper, and handed it to Amy. "While you're getting the groceries, I'll take a walk and see if I can pick up any information."

Butch ambled down the street, stopping at a rusty newspaper dispenser. He dropped seventy-five cents into the slot and yanked out a copy of the Minneapolis Star & Tribune. The headline caught his attention.

LONGVILLE CITIZENS KILLED BY WOLVES

Sheriff McCarthy of Walker reported Thursday that at least two packs of wolves entered the city of Longville Wednesday night and were likely responsible for attacking its citizens. Twenty men, women and children are dead and thirty-four are missing from this northern Minnesota resort community.

According to Sheriff McCarthy, "It is the most devastating thing that has ever happened in Cass County."

The sheriff, with the cooperation of the National Guard unit from Grand Rapids, is sweeping the wooded areas around Longville, hunting the wolves.

John Regan, animal zoologist from the Minnesota Zoo, said, "It's very rare for wolves not suffering from rabies to attack humans on the scale that occurred in Longville. I still can't believe that wolves are responsible for killing those people. There has to be another explanation."

Relatives are still pouring into Longville to help arrange for the burial of family members and to console the living.

Butch turned to the inside pages and looked at vivid color photos, graphically depicting the savagery of the slaughter. He glanced up, with concern as

Amy and Carey came out of the grocery store, then leaned against the door of the Explorer and waited for them.

Carey opened the back door of the Explorer and set the groceries on the seat. Amy saw the troubled look on Butch's face. She didn't say anything, and started to get in the back seat.

"Wait Amy," Butch said, looking up the short main street. "We came to town to find out what the people are saying about what happened in Longville. Let's go in Kramer's Drug Store and see if we can learn anything."

The drug store was in a red brick building in the middle of the block. Without waiting for agreement, Butch headed for it. Carey and Amy jogged to catch up.

Along the far wall of the store was an old-fashioned counter with real swivel stools. They sat down at the counter. A tall, hairless clerk, with a stained apron tied around his waist, asked what they would like. Butch ordered a Pepsi, Carey a Coke, and Amy asked for a strawberry malt. Butch twirled his stool around and glanced down the aisles of merchandise. Towards the back of the store, several men sat around a glass-topped table drinking coffee.

Butch leaned toward Amy and Carey and said. "Hey those guys are talking about Longville. Hush up."

He heard a grizzled old man say, "We need to organize a posse and hunt down every son-of-a-bitching wolf in the county."

A second man with faded red hair, long overdue for a haircut, replied, "I don't think wolves done it, do you Hank?"

Butch glanced at Amy and Carey. He whispered, "Oh-oh, Here it comes."

Hank, a third old man in a red flannel shirt, with a hole in the toe of his right boot, injected, "Shit, you know it was some kind of military attack. The damn army was trying out some new-fangled weapons. They don't give a shit for us civilians, you know."

"Bullshit," interrupted a fourth man at the table. He was short, just over four feet tall. His hair was cropped short except for long sideburns that stopped at his chin. He sucked in a big breath of air and continued, "It was werewolves that done it—that's what the news people are saying."

Butch choked on his Pepsi.

The man in the bib overalls laughed and said, "Ah, shit, Carl, there ain't no such thing as werewolves. Reporters are saying it was plain old wolves that killed everybody. That's what they're saying."

From that point, the conversation among the men degenerated into mindless talk and more wild speculation.

On the drive back to the cabin, they listened to WCCO radio's Eric Winstrom, who said, "The Minnesota Legislature was called into special session this morning by Governor Anderson. The seriousness of the killings in Longville prompted the governor to take action. The legislature met in a joint session called for the express purpose of dealing with the killings in Longville. They passed a proclamation demanding that the federal government appoint a special commission to look into the Longville deaths."

* * *

Within two days, President Thompson appointed Federal Marshal Ralph Morsching to head up the investigation of the 'Longville Massacre'. Headquarters for marshal Morsching was in Madison, Wisconsin. Ralph was a decorated officer, widely respected throughout the law enforcement community. Unknown to anyone, Ralph had called in a few favors in order to receive the appointment.

Ralph Morsching and his team flew to St. Paul on Monday to meet with Minnesota's governor. Ralph took a cab to the state capitol. The rest of his team went on to the Radisson Hotel.

A security guard escorted Ralph into the governor's waiting room Within several minutes, a young, dark-haired man approached him. "Mr. Morsching?"

Ralph nodded.

"Please come with me, the governor is ready to meet with you." The aide escorted him into the governor's office.

Governor Anderson sat with his back to the door looking out a picture window, which provided a scenic view of the city. To the south, pieces of the Mississippi River, like a blue ribbon, sparkled and flashed between buildings.

The governor's office was immaculate. A polished oak desk was bare, except for one sheet of paper. On the walls hung two pictures, one of President George Washington, the other of Governor Anderson's wife.

Ralph looked at the gray-haired, overweight man behind the desk. He fought the superior attitude that was a major part of his personality. "Governor," Ralph said, and then waited for Anderson to swing his chair towards him.

"Ah, Mr. Morsching," the governor said, "I'm glad you've arrived."

Ralph nodded.

The governor crossed his legs and smoothed out his tie. "I was informed that the president appointed you to investigate the deaths of those folks in Longville."

"Yes sir. It was a horrible waste of life. I extend my sympathies to the people of Minnesota. It was such a ridiculous, senseless slaughter. If you will give me a month to conduct my investigation, I'll provide you a complete and accurate report of my findings."

The governor looked at Ralph over the top of his glasses. "You've got three weeks—twenty-one days—to lay your report on my desk," the governor said sternly. Then his face softened and a smile broke out. "The citizens of Minnesota want immediate action. They're screaming for my scalp, as though the wolf attack was my fault."

Ralph seethed internally, but his face was a mask, hiding his true emotions, as he stared back at the governor. "I guarantee you one thing governor. The investigation will proceed quickly and efficiently. I'll have my report on your desk within your time frame."

Ralph was not happy with the short time permitted, but apparently there were no other options.

"Then, get to it," the governor said, jumping up. "My constituents want the answers yesterday."

CHAPTER 12
INVESTIGATION NORTHWARD

Ralph Morsching sent the rest of the team to the parking lot to bring the rental cars around to the front. He and Tom Jarvis, his brother-in-law, paid their hotel bills and headed for the street.

They waited on the sidewalk in front of the Radisson. Tom was Ralph's chief deputy. He was tall, skinny, and possessed a big curved nose. He'd served in Vietnam as a Special Forces assassin.

"You know, Tom," Ralph said, staring across the street, "something is funny about this whole deal in Longville."

"What do you mean?" Tom took a step forward and turned to face his brother-in-law.

Ralph brushed his hair back before answering, "If you go back in history, there are numerous accounts of wolves attacking people. The majority of fatal attacks have involved wolves that had rabies. Surprisingly, Europe has all kinds of documented wolf attacks. For example, in France from 1580-1830, wolves killed over three thousand people. One-third of those people were killed by non-rabid wolves."

"That kind of supports the claim that wolves attacked the people in Longville," Tom said.

Ralph wrinkled his nose. "Not so fast. The funny thing is, North America has had very few documented attacks by wolves on humans."

"Why is that?"

"The experts think it's because most of the people over here had guns and shot the wolves anytime they saw them, thus teaching the wolves to fear humans."

Tom looked impressed, "Where did you learn all of that?"

"Wikipedia—on-line. They have pages of information."

"Guess I better start reading again."

Ralph's eyes grew smaller as tiny wrinkles appeared at their corners. "What I can't understand is what would cause two or three packs of wolves to join together in an attack? Why didn't they attack each other?"

"Maybe they were related," Tom said.

Ralph smiled, "Naw, something is weird. Something we aren't seeing."

Just then, the cars came around the corner of the hotel and pulled to a stop in front of them. Ralph and Tom jumped into the lead car. The caravan headed for highway 169 and the first leg of the journey to Longville.

Ralph's team consisted of ten handpicked professional law enforcement officers. Each deputy was a specialist in several different fields of investigation. Ralph worked with all of them before and was aware of each man's abilities.

He leaned his head back on the headrest and closed his eyes. Before he fell asleep, he promised himself that his team would uncover what really happened in Longville.

CHAPTER 13
TESTIMONY

Several hours later, the four-car caravan pulled into Longville. Mayor Stimpson met Ralph on the sidewalk in front of the bank and led him to a vacant building that was a former gift shop. This was to be their base of operations. The building stood on Main Street. Faded-green wood siding showed years of neglect. The big picture window in the front of the building was covered with dust. Ralph didn't know if the lights were on inside until someone cleared a spot on the window and peeked out.

Ralph walked into the building and saw a bunch of volunteers cleaning and arranging old desks and other furniture behind a long oak counter. He heard a vacuum cleaner humming from a hallway to the left. Down a second hallway, a flurry of pounding created a deafening racket. From the back of the store, the sound of a saw tearing through wood added to the chaos.

A man with a shirt reading Johnson Telephone Company pulled a cable up the left hallway to a counter in the main store. He threaded the cable through a hole in the side of the counter, and then pulled it along the middle shelf to a distribution panel.

Mayor Stimpson touched Ralph's sleeve and said over the din, "We're having them install phone jacks in the back rooms, along with high-speed Internet hookups." He cupped his mouth, leaned closer to Ralph, and added. "We assumed you would want some offices to work out of. Am I right?"

Ralph glared at the mayor, but then switched to a smile. "That's right mayor. We'll need offices and rooms to interview witnesses. Thanks. Now if you will excuse me, I need to get my team settled."

* * *

Unknown to all but pack members, Ralph Morsching was the Alpha of a werewolf pack located in Wisconsin. They believed they were the only werewolf pack remaining in the world. Occasionally a single werewolf would show up in the United States, and then they would move to eliminate him from endangering their pack. His position as federal marshal gave him a perfect vantage point to learn of any strange deaths in the United States—deaths that could possibly have been caused by werewolves.

* * *

Ralph's team marched in carrying boxes of equipment they had brought from Madison. Each member scattered down the two hallways, as if they knew where they were going. Each began to claim a vacant room.

Tom followed the crew down one of the halls and shouted out orders over the noise. He stuck his head in one of the larger rooms and said, "Bubba, I want this room for interrogation. You gotta move."

Bubba Anderson was a barrel-chested, non-family werewolf. His real name was Horatio, but you had to defend yourself if you called him that a second time. Once he was selected, he'd been given the 'were-blood' from the Alpha.

Bubba nodded, picked up his box and hurried farther down the hall to another empty room.

Tom followed. He peeked into the next room. "Kurt, let's leave this room for Ralph. Okay?"

"You bet, boss," Kurt said, picking up the box he'd set on the desk and hurrying down the hall to claim another room. Kurt Fleming was another non-family werewolf. He was an up-and-coming police officer in Madison—a weapons specialist. Tom had recruited him. After Ralph had approved of him, Kurt soon became a valuable member of the pack.

The rest of the team wasted no time moving in and setting up their base of operations.

Later in the afternoon as Ralph was working out the initial assignments for his team, Tom Jarvis walked into the office and sat on a wooden chair across from Ralph. Tom's hawkish nose dominated his round face, and his protruding ears added to his comical appearance. Despite his looks, Tom was an intelligent peace officer. A few people would have added the word ruthless to his description.

Ralph leaned back and rubbed the crew cut bristles on his head. He looked at Tom and said, "I still can't believe this happened, Tom. As I told you earlier, wolves do not normally attack humans. Now, all of a sudden, we have possibly fifty-four people killed in one evening by wolves." A look of disbelief grew on Ralph's face. "It's even harder to believe when you see that it was a coordinated attack involving several different wolf packs. It just doesn't make any sense."

Tom stood up and moved to the one small window, letting in light from outside. He peered through the smeared glass and watched two boys playing with small metal cars in the dirt between the sidewalk and the street. Tom turned back to Ralph. He glanced out the open office door to see if anyone was within hearing range. He walked over to Ralph's desk, leaned down, and whispered, "If I didn't know better, I'd say our pack carried out the attack."

Blood drained from Ralph's face and he slouched back in his armchair. "Christ, you might be right." Ralph slid forward in his chair and slapped his forehead. "This had to be a feeding. I should have thought of that myself. Over the years, there have been a number of killings in Minnesota that made me wonder if someone from our pack was coming over here and feeding. I never found any evidence to prove that was happening. Seven or eight years ago, a report of wolves killing six people in a town in northern Minnesota hit the wires. The witness was finally declared insane, and I didn't give it another thought until now. Maybe he wasn't insane."

Tom beamed. He was proud he came up with an idea that excited Ralph. "Yeah, maybe he wasn't."

"Oh, shit," Ralph said, squeezing the edge of the desk with his hands. Ridges of wrinkles covered his forehead. "If that's true, it means there's another pack of werewolves in the U. S. That can't be possible!"

Tom's face turned white. "It must be."

Ralph cupped his chin and then looked into Tom's eyes. "If there is another pack, we can't allow them to survive," he said, matter-of-factly.

"I agree," Tom's lips curled in a wicked smile. "They've already endangered our pack by their wanton slaughter. It's lucky we're in charge of this investigation, otherwise the findings could end up exposing their pack. And in the long run, maybe ours, as well."

Ralph slapped both of his palms on the top of his desk. "We can't let that happen."

* * *

The next morning, Ralph checked the schedule of activities for the day. He saw that his inspectors were going to interview two surviving witnesses from the massacre. A note at the bottom of the page suggested that one of them was understandably suffering from emotional issues. Ralph's eyebrows rose as he wondered what information the interview would reveal. He decided to sit in on the sessions, so he walked down the hall and entered the interrogation room.

Joe Petrie, the team leader in charge of interrogations, was a former private investigator. He had come to Ralph's attention six years ago when he'd been getting too close to the pack during his investigation of a homeless woman's death in the railroad yard. The pack either had to kill him or bring him into the pack.

Joe pulled open the door leading into the hall. He looked out and saw a woman in a white uniform holding the hand of a small, nervous boy. The woman turned toward the opening door. "Ma'am, will you please bring the boy in?" Joe said.

"Let's go, Jimmy." The nurse stood and pulled five-year-old Jimmy by the hand. Jimmy held back for a moment and then slid off the chair and let the nurse lead him into the room. Jimmy's dark, wavy hair hung over one robin's-egg-blue eye, which looked around the room, alert and intelligent.

Ralph read the report of the boy's story—how he had survived the attack on his family by crawling under the front porch of his home. From under the porch, he had witnessed the 'wolves' attack and kill his sister and mother.

Ralph Morsching sat next to Roger Stringley at a chewed-up, oak table. Roger was a member of the investigative team, but he wasn't a werewolf. The nurse and Jimmy settled on two mismatched folding chairs in front of the table.

Joe Petrie stood beside the table closest to Jimmy. He leaned against the corner of the table and said, "Hi, Jimmy," as cheerfully as he could, trying to put the boy at ease. "My name is Joe and that big guy over there is Ralph, and the man sitting next to him is Roger. They want to hear the story of what you saw the other night."

Jimmy looked with a shy glance at the two men behind the table and then dropped his eyes back to the folded hands on his lap.

Joe frowned and said. "We've been directed by Governor Anderson to find out what happened in your town and tell all the people in the United States the truth." Joe walked over to where Jimmy sat on his folding chair, and knelt down so his head was at the same level as Jimmy's. "Now, to do the job your governor wants us to do, we need your help, Jimmy. Four people saw what happened a week ago on Wednesday night, when all those people were hurt. Four people in your town saw the wolves. Of those four, Jimmy, you're the most important witness."

Jimmy's head bobbed up and his face showed a slight smile on his lips, "I am?"

"Yes you are. Two of those people are sick and can't talk. You saw the wolves and you *can* talk." Joe hesitated. "Jimmy, can you tell me what you saw?"

Jimmy stared at his folded hands. Ralph watched the boy's face contort, and tears begin to flow down his cheeks. Jimmy started to shake as he remembered.

"Jimmy," the nurse said, "tell these nice men what you told the doctor and me about the wolves. If you don't they can't help us get rid of them."

Roger glanced at Joe, caught his eye, and then said, "Maybe Jimmy didn't see anything."

Jimmy sat up in his chair and glared at Roger. "I did too see something. I—I—saw great big wolves kill and eat my mommy and my sister, Becky."

The nurse pulled him back on the chair and patted his leg. Tears continued to cascade down his cheeks.

Joe patted Jimmy on the back, "Will you tell us the first thing you saw?" Joe said.

Jimmy sniffed a couple of times and the nurse handed him a Kleenex. He wiped his eyes and face, blew his nose, and handed back the wrinkled tissues.

"My daddy made me go outside and sit on the porch."

Ralph asked, "Why did he do that?"

Jimmy squirmed, "Because I was naughty. I made too much noise when he was watching TV. That was before the lights went out."

"Okay," Joe said, "then what happened?"

"It was dark out, but I saw one of those big wolfs run from behind our garage to the side of my house. At first, I thought it was Cracker."

Joe asked, "Who is Cracker?"

"Our neighbor's dog. But I knew it wasn't Cracker. The thing I saw was too big. Then the first wolf went behind my house."

Joe interrupted Jimmy. "You mean you saw more than one wolf?"

"Yeah," Jimmy said, "I saw another one run after the first one. They were real big."

Ralph said, "How big Jimmy?"

Jimmy slipped off the chair and raised his hands over his head.

Ralph nodded, "Four feet tall. Did they run on two feet or four feet?"

The nurse's eyes squinted together and turned to stare at Ralph's face.

"Wolves can't run on two feet," Jimmy said, looking at Ralph as if he was a dummy. "They ran on four feet, you know, like a dog." Jimmy's voice cracked with excitement.

"Good, Jimmy," Joe said. "You're being a big help, telling us just what we need to hear. Go on, what else happened?"

"Then I heard a window break. I know what that sounds like, cuz I threw a ball through our garage window last week." He smiled and then said. "I looked in through the screen door and saw one of the wolves bite my daddy on his head and make him bleed. My daddy started to scream and that's when I ran and hid under the porch. My sister Becky started screaming, and then she ran out the screen door. I looked between the steps and I could see her and mommy running across the grass." Jimmy stopped and wiped his nose on his hand.

Joe leaned forward. "And?"

"Then I saw two big wolfs run after them," Jimmy said. "They caught Becky and mommy, and then...." Tears flowed down his cheeks and sobs shook his body.

The nurse pulled Jimmy's head down on her lap. Jimmy's shoulders shook as he cried into the nurse's white skirt.

Ralph shook his head. He was now sure that werewolves were responsible for killing the people of Longville. What Jimmy described fit the werewolf size and mode of attack.

As Jimmy sobbed, the men discussed Jimmy's account of what had happened.

Ralph caught Joe's eye and then communicated telepathically, *Son of a bitch, this confirms it. There is another werewolf pack in the U. S.*

Joe shot back, *Tom warned me there might be.*

Roger was not a member of Ralph's werewolf pack, so Ralph and the other pack members had to be careful what they said around him.

Ralph stood up and moved toward the door. "It looks like the reports are correct," he said, "Wolves were responsible for killing all those people."

Roger nodded and looked at Ralph with a question on his face, "Yeah, I guess so, the only question I have is, do wolves get that big—over four feet tall?"

Ralph chuckled, "Maybe they weren't quite four feet tall." He winked at the nurse and smiled. She smiled back at Ralph, and then escorted Jimmy from the room.

The second witness's account provided no useful information. His ramblings, however, did support the theory of wolves being responsible for the killings.

The other two witnesses were still in a state of shock. They were unable to give any kind of coherent statement. One of them babbled repeatedly about a "big, big wolf." The other witness said, "Stand up—head flew through the air—eat mama."

According to the doctors, it would be months before they might regain their sanity, if ever.

* * *

The next afternoon, Ralph left the interrogation room as Tom was talking to one of the hunters. He walked down the hallway to where another interrogation was taking place. Ralph opened the door and saw Sergeant Michel talking to a man that fit the description of Sheriff McCarthy.

Sergeant Stan Michel was a forensic whiz. He was responsible for solving over half the U. S. Marshal cases in the four states that Ralph's team covered. He didn't like anyone calling him Stan, so everyone that knew him referred to him as Sergeant or Michel.

The Sergeant saw Ralph peeking through the doorway and motioned for him to come in. "Sheriff, I'd like you to meet Marshal Morsching. He's in charge of the investigation. He was appointed by President Thompson."

Ralph offered his hand to the Sheriff, who grabbed it with both of his hands and nervously shook it up and down.

"Hi, Mr. Morsching, sir," Sheriff McCarthy said, with a nervous tick causing his left eye to quiver. "I was just telling the Sergeant here what we've found so far."

"Go on, don't let me interrupt you," Ralph said, taking the Sheriff by the elbow and escorting him back to his chair. "If you don't mind, I'd like to sit in and listen."

The Sheriff nodded with a nervous twist of his head, exposing his awe of the Marshal. Ralph smiled and sat down on an old-cushioned living room chair.

"Well," the Sheriff said, looking directly at Ralph. "We found thousands of wolf tracks all over town. In gardens, alleys, and in muddy areas at the edge of town. We found some weird-shaped wolf prints inside several homes. You know, where the animals stepped in the blood of their victims."

Ralph nodded.

Sheriff McCarthy said, "The prints in the houses were like those of a wolf, but much larger, with longer claws. Some of the trappers in the area said the prints were those of wolves, the same number of toes and everything. Man, I tell you, some were gigantic, ten to twelve inches across. A couple of experts from the Minnesota Zoo came in a couple of days ago, and even they were hesitant to identify the real big ones as wolves."

Ralph leaned forward and rested his head on his two fists. "Did they say what they might be, if they weren't wolves?"

The Sheriff swallowed and then said, "Naw, they weren't sure. They suggested the tracks could have been from some larger crossbred form of a wolf. I'll tell you, the trappers around here have never seen prints that big, but they all agreed they were wolf tracks."

The Sheriff glanced down at the paper in his hand and then said, "Twenty bodies of residents are accounted for. Some of them were missing a few parts. What confounds me is that we have not found any evidence of what happened to the other thirty-four people. I'm sure you've seen pictures on TV and in the newspapers. Some of the victims were dismembered, and all of them were partially eaten."

"Are conditions in the forests that bad?" Sergeant Michel asked. "What I mean is, could the wolves have been that hungry to attack people in a town?"

"No," the Sheriff said. "The trappers tell me there are abundant deer in the woods, along with rabbits and mice. No, the wolves were not lacking for their normal food sources." The Sheriff glanced down at his list and went on, "We have four National Guard helicopters carrying sharpshooters flying over the area. As of this morning, they've shot twenty-eight wolves. The wolves were concentrated in three separate areas, suggesting they were from three different packs. The shooters tell me they've annihilated the two wolf packs closest to town."

"How many wolves do they figure are left?" Ralph asked.

"There might be ten, maybe fifteen still running around. Most of those belong to the third pack."

Sergeant Michel asked, "Sheriff, if we kill off those wolves, do you think it will prevent the same thing from ever happening again?"

"There's no doubt in my mind," the Sheriff said. "These wolves must have gone off the deep end to come into town and attack people."

"Your assessment of the situation should satisfy the people of Minnesota," Ralph said.

"It has to—what else can we do? Once we kill off all of the wolves, we've eliminated the problem," the Sheriff said, shrugging his shoulders.

* * *

A week later, the special investigation was completed. The team compiled their final report. Ralph scheduled a public meeting at which he'd inform the people of Longville what most of them knew and already believed. The mayor arranged for them to use the VFW Club, reserving most of the seats for residents and saving a few spots for members of the press and TV.

* * *

The next evening Ralph Morsching stood behind the podium waiting for his cue. The Channel 4 news director pointed to him, counting down with his fingers: *three, two, one...*

"Ladies and Gentlemen," Ralph said, to get everyone's attention. The room hushed. "Our investigation into the killing of twenty residents of Longville is now complete. Thirty-four other residents are still missing and presumed dead. We have not found any clues as to their whereabouts, but I assure you we are still searching. What we have found can in no way make up for the loss to Longville of so many of their friends and neighbors."

"I hope what my team has learned from the evidence will satisfy the living. With the expert assistance of the Cass County Sheriff's Department and Sheriff McCarthy, the Minnesota National Guard, the Minnesota Highway Patrol, and the Longville Police Department, our team has gathered all of the available facts in this case. The evidence we have is in the form of footprints, medical evidence, and the testimony of experts."

"All of our information supports the conclusion that the attack on the residents of Longville, and the subsequent deaths of its residents, was caused by three separate wild packs of wolves. We can't explain how or why three wolf packs happened to attack Longville at the same time. We found human tissue in the digestive systems of wolves from all three packs."

"Wolf behaviorists suggested to my team the possibility that there was a territorial fight between the three wolf packs, and that the people of Longville ended up in the middle of that fight. In addition to the fight between the packs, we have found another contributing factor which may explain the savagery of the attack." Ralph hesitated and then said, "Veterinarians performed autopsies on all of the wolves shot. Some of the wolves had an unusual brain infection, similar to, but not the same as rabies. There is a possibility that this infection may have exacerbated the attack."

The reporters in the crowd leaned forward. Several of them laughed. One of them yelled, "That's kind of a big word."

Ralph smiled. "I heard one of the scientists use it. Sounded impressive."

Here was something newsworthy, something to explain why the wolves attacked and killed that many people.

Ralph noted the heightened interest and said, "The veterinarians suggest these infections may have something to do with the attack on the people of Longville, but of course we cannot say it definitely caused the attack."

Everyone started talking and asking each other questions.

Ralph shouted, "Hey, quiet down and let me finish." The noise faded and Ralph continued, "Because all of the infected wolves have been killed, nothing like this should happen again." Ralph stepped back. "This is what I will report to Governor Anderson and a joint session of the Senate and House tomorrow. Thank you all for coming."

The reporters all dialed out on their cell phones. Ralph didn't mind. They would help spread his version of the cause for the 'Longville Massacre'—just what he wanted.

"Hey, Mr. Morsching," a reporter from the side of the room called out. "Are you sure you killed all the wolves?"

Ralph smiled, "Major Hendrickson of the National Guard assures me they killed them all. To make sure, I'll recommend in my report that they hire a core of special hunters and trappers, who will continue scouring the woods for any wolves we might have missed."

Ralph gathered his papers from the podium and started to leave when another reporter asked, "Will you be providing a written summary for us?"

Ralph turned back, "Our team will provide written copies of our full findings to the news media following our presentation to the Minnesota legislature on Wednesday, which is three weeks to the day that the atrocity occurred. I might add I am within the time frame Governor Anderson insisted on."

The eyes of Morsching and captain Tom Jarvis locked. A secret message flashed between them. They nodded their mutual understanding. They knew *what*, or rather *who*, was really responsible for the Longville Massacre, and it was not wild wolves.

* * *

Sergeant Michel, one of Ralph's top inspectors, left the VFW and headed back to the motel. He walked along the sidewalk, watching out for irregular pieces of concrete. He heard the clatter of footsteps coming up behind him. A chill raced down his spine. His werewolf senses screamed danger.

The word 'werewolf' raced through his mind. He started the steps that would bring on his own change. Hair had already sprouted on the back of his hands, and muscles had begun to enlarge, stretching fabric to the tearing point, when he heard a female voice behind him, "Excuse me, Sergeant Michel, could I ask you a couple of questions?"

Sergeant Michel stopped his transformation and whirled around, a frightened mask covering his face. He saw a woman with a press badge hanging from her jacket pocket. She was silhouetted against the light from the VFW. She wore a gray sports jacket. Long, blond hair cascaded over her collar. Even in the dim light, he could see that she was very attractive. He gulped and tried to speed up his return to normal. His hair reabsorbed, the follicles tightened, and muscles returned to normal. He had almost let his imagination expose him for what he really was.

A whoosh of air escaped from Sergeant Michel's mouth. He tried to assume a relaxed pose by placing his hands on his hips. It didn't work, but he felt better. "Sure, why not?" he said in a deeper than normal voice.

The female reporter advanced, pulling a tape recorder from her pocket.

"Hi, I'm Karen Foster with WCCO-Channel 4 news. I have been talking to some of the townspeople, and a few of them wondered if there was a link between the wolf attack and the digging up of the main roads leading into Longville. They told me that the disruption of Highway 84 on the north and south sides of town prevented any traffic from entering or leaving Longville. How was it possible that the telephone, cell phone, and electric services all went dead at the same time? The people I questioned think someone was behind all of these things happening concurrently. Would you care to explain?"

Sergeant Michel smiled. He thought to himself, *just like a nosy reporter*. "Let me address your last question first, regarding the telephone lines, cell phone and electrical disruptions. The electric company found a major short occurred at the substation on the edge of town. It happens that a gray squirrel shorted a critical transformer shutting down all electricity to Longville."

"Okay, I didn't know that," the reporter said contritely, and then added, "How about the cell phones?"

"That's easy. The towers require electricity to relay messages in and out of the tower."

"Okay, and how about the telephones, do they need electricity?"

"There is even a logical explanation for the telephones not working. A tree fell on the building which contained the switchboards for incoming and outgoing calls—just a freak accident."

Angrily the reporter said, "Okay—okay, I understand."

Sergeant Michel was actually enjoying putting this bitch in her place. "Now to the first part of your question. We heard that cock-eyed idea before. Let me lay it to rest for you. The digging of the roads was in no way related to the wolf attack. To believe that would suggest a coordinated, planned, intelligent operation conducted between humans and wolves. Let me assure you wolves are not that intelligent or cooperative. In the first place, how in hell could any human control three wild wolf packs? What benefit would any humans have, assuming they could control the wolves? Nothing was stolen, just innocent people killed."

The reporter interrupted, "Yeah, but…."

Sgt. Michel spoke louder. "Hold on now. Let me finish. The attack and the digging up of the roadway were coincidental. The buyers of the land on either side of town applied to Cass County and the State two months ago for building permits."

The reporter asked, "Why did they have to dig up the road?"

"The group that bought the property is planning to construct an office building on the south end of town and storage facilities on the north. The culverts were needed to drain the water from the upper side of the highway. The work on the culverts and roads just happened at the same time the wolves attacked the town. The road work was repaired Thursday morning, the day after the attack."

The reporter asked. "Care to explain another unusual feature I dug up?"

"And that is?"

"Three ham operators in town were killed," she exclaimed.

Sgt. Michel grabbed his chin with his right hand and said, "Hmm, there were a lot of people that were killed. We knew the Ham operators died and didn't see it as significant, so I guess I don't have an answer for you. It must be another coincidence."

"There are a lot of coincidences in this whole mess, if you ask me," the reporter huffed.

"Come on now," Sgt. Michel said. "To accept what you are suggesting would mean just what I said earlier. Humans and wolves would have been working in concert. Do you believe that?"

The reporter nodded. "No, I guess not. That would be absurd." She held the tape recorder closer to Sgt. Michel and said. "That brings up another question I have."

Sgt. Michel said with irritation coloring his words, "C'mon now, I must be going."

The reporter said. "Just one more question, please?"

"Okay."

"If three wolf packs were fighting each other over territory, why weren't any dead wolves found in town?"

Sergeant Michel's face paled. "Well—ah—ah—I suppose because none were killed in town. If there were any wounded ones they must have been able to make it back to the woods."

"Yeah, sure," the reporter said, "According to the release from the Sheriff's Department, all the wolves brought in died from bullet wounds, none from other causes." The reporter grunted, "Something in this whole story just doesn't add up." She turned and walked back towards the VFW Club.

Sgt. Michel wondered why no one on the Investigation team had thought of some of the reporters concerns. He decided he would talk to Ralph tomorrow.

As the reporter walked away, the sergeant forgot the dead wolves for a moment as he admired the swing of her hips.

* * *

Ralph sat alone in his makeshift office. A single light bulb made an effort to illuminate the room, but was not having much success. The shadows still controlled the perimeter of the room and the area behind the file cabinets.

In a few hours, the town of Longville would lose half its population when the press, National Guard and other police officials left. The human invaders would all go home and soon forget the sinister events that happened in Longville. The people of Longville could finish grieving and go on with their lives.

Ralph sat up and rested his hands on the old school desk. They may be able to put all of this behind them he thought, but when I go home, I will be starting my own hunt.

CHAPTER 14
A HUNTING WE WILL GO

Ralph swiveled his chair around and gazed out the window of his office on the tenth floor of the Bradbury Building. His eyes followed a Delta jet as it floated across the sky. Gazing at the skyline of Madison always brought him a feeling of inner peace and contentment. After all, this had been his home for over two hundred years.

Tom Jarvis burst into Ralph's office. The door crashed against the wall.

Ralph jumped. Tom's abrupt entrance had scared the heck out of him. He tried to hide the fact that he was momentarily frightened by continuing to stare out the window.

Ralph admonished himself. *I should have heard him coming down the hall. I need to pay more attention to what goes on around me.* He turned slowly from the window, keeping his shaking fingers on his lap. He glanced calmly at Tom, who stood puffing in front of his desk.

Tom, always the military man, stood with his legs apart and hands locked behind his back. He said, "Ralph, what in the hell are we gonna do about that other pack?"

Ralph slammed his fist down on the top of his desk. "That's simple, we are going to find the other werewolf pack and exterminate them. They bungled that Longville raid. If it wasn't for us conducting the investigation, there is a good chance werewolves could have been blamed for the Longville attack."

His face turned ashen. "Chances are our pack would have eventually been found out as well."

Tom said, "Doesn't that blow your mind?"

"What do you mean?"

Tom's eyes grew round, "Ralph, weren't you surprised to find out another werewolf pack exists? Where did they come from?"

Ralph rotated the chair toward Tom. Ralph's nostrils flared and the artery in his forehead pulsed. "Surprised? I was flabbergasted! I have no idea where they came from. Of course, that's not important. Our main problem is our survival." He shook his head. "We can't afford to let them repeat another feeding like that. They were stupid and reckless." He swung his chair back to his desk and slammed his elbows down. "Can you imagine what would happen to our pack if humans found proof that werewolves existed?"

Tom walked to the couch and sat down. He picked at his fingernails with a small pocketknife. "Jeez, I suppose we'd have to run for it. But Ralph, I'd still like to know where they came from. I thought our family was the only werewolves left in the world."

Ralph spread his fingers out on the desk. He did not want to worry about where the werewolves originated. They were here and that was enough. He knew Tom would keep bugging him until he found out where they came from.

"Okay, Tom. It might be possible someone survived the Belgrade massacre. Grandfather Adolph figured he and grandmother Rachel were the only ones to escape alive, but he always thought it possible the werewolf that infected him could have also passed on the curse to one of the other hunters before it died.

"In all the years of following the destruction of the werewolves that infected him, he never ran across any evidence of another werewolf in the Belgrade area. Of course, he finally fled Belgrade when his pack was exposed. He and Rachel ended up in Bavaria, Germany, before immigrating to America. He settled just outside of Madison and farmed until he died a hundred years later."

Ralph's eyes glazed over as his mind wandered, taking him into the past. He saw the inside of his grandparent's old homestead. Without trying, a picture of his great-grandmother Rachel popped into his mind. She was standing at the sink, peeling potatoes and humming to herself. Ralph's mind focused on that time, so long ago, when he had sat on great-grandpapa Adolph's lap. Ralph's father Adolph had been named after him. His father and grandfather Wilhelm were still working in the fields, but were expected home for supper soon.

He could hear the hoarse, rasping voice of his great-grandfather Adolph as he told the story of the killing of his pack in Belgrade.

"Listen, Ralphie," great-grandpa had said, "I'm going to tell you a story about our first pack. It happened a long time ago when Rachel and I lived in Europe."

Ralph felt a shiver of warmth similar to the one that radiated from his great-grandfather's body those many years ago. Every time he pictured his great-grandfather holding him, he felt safe and secure.

"Back in 1580 our pack was well established," great-grandfather had said. "Pack members owned a number of farms near Belgrod, as it was called back then. We were very careful in choosing our victims, so no one became concerned and looked for them. It was difficult staying hidden until our pack discovered a drug that held back the madness. The drug reduced the desire to kill and devour human flesh for long periods of time. We were ecstatic. In spite of the drug, at regular intervals, the desire for human flesh still rose up, overwhelming our control. When that happened, we had to satisfy our needs or experience the madness. On those occasions, the pack would venture into Belgrade or travel to another large city to hunt.

"Ralphie, we needed to satisfy the craving. Do you understand? We would hunt as a pack with all members participating. The important thing was that individuals did not have to kill their own victim. One victim satisfied all of our needs. We always chose our victim from the streets, someone single, with no attachments. We would often go down along the river, where the homeless people lived, and choose a victim.

"The start of our demise began when the pack entered Belgrade hunting for a derelict to feed on. Three members of my pack lost control. They became crazed and uncontrollable. They slipped over to the wild side. They ran off down the street toward the populated part of the city. We chased after them to stop them, but were too late.

"On a corner outside a tavern, the crazed ones came upon a group of people. They attacked and killed all but one. The survivor ran into the tavern screaming for help.

"We were a short distance away when we heard the screaming. We raced toward the noise, fearful of what we would find. Even though we expected the worst, we were shocked to see what the three had accomplished in such a short time.

"Four dead humans lay scattered on the cobblestone, blood splashed everywhere. The three out-of-control werewolves were feeding on the dead. They were engrossed in feeding and did not even know we had come up behind them. We attacked the renegade werewolves and killed them. Freed from their madness, their wolfish features changed back into their human forms.

"We raced off into the night before anyone saw us. From a dark alley a block away, we watched a crowd of people pour out of the tavern. The screams carried to where we hid as the humans circled the dead. Our three relatives lay among the dead humans and drew no special attention. They were just three more of the many torn and mangled bodies.

"The next day a group of angry townspeople used blood-hounds to follow our trail back to your Great-Uncle Frederick's farm. The armed group of people attacked the farm. They killed Frederick, Alicia, and their children. Their son, Grappli, escaped and fled through the corn fields to Herman Morsching's farm located on the other side of the valley.

"The mob set fire to Frederick's farm and then followed Grappli's trail across the valley. By mid-afternoon, the armed mob reached Herman's farm. Grappli continued down the valley, warning everyone. He arrived at my farm with a small group of werewolves. The members of my pack wanted to rally and fight the humans. Rachel and I tried to encourage them to flee, but they insisted we lead them in the battle.

"While we rallied the remaining pack members, two of Herman's older sons changed into werewolves. They fought the city mob and killed several humans before dying themselves. In the end, the mob killed all of Herman's family and decapitated the bodies.

"The citizens, incensed at finding out that werewolves existed, continued down the valley attacking and killing anyone with the name of Morsching. We tried to fight them, but it was no use. There were too many of them and they knew what to expect. Rachel and I were wounded, but were able to escape with our lives."

Tears ran down Ralph's cheeks. He blinked, flushing more tears from his eyes. The daydream was vivid. He pictured the burning buildings, the maddened mob, and the beheading of his ancestors. He pictured his wounded great-grandfather Adolph and great-grandmother Rachel as they had escaped into the forest. Every single one of great-grandfather's relatives died in the Belgrade Massacre. His great-grandfather had left Belgrade and later settled in Bavaria, Germany. Years later, they immigrated to the United States.

Ralph's body shook with empathy, as he wiped the tears from his face. The picture of his sobbing great-grandfather faded and his daydream ended. The memories left him saddened and feeling drained.

Ralph thought of his daydream, hoping to learn from the memories. "Tom, see if my reasoning is correct," he said. "First, we know this new pack does not use the drug or they would not have killed so many humans."

"Do you think they have fifty-four pack members?" Tom said.

Ralph said. "Jeez, I didn't consider that. It is unbelievable any pack leader would allow his pack to get that big."

Tom replied, "Don't forget, they are not us. Anything is possible."

"You are right. They can't be related to us or they would be using aldopamine."

"True." Tom folded the blade of his pocketknife and slipped it into his pocket. He stood, walked over to the desk and sat on a corner, placing a hand on Ralph's shoulder.

"You know," Ralph said, still finding it hard to believe his pack was not aware of other werewolves, "It's even more amazing that we've not run across the other werewolves. We've been in Minnesota many times."

"What makes you think they live in Minnesota?"

Ralph looked up with a startled look. "I just assumed it."

"Why not North or South Dakota, or for that matter, they could have come from anywhere."

Ralph shook his head and stared out the window. After a minute, he swiveled his chair back toward Tom. "They could have, but we have to start looking for them somewhere."

"I agree," Tom said. "We've got to stop them before they have to feed again. The next time they might be seen, and that would pull us into the mix." He walked over to the sofa and dropped like a lead weight.

Ralph made up his mind. "Here is what we are going to do. We will start with Minnesota, which in my mind is the logical place for them to be. Next Monday, I'm going to take a team to the Twin Cities. We will hunt for them and if we find them, we will destroy them. We have to be careful not to attract any attention to ourselves or to the fact werewolves are involved in the killings." He turned to the window again and placed his elbows on the arms of the chair. He formed his fingers into a pyramid in front of his chin and looked out the window, formulating the details of the hunt in his mind.

A few moments later, he murmured, "Tom, I want you to stay in Madison and run the office. I've got some vacation time coming. I'll handle the away team."

CHAPTER 15
BACK TO MINNESOTA

Ralph watched the gusting north wind lift several shingles on the garage roof across the street. The shingles tapped out a cadence of a long forgotten death march that played in the back of Ralph's mind.

Black clouds rolled out of the north. Ralph's eyes searched the horizon looking for the sun, which was nowhere in sight. He wondered if the sun would show up and chase the ominous clouds away. If the sun would shine, it would lift the momentary depression he was feeling. Ralph shook his head and thought, *It doesn't make any difference if it's sunny or cloudy, we have to leave for Minnesota.*

The thought of embarking on this mission excited Ralph. The werewolf pack could be headquartered anywhere, but he had a feeling their home base was somewhere in Minnesota. The Twin Cities was a good place to start looking.

The thrill of the hunt flowed through his body. He hoped this dismal weather was not an omen of what lay ahead. A touch of fear plagued him and rode the edge of his consciousness. Was nature trying to tell him something?

Ralph gave a lot of thought to starting a war between werewolves. He knew some of his pack members would be injured or killed in the next several weeks. Nevertheless, today would mark the beginning of his search for the out-of-control werewolves in Minnesota. After all, he had a responsibility to protect his pack.

Looking out the kitchen window, Ralph saw five of his handpicked team members standing next to the dark blue Chevy Suburban. Alice Jarvis, with her pitch-black hair and dark complexion, leaned against the front fender. She was Tom Jarvis's daughter-in-law, forty-seven years old and the most vicious killer in Ralph's pack. All of the other werewolves left her alone.

Pete stood near the rear door of the vehicle, avoiding the blustery wind. He was Ralph's second oldest son and slated to take over command of the pack if anything happened to Ralph. Pete was intelligent, built like a bull, and had a weird sense of humor.

Selected because of her role in the last feeding, Pete's seventeen-year-old daughter, Gretchen, was part of the team. On her own, she had prevented Bernie from losing control and going over to the wild side. Six months ago, Bernie had started to go crazy and Gretchen jumped him, biting him on the back She did not let go until Ralph came to her aid.

Ralph chose Joseph, also seventeen, because of his special ability to see into the future. With more experience, Joseph's unusual talents would be a tremendous asset to the pack. He had told Ralph yesterday that the expedition was going to be successful as long as they didn't stay in Minnesota too long.

The last member of the away team was Will Franzen. He was eighteen and another of Ralph's grandsons. Will showed the greatest promise of any member in the pack. He was intelligent and possessed excellent leadership skills. Will had played a major role in planning the last two human feedings by the pack. He had provided logistics and timing for both events, which had gone off without any problems.

Excitement radiated from the faces of the team members. Ralph knew they were thrilled at being included in this different kind of hunt—a hunt for their own kind. Ralph put on a light jacket and exited the house through the kitchen door. He walked toward the Suburban. "Okay, Pete, let's get going," he said, slapping him on the back.

The rest of the group scrambled for a seat.

Pete jumped behind the wheel. He turned the key and the vehicle coughed to life. He pointed the vehicle toward Interstate 94. A few minutes later, the Suburban crawled up the ramp onto the freeway and headed west for Minnesota.

With a yawn, Ralph said, "Wake me when we hit St. Paul." He slouched down in the passenger seat and closed his eyes.

A moment later Ralph opened his eyes and slid erect in his seat. He pivoted to look back over his shoulder. "Will, you did find us a place to stay didn't you?"

"Will stretched and shoved a pillow behind his head before he answered. "I booked us at the Hilton."

Pete glanced at Will in the rear view mirror. A smile crept across his face as he asked, "Where's it located?"

"South of the Airport, ah, just off of I-494." Will was annoyed at the second degree.

"Will," Pete grumbled. "I don't like the Hilton."

Will bounced up off his pillow. "Well, tough shit. If you don't like it, then you should have made the reservations." Will's face was red and his jaw muscles moved back and forth.

"Hey kid, take it easy. I was just kidding," Pete said, faking fright. He enjoyed the rise he got out of Will.

Ralph said, "Okay you guys, that's enough. Will, why not take a minute and explain to my bone-headed son why you chose the Hilton."

Will calmed down and said, "The biggest reason is that the hotel is centrally-located close to Minneapolis, St. Paul and the surrounding suburbs."

"Do you see now the wisdom of trusting Will to do the right thing rather than you?" Ralph smiled and slid back in his seat. Ralph knew everything was set. He closed his eyes and fell asleep.

* * *

Late in the afternoon, they crossed the bridge over the St. Croix River at Hudson, Wisconsin, and followed I-94 into the East side of St. Paul, then pushed down I-494, through Woodbury, Newport, and South St. Paul. It was not long before they spotted the Hilton, across from a bunch of planes and hangars on the north side of the freeway.

They checked in and rode the elevator to the tenth floor. Will had reserved three adjoining suites. Ralph and Pete chose the middle room. Their windows looked south, out over the Minnesota River bottoms that meandered behind the strip of hotels and business places.

The river ran through Fort Snelling State Park and emptied into the Mississippi River. Looking to the left, Ralph saw airplanes coming in for a landing at the Minneapolis-St. Paul International Airport.

Everyone unpacked and then gravitated to Ralph's room. Will was the first one through the door. He walked to Pete's bed and sat down, then looked at Ralph and said, "Well, what do we do now?"

Ralph shrugged his shoulders. "The first thing we do is take a ride and get acquainted with the Twin Cities."

Ralph called the desk and arranged for the rental of two automobiles. He then explained everyone's assignments.

Ralph and Pete took the Suburban and headed for Minneapolis.

Will and Pete's daughter, Gretchen, grabbed the red Chrysler convertible and headed east on I-494 toward St. Paul.

Alice, Tom Jarvis's daughter-in-law, and Ralph's son, Joseph piled into the more conservative Escort and followed I-494 east to 35E and then south toward Inver Grove Heights. The three teams spent the next few days exploring different areas of the Twin Cities.

Monday night arrived with a loud bang. Lightning raced across the sky from cloud to cloud. Other brilliant bolts followed a jagged path to the ground. The hotel windows rattled with each booming crash of thunder. Rain and sleet came down in sheets and pounded against the windows.

Ralph looked into the sky thinking that November was late in the season for thunder and lightning, but he wasn't going to stand on the balcony arguing the point. He hurried in and slammed the door to the rain. He left wet footprints on his way to the bathroom, removed his wet robe, and wiped his body dry. After putting on another robe, he walked out into the main room and plopped down on the sofa with a loud sigh. "Well, tomorrow we begin the search for the werewolves. It looks like we'll have to search each city and suburb until we find their lairs."

Will slouched on the other end of the sofa. His face brightened. "Good, I'm tired of all this aimless wandering."

A familiar theme jumped into Ralph's thoughts: what would happen to the pack if he and Pete died? Concern over a leaderless pack occupied his thoughts a lot. Ralph decided it was time to begin grooming someone else as a back-up to take over the pack. He was fast coming to the conclusion that Will was the logical werewolf to assume leadership if he and Pete were killed.

Now was a good time to start grooming him for his future role.

Ralph stared at Will. He was proud of his eighteen-year-old grandson. Several times in the recent outings, Will had demonstrated exceptional leadership. Most pack members were willing to listen to what Will thought about the way things should be handled. That was why Ralph went out of his way to give Will as much responsibility and experience as possible. The Minnesota excursion would be a good chance for him to learn what it takes to lead.

He turned to Will. "The past few days have not been a waste of time. It gave all of us a chance to learn the layout of the Twin Cities. It'll help in our search."

Will blushed as he said, "I know, Grandpa. I guess I'm just anxious to find the stupid werewolves and put an end to them."

Ralph smiled. "I know how you feel." Then he turned to the rest of his team. "Any questions regarding your assignments for tomorrow?"

Pete said, "Naw, we've gone over them enough."

"Okay, then let's get a good night's sleep," Ralph clapped his hands together. "Tomorrow the search begins for real."

Joseph and Will went to the room they shared. Will finished using the bathroom and changed into his pajamas, then crawled under the sheets and stared at the ceiling. Joseph headed for the bathroom.

Will turned toward the bathroom door and said," Joseph, if those werewolves are anywhere in the Twin Cities, their days are numbered."

Joseph appeared in the doorway. "I hope you're right, but aren't you worried some of us might be killed?"

"No, I'm not. They won't know what hit them. I'm looking forward to hunting and killing them."

"But, remember they're also werewolves, and they'll fight to protect their pack. Think about that, Will. Would you like someone like my dad coming after you?"

Will's eyes grew large, "Hell no!"

Chapter 16
Hanging Out At University & Rice

Across the street was a sign marking University Avenue. The cross street was Rice, which ran north and south. Will's gaze followed University Avenue to the east until his eyes locked on a white-domed building, topped by golden horses pulling a chariot. From his studies of St. Paul, he knew the building was the Minnesota state capitol.

Will rubbed his eyes and squinted as he attempted to read the small letters on the harness of one of the horses. He was surprised he couldn't make out all of the letters.

The November sky was overcast and hazy. A cool breeze blew up from the Mississippi River and sent a shiver through his body. He should have worn a heavier jacket.

Will leaned against the brown brick wall of the building behind him and felt cold from the bricks penetrate his jacket. He studied every person that passed by him. Some of the people caught him staring, diverted their eyes, and hurried by. He ignored the peculiar grimaces on their faces and wondered if he looked different to them. Maybe that was why they looked at him with weird side-glances. He caught himself sniffing like a dog, which would account for the strange looks he was getting. Strange behavior like that would make anyone nervous.

A tall man in a dark blue suit walked by carrying a leather briefcase. He stared at Will with a disgusted look before shaking his head and looking away.

As he passed by, Will heard him mutter, "The crazies you see on the streets nowadays."

Will smiled and thought, *If only you knew.*

Will spent the morning glued to the corner of University and Rice. The weatherman's prediction proved accurate. By late afternoon, the weather became colder and windy.

Traffic increased as people began to head home from work. Car exhaust polluted the air and made it difficult for Will to filter out the specific scent he was searching for.

A middle-aged woman shuffled toward Will from up-wind. She was a block to the east, yet he was able to detect the faint scent of blood. Under normal conditions that would excite him, but today he was looking for more important prey. He looked away, hoping he would be the one to locate the werewolves.

A few minutes later, a man driving a brown, rusted-out Chevy passed Will, traveling west on University Avenue. The exhaust smoke swirled on the breeze and blew toward Will. He smelled the strong scent of alcohol coming from the vehicle. Will gagged and swiveled his head to focus on another man in a gray suit standing on the corner of University Avenue and Rice Street.

The man waited for the lights to change. Will got a whiff of old urine and knew the man had wet his pants earlier in the day. From the strength of the ammonia, he guessed it had happened close to nine o'clock that morning. It would take that long for the bacterial decomposition of urea to produce such a strong stench.

The pleasing smell of yeast and bread wafted on the currents and eddies of the breeze. He knew the odors were coming from the Taystee Bread Day-Old Shop a few blocks away. His stomach growled. Wrapped up in his search for some sign of the other werewolves, Will had forgotten to eat anything all day.

Will grinned and leaned back against the building that housed AAA Vacuum Cleaner. The store was two buildings from the intersection. He closed his eyes. A scowl grew on his face as he told himself, *Shit, this is a waste of time, standing around waiting for a werewolf to walk by. Chances are one in a million that is gonna happen. Here I stand waiting for an odor to awaken my primordial senses.* He smiled and said out loud, "Hey, that's kind of poetic, but to locate the other werewolf pack will take more than my primordial senses."

He felt better after complaining and pushed away from the wall. He strolled toward the corner, hoping his patient efforts would bring results.

All of a sudden, his instincts kicked in and Will's head snapped erect. He could not prevent the growl that escaped from his throat or the sniffing sounds that was coming from his nose. Like a hunting dog, his head swiveled back and forth, his nose testing the wind.

He honed in on a faint, but distinct smell. It was werewolf. His nose pointed eastward. Mixed in with the exhaust-laden currents, urine, baking bread odors, and a hundred other scents, swirled a few molecules of werewolf musk. There was no mistaking the distinctive smell.

Will jogged down the sidewalk toward the State Capitol, his nose leading him. He didn't notice the deliveryman until he bumped into him. Two boxes of drugs tumbled from the man's arms. He did a funny dance to keep the other three boxes from dropping. Will ignored the string of curses that followed him as he ran east on University Avenue.

Will was no longer in charge of his actions—his nose was. He did not even know that he had crossed Rice Street against a red light until he heard brakes screeching. Out of the corner of his eye, he saw a fat woman bounce back from the steering wheel of her mini-van, which had stalled in the middle of the crosswalk. In a daze, the woman reached over and pulled a bleeding child up from the floor. Will saw that the passenger side windshield was shattered.

As he mounted the curb on the other side of the street, Will said. "Way to go Lady. It's your fault for not making your kid wear a seat belt."

Frightened, people parted on the curb to let Will through. Halfway down the block toward Park Street, Will sniffed the air. "Shit, I've lost the scent," he said, twirling in a circle.

His mind sought a solution. *They could have passed me on the other side of the street or driven by me in a car. If they are west of me, that means they can smell me by now.*

A chill caused the hair on the back of his neck to stand erect. They could have gone north or south. What do I do? He shrugged his shoulders and without hesitation turned south on Park Street.

Will jogged down the street to where it curved in front of the state capitol and then stopped. The 'were-odor' once again assaulted his nasal passages. He looked upwind and saw fifty people walking in all directions. Most of them were heading for Robert Street. Will raced down the street and lost the scent again.

He stood at the Robert Street intersection wondering if he should follow it to the northwest or southeast. He threw up his arms and then turned to the southeast. He passed over I-94, toward downtown St. Paul.

A block ahead, three men were walking on the other side of the street. Will saw their lips moving and one of them was using his hands to emphasize a point as he talked.

Will ran down the street until he was across the street from them. The werewolf scent hit his nostrils and overpowered him. He stumbled, surprised at the strength of the odor. He regained his footing, afraid they might have noticed him stumbling around. Will slowed to a walk and took several deep breaths. He shivered from the emotional drain he was experiencing.

He was afraid to glance across the street, because he knew they were staring at him. He felt their eyes boring through him. He steeled himself and stole a furtive glance across the street. The men were walking and talking as before, paying no attention to him.

Will glanced at the men. Two of them were dressed in dark blue business suits. One man was gray-haired, while the other man was around fifty years old. The third person was a young man dressed in a Twins' team jacket and baseball cap.

To Will, they looked like two ordinary executives walking from one business meeting to another. He did not understand why the younger man was with them. The distinctive smell of werewolf identified them as being very different from ordinary humans. To avoid drawing attention to himself, Will dropped further back and continued to follow them at a more leisurely pace.

* * *

Across the street, oblivious to the presence of another werewolf, Jerrold, Richard, and Butch walked along discussing the meeting they'd just had with Senator Bob Johnson. They had met with the senator to discuss issuance of the new state highway contracts. The senator had assured Jerrold the contracts would be forthcoming for the Guhl Construction Company.

At the corner of Robert and 10th, the three checked traffic and crossed to the other side of the street.

* * *

God," he screamed to himself. *They're coming after me.* He began to shake. He wanted to run away, but his legs would not respond.

The three men turned in front of Will and continued walking toward downtown. A half a block later, they turned into a three-story parking ramp. Will relaxed, feeling his heart beat drop.

Cracks and fissures covered the cement walls of the ramp. It looked like the building could collapse at any time. Will walked to the corner and peered down the side of the building. He looked for another exit. Seeing none, he walked back to Robert Street and watched the exit. From his vantage point behind a garbage dumpster, he would see any vehicle leaving the ramp.

Will heard a vehicle coming. He bounced his fist off his forehead. "Just great," he said aloud, then turned to the building behind him and hit the wall with his fist. "How in the hell am I going to follow them?" He kicked the wall with his foot.

Will recognized the three men in the red sports car when it emerged from the ramp exit. The driver waited until three cars had cleared the lane and then pulled out toward downtown St. Paul. Will committed the license plate number to memory—385-ERW.

"That's all I can do for now," Will said, clenching his fists at his side. He pulled a cell phone from his pocket and made a call.

CHAPTER 17
'WERE' SCENT REPORTED

At the table in his hotel room, Ralph studied a map of the Twin Cities. He used a stubby yellow pencil to mark the areas they had already searched. Closed windows and patio doors trapped the smell of old sweat in the room. In the corner, the beds were unmade and half-filled glasses of wine sat on the bedside stand.

Ralph jumped when his phone rang. Wiping beads of sweat from his forehead, he picked up the call. "Yeah!"

Ralph listened. A broad smile creased his face. "Good job, Will. This is the break we've been waiting for." He was quiet for a moment and then said, "Why didn't you follow them?"

"My car was blocks away so I chose to follow them on foot. When I first got the scent, I felt I needed to stay on it or risk losing it. I managed to get their license number."

"Will, you've done a great job," Ralph said. "At least we know they're in Minnesota. If you were here, I'd give you a big hug. Come on in. We have plans to make."

Ralph slammed the receiver down and jumped up from the table. He raced to the balcony door and threw it open. He screamed into the winds, "We got the bastards now!"

CHAPTER 18
WHO IS THE OWNER?

Ralph wore a pair of gray shorts with a green paint streak on the left leg. A faded green T-shirt, with a Green Bay Packers logo on the front completed his wardrobe.He drummed his fingers on the table, picked up his phone, and placed a call to Madison. A woman's voice answered. "Good evening. This is the U. S. Federal Marshal's office. How may I direct your call?"

"Hey Marge, this is Ralph. What are you doing at the office so late?"

"Oh, I was just finishing up a few things before going home. How are you? How is your vacation?"

"I'm enjoying Minnesota," Ralph lied. "Did you know this is the fifth time I've been here?"

"No, is that right? I knew you just came back from there a couple of weeks ago. You must like it, to go back."

"Yeah, I like it all right, but I'm also doing some business over here." Ralph said. "Say Marge, is Tom still there?"

"I'll put him on." Tom picked up.

"Tom—Tom is that you?"

Tom sounded surprised, "Ah, Yeah."

"Good, listen, I want you to check a vehicle license number for me. I want the request to come from the office rather than from me. You will have to call the Minnesota Motor Vehicle Department."

"Hold on, let me grab a pen," Tom said, excitement shaking his voice. "Okay, go ahead."

"385-EWR."

Tom said, "It sounds like you might have something."

Ralph knew Tom was dying to hear what they had found, but Marge sometimes listened in on calls, so he needed to watch what he said. "Yeah, this is a definite link to the case we've been working on. Will's the hero, he eyeballed the lawbreaker."

Excitement flowed through Tom. He couldn't contain himself as he jumped up and down in his chair. "Should I bring the rest of the marshal's to Minnesota?"

"Not yet," Ralph cautioned. "Give me time to check everything out and get surveillance set up. I'll call you in a day or two if we need backup. Get on that license number and call me back as soon as you get a name and address to go with it."

"Okay, talk to you later," Tom said.

Ralph felt Tom's excitement over the phone, but he couldn't tell him any more of the details and hung up. It had been years since Ralph felt this much excitement.

A challenging hunt was ready to begin. He was exhilarated over the prospect of a fight to the death between his pack and the out of control Minnesota werewolves. Nothing was more stimulating than a hunt for his own kind.

* * *

When Will finally walked into Ralph's hotel room, Ralph jumped up with a big smile and threw his arms around him. He hugged him tight and Will started to cough. Ralph loosened his grip, but the excitement was contagious. They both jumped up and down, with arms around each other, like a couple of football players who had just scored a touchdown.

"We got them now Will," Ralph said in his ear. "Those sons-of-bitches are gonna die soon."

CHAPTER 19
INTO THE ENEMIES LAIR

Pete called out directions, pointing to a side street that came up just after the sales office for the Wedgewood Development. "385-EWR is registered to a Jerrold Guhl who lives at 9297 Wedgewood Lane. So according to this map, we need to take a right, just ahead . . . there on Lake Road."

Will signaled and slowed for the turn. The dark blue Suburban leaned around the corner. They passed between ponds on both sides of the street. Large homes circled the pond on the left.

"Take a left at the next street," Pete said.

To the right was a small park with some basketball hoops, a tennis court and playground equipment. A small pavilion overlooked the south end of Colby Lake. Will turned at the corner and proceeded down the street.

"Good, now look for 9297 Wedgewood Lane," Pete said, checking house numbers, and then glancing at the GPS. "The house should be six blocks ahead."

They passed by impressive homes laid out on spacious lots. Some of the homes were three-story mansions. All of the homes possessed well-manicured yards, with the right shrubs in the right places.

"I see it, Will," Ralph said, tapping him on his shoulder and pointing.

Will slowed. On the left side of the road, the sun reflected from the roof of a massive three-story brick mansion with a four-car attached garage. A paved drive circled in front of a pillared entrance. The drive looped back to complete the circle just before the street. A bean-shaped pool with a magnificent bronze statue occupied the center of the drive circle.

Ralph peered between the neighboring houses and saw a few people golfing—probably the last chance they would have this year. Large homes ringed the Wedgewood Golf Course. Ralph leaned back, impressed. "Keep going, Will," he commanded. "We'll turn around up ahead and come back to take a look at the house again on our way out."

Will looked at Ralph with a puzzled expression.

Ralph noticed this and said in a gruff voice, "We don't want to leave our scent. Do we?"

Will shook his head, not understanding. "But Grandpa, the wind is blowing from the south, and we're north of the house. They can't smell us."

"Not now, Will," Ralph said. He was busy looking at everything he could see and paid no attention to what Will said.

In the passenger's seat, Pete was busy videotaping the mansion and surrounding homes. Will sat behind the wheel feeling that if he moved he would draw attention to himself from the werewolves inside the house.

Pete focused the camcorder on the security emblem sticking out of the ground beside the front door. It reminded him of a limp, yellow flower. He panned the camera to show the curved metal bars decorating the windows on the first and second floors. *It would be one tough house to break into,* he thought.

The shadows created by the afternoon sun cast a black and foreboding picture of the house from the street. The scene sent shivers down Ralph's spine. The mansion was heavily fortified. It would be too dangerous to attack. He decided this would not be their primary objective.

Ralph reached over the front seat and touched Will on the shoulder, "Let's go up a ways and turn around. We'll come back for another look."

CHAPTER 20
I SPY

Jerrold and his sons Richard, Bruce, and grandson Butch relaxed on the deck at the back of the house unseen by the three men in the car. They had finished nine holes of golf and were enjoying a beer and watching the few golfers still on the course.

Richard winked at his father. "Too bad Bruce bogeyed the ninth hole or I would be paying for dinner tonight."

"You know, being the pack leader," Jerrold bragged. "I have the power to control the ball."

"Oh, shit, Dad, you can't do that, can you?" A disbelieving look spread across Bruce's face.

Jerrold said. "Of course not, son. If I could, I would not have let Butch embarrass all three of us. 'Were' beings cannot...."

Richard heard the sound of a car stopping. He growled, interrupting the playful banter between Jerrold and Bruce. The others froze.

Richard lifted his head high, sniffing a breeze that gusted and swirled around the house. The hair on the back of his neck bristled and then stood erect. "I smell 'were-scent', and it is not from our pack."

Butch, Bruce and Jerrold thrust their flaring nostrils into the air. Butch and Jerrold snorted when they caught a few molecules of foreign were-scent. Bruce sniffed, but did not smell anything unusual. In unison, Richard, Jerrold and Butch vaulted over the railing of the deck, followed by a bewildered Bruce. They raced around the corner of the house.

Jerrold skidded to a halt when he saw a dark blue suburban stopped on the street in front of his house. His eyes locked on a man sitting in the back of the Suburban. Even though separated by a hundred feet, Jerrold could see the man's dark blue eyes.

Jerrold snarled, shocked at the brazen invasion of his home territory by another 'were-being'. *Who were they?* Jerrold and the man growled at each other like two German shepherd's ready to do battle.

Coming into another werewolf's territory uninvited was an invasion of privacy, a direct challenge. Jerrold acknowledged the violation with a low bark. From this moment on, one of the invaders would have to die before this insult was resolved.

Jerrold snarled his willingness to meet the man in a battle to the death.

The man growled in response, but realized this was neither the time nor place, and bowed his head. They would meet again.

The Suburban accelerated away from the house.

* * *

When the vehicle was a half a block away, Ralph Morsching said, "Shit!" and hit the back of the driver's seat with open hands.

Will's head bounced forward.

Ralph continued, "I wasn't ready for this. I didn't want them to know we were hunting them—not yet." He shrugged, accepting the deal fate had handed him. "Well, there's nothing we can do about it now. They'll be on guard from now on and hunting us. We no longer have the advantage of surprise."

Pete snarled and dropped the camcorder on the seat. "That's okay, Dad, it will make the fight and the outcome that much more exciting."

Ralph shrugged his shoulders. "Let's get out of here, Will. We don't want to make it too easy for them to follow us back to our hotel."

Will accelerated and the Suburban roared like a charging lion.

* * *

As Jerrold raced toward the red Corvette sitting in the driveway, he called back over his shoulder, "Richard stay and warn the rest of the family. We'll see if we can catch them. Bruce, you and Butch come with me." He tore open the door of the Corvette. Bruce jumped behind the wheel and buckled up and Butch vaulted into the back seat. The Corvette growled and Bruce squealed out in pursuit of the dark blue Suburban. Jerrold glanced at his watch, "Shit, they have a big head start."

The Red Corvette flew north on County Road 19 and then turned left on Valley Creek Road, heading toward Woodbury City Center. Bruce circled through the streets of Woodbury, attempting to pick up the 'were-scent'.

Fifteen minutes later, Jerrold shook his head and said, "We lost them. Let's go home, Bruce."

CHAPTER 21
VICTORY ANTICIPATED

The six members of the Morsching pack crowded into Ralph's hotel room. Will and Pete sat on the sofa, finishing a pizza.

"Okay, my family," Ralph said. "What we did this afternoon was stupid, but we stll managed to locate one of their hideouts. It must be their headquarters, and it's well protected, so we won't attack them there. We'll keep them under surveillance until a good opportunity to eliminate some of them presents itself."

He opened the French doors leading out to the balcony and walked into the darkness. He looked out over the Minnesota River bottoms and then swung around with a dramatic flair and reentered the room. "Remember, as we eliminate them, none of the killings can leave any evidence linking their deaths to a werewolf. You can rob, beat, shoot or strangle them, just as long as you kill them in human form. In no way, will any of the killings be in werewolf form." He walked back to the table and banged his fist down. "Am I understood on this point?" Ralph scanned the room and gathered the nods and grunts of acceptance.

Ralph picked up his glass of Southern Comfort from the table and raised it to the other pack members, who raised their glasses. An air of confidence permeated the room. Ralph said, "I propose a toast to the success of the Morsching pack, and to a victorious hunt."

A giggle escaped Will's lips, betraying his nervousness. His body shook with excitement at the thought of killing another werewolf. A trickle of red wine spilled over the side of his glass and ran down his fingers. "Shit," he said. "I'm going to hunt werewolves. I can't believe it." He blanched when he remembered they would be hunting him as well, and would be just as dangerous.

"To victory." Alice Jarvis saluted.

Will looked at Alice and shivered. She scared him. She was the deadliest female killer in the pack, in part because she lacked a conscience. Will had seen her in action during their last hunt and knew how vicious she was.

"To a safe and successful hunt," Joseph Morsching said.

With a broad smile, Ralph raised his glass and, tipped his head back craining it, "To the Morsching pack."

Will lifted his glass and said in a high squeaky voice, "To the High Wolf."

All started chanting, "Ralph—Ralph—Ralph—Ralph—Ralph," as they began to remove their clothing. Groaning, snapping and crunching sounds filled the room and then the room went silent, except for the heavy breathing of six hairy werewolves. Five sat on their haunches within a circle of clothing around Ralph, the leader of the pack. Ralph stood before them with his hairy chest jutting forward. He stared at the ceiling, eyes gleaming with excitement.

CHAPTER 22
THE FIRST KILL

Streetlights illuminated the exterior of the parking ramp. Every hundred feet, cement pillars on either side of rectangular openings, admitted light into each floor. Between these faint blocks of light, shadows of tree limbs scratched against the cement walls. On the fifth floor, a shadow moved among the cars. One of the security lights went out. Broken glass tinkled to the cement floor, as light after light was extinguished. Shadows were no longer visible.

Something at home in the darkness moved down the center of the aisle, no longer inhibited by the light. The entire fifth floor was now dark, except for small slivers of light from the streetlights. A presence waited.

* * *

Three blocks away, on the eighth floor of the Cancer Institute, evening classes were ending. Students dribbled out of the lecture hall in twos and threes, going off in various directions. In an hour, the hallways would be abandoned.

Marsha Guhl, daughter of Jerrold's son, Bruce, was a tall, blonde woman of twenty-two years who possessed a bubbly personality to go with her large breasts and narrow waist. She was attractive, but not beautiful.

Stuffing her book and notes into her backpack, she exited the lecture hall. Following a group of younger students, she walked down the hallway and entered the elevator with three of them, riding it to the ground floor.

Marsha walked out the exit into misty darkness. She hurried down the five steps to the sidewalk. A chill crept down her back, causing her to shiver. She walked from streetlight to streetlight, not afraid, but feeling something was not quite right.

Marsha heard a group of students walking ahead of her, and then saw them appear out of the mist. Feeling alone and vulnerable, she walked faster to close the distance to the group, thinking there would be safety in numbers.

A premonition that something evil was out tonight, traveling the darkness, flashed through her mind. Even so, she was not afraid. After all, she came from a family of werewolves. She was not one, but being around them gave her a different slant on fearful things.

Looking up, she saw dark clouds swirling overhead, moving to the southeast, pushed by a cool northwest wind. Humidity hung heavy in the late November air, sending another chill racing through her body. She pulled her jacket tighter around her neck, appreciating the warmth of the down lining.

The warning her grandfather had issued last week popped into her mind. Jerrold had told the family that a foreign werewolf pack was in the Twin Cities area and everyone should be careful until the Guhl pack discovered their intentions. She wondered why she thought about the warning just now and shivered again, but this time not from the cold.

She walked faster.

At Union Street, Marsha crossed ahead of two cars that were racing toward her. She jumped up on the curb just as they zoomed by and followed the sidewalk toward the parking ramp. Through the fog, the open mouths of the parking ramp yawned before her. Over the entrance, a florescent light illuminated a hazy circle of light around the door.

The brightly lit elevator room promised a safe haven. As she opened the door and walked into the small waiting room, a cold, eerie feeling raised goose bumps on her arms. She thought the response was from the cold.

She pushed the call button for the elevator and the door opened, giving her a start. Feeling jittery, she peeked into the bright elevator car.

No one, she sighed. "Quit being such a chicken," she admonished herself. She stepped into the elevator car and pushed the button for the fifth floor.

In the well-lit elevator, her stress dissipated and her thoughts turned to her newest boyfriend, Frank Williams. He was handsome and sexy. She had met Frank a week ago at the Gold Rush in Cottage Grove, a hangout for college kids and young adults. Sex had occurred on their second date, and she was anxious to see him tonight for more.

The elevator jerked to a stop on the fifth floor and the door slid open. The rest of the ramp was dark, except for the small amount of diffused light from the streetlights below. She noticed that all the overhead lights were out. Marsha stared into the darkness and saw bits and pieces of other cars parked along the sides of the ramp. For a moment, she considered turning around and taking the elevator back down to the first floor. From there she could call for an escort. However, that would take time, and she was in a hurry to see Frank.

Marsha stepped out. The elevator doors slid shut behind her, committing her to the darkness. Her Pontiac convertible was at the far end of the ramp.

She wondered, *Why in the hell did I park so far from the elevator? I have to stop being such a coward.* She took a deep breath and took a tentative step away from the safety of the elevator. She lifted her backpack to her breast, folded both arms around it, and hurried toward her car.

Marsha recognized the outline of her Pontiac. She fumbled in her jacket pocket for her car keys. She didn't want any delay in getting into her car. As Marsha rounded the back fender of her car, she heard something crash behind her.

With a scream, she turned toward the threat. She couldn't see anything. The same crashing noise occurred again. It came from the street below. Trapped air whooshed from her lungs. There was nothing for her to be afraid of, but her heart fluttered in her chest anyway. A sigh escaped her lips, marking an end to this nonsense.

The moment Marsha turned back she felt, rather than saw, a dark shape rise up in front of her. She gasped, unable to move as the presence darted toward her. Strong arms grabbed her hair. A fist smashed into her face. She screamed from the pain, and sagged. The fist pounded her until the hurt went away and unconsciousness overtook her. She slumped to the concrete floor.

It wasn't that hard to find his prey. He used the University of Minnesota web site to locate her and once he knew which classes she was signed up for, the rest was simple.

Will Franzen, stood over Marsha's unconscious body. He glanced around, listening for the presence of anyone, but no one was there. They were all alone.

As though he didn't have a worry in the world, Will pulled a pair of latex gloves from an inside jacket pocket and slipped them on his delicate hands— the hands of a pianist, or a surgeon. He dropped down, his knees on either side of Marsha's body, and began to rip her clothes off. When Marsha lay naked before him, he unbuckled his pants, dropped his shorts and slipped a condom on his erect penis. He spread Marsha's legs and savagely raped her.

Will was nothing more than a smudge on a black background. He rose up from Marsha's limp body, removed the condom, and stuffed it into a plastic sandwich bag. He pulled his pants up, taking his time buckling his belt. He slipped the plastic bag into his jacket pocket and brushed off his clothes. He picked up Marsha's purse and stuffed it in a pocket on the inside of his jacket. In a high-pitched nervous voice he said, "I dedicate number one to Grandfather Ralph and the pack."

Will bent down over Marsha's unconscious body and wrapped his gloved hands around her throat. He squeezed until he heard the cartilage rings crack and felt her trachea collapse. Marsha convulsed, as her lungs tried to take in air. Will felt her spasm again, and then she was quiet.

Will's shoulders moved up and down as he laughed, proud of what he had just done. He had struck the first blow for his pack. Will peeled the latex gloves from his hands and stuffed them into the bag with the condom, and then he turned and walked up the ramp to the elevator and pushed the down button.

Marsha had become the first victim in the 'Werewolf War'.

Chapter 23
Dig 'Em Out

Butch guided the green Chevy Malibu down the off-ramp unto Long Lake Road. A block ahead, the Park and Ride Lot sign glowed white on green through the swirling snow. He signaled and turned into the lot. Five cars were scattered across the pavement. He headed for a dark corner, killed the engine next to a large snow bank, got out of the car, and walked around to the trunk. He glanced back as Brad stepped out and slammed his door.

Butch shook his head, "Jesus, Brad, be quiet."

"Oops, I'm sorry."

Butch turned and headed down a snowy embankment behind the car, waiting behind some bushes for Brad to join him.

For several nights, Guhl teams—angry over the death of Marsha—searched different suburbs for some sign of the other werewolf pack. They knew the rival pack was somewhere in the Twin Cities. Tonight Butch and Brad were going to search New Brighton, a northern suburb.

Butch punched Brad on the shoulder. "Well, let's do it."

They undressed, folded their clothes, slid them under the bushes and covered them with snow. They were proficient at making the change.

In less than three minutes, two werewolves trotted away from the shrubs. Butch melted into the second row of foliage and disappeared into the darkness, headed north along the west edge of Long Lake. He wasn't worried about the large tracks they were leaving behind, because it was snowing and was supposed to do so all night. By morning their tracks would be covered.

Butch and Brad loped across a field. In the distance, a dog howled. Butch turned toward a large housing development. When they got close, Butch moved toward a yellow house surrounded by a chain link fence. He jumped the fence and angled across the back yard. He thought of the occupants sleeping inside. If they knew of the danger passing by, they would never sleep again without leaving their lights on.

Ten minutes later, Butch stopped behind a house surrounded by Styrofoam cones protecting dormant roses. Dozens of odors inundated his nose. He was able to ignore the everyday odors of cat and dog waste, frozen garbage, gas, and oil.

Butch snorted and shook his head with disappointment. The one odor he was hoping to detect was not there. Butch trotted out of the yard and turned upwind from the houses.

They were careful not to travel downwind and give the other werewolves a chance to pick up their scents. If the other pack got a whiff of them, they could be the hunted down and killed.

Butch came to the north end of the Long Lake. He stopped and waited for Brad to catch up. Brad stopped and sniffed the night air, searching for the elusive werewolf scent. Butch knew it would take only a few molecules of the 'were-scent' for them to locate the enemy.

Butch glanced at Brad and said, "I hope the other teams are having better luck than we are. We can't let them get away with killing Marsha."

"Yeah—the bastards! But we won't know what kind of luck they're having until we get back to the car."

"I can't believe no one has found them—yet."

"We just have to keep trying."

"I've got a feeling tonight is the night."

What Brad said reminded Butch of what Grandfather said earlier tonight. "I'm confident, that if we persist and do not falter, we will find their lair. It's a matter of time and then we will destroy them."

Butch had told Grandfather earlier in the evening that "he was not going to stop searching until he'd found the killers of Marsha and then...."

Butch blew out a large volume of air and took off. Brad followed him in their dash across a street over a snow bank and down into the ditch. They turned southward back toward Pike Lake and their car.

It took Butch and Brad two hours to come full circle. The two werewolves stood in the bushes at the back of the Park and Ride lot, reversed the "change" and retrieved their clothes. It was below freezing, and they shivered as they dressed. Butch trotted through the bushes to the car and reached down along the driver's seat for the trunk release. He walked to the rear of the car and removed two beers from an Igloo cooler. He threw a can to Brad and then leaned against the rear fender of the Malibu.

Brad joined him and let out a big, dejected sigh. "Shit."

Butch downed half the can in one gulp. "Ah, that hits the spot." He turned and slammed the cooler lid, closed the trunk and boosted himself up on the back of the trunk. Leaning back against the curve of the rear window, he said, "Well Brad, at least we know they're not in the New Brighton area."

"Yeah, but I was hoping we'd be the ones to find them," Brad shrugged his shoulders. "Ah hell, let's go home."

They finished off their beers and threw the cans behind a clump of bushes. As Brad started the engine, the cell phone buzzed.

Butch looked at Brad and then at the cell phone. He picked it up as if it was a hot coal. "Hello," he said, grabbing the dash with his left hand.

The elated voice of Jerrold said in his ear, "We've located the prize. Come home."

The phone went dead.

"They found them!" Butch was no longer tired. He reached over and messed Brad's hair. "Come on, let's go. Grandfather wants us home."

Brad grinned and jammed the accelerator to the floor. The car shot toward the exit.

"Slow down, Brad," Butch cried, balancing himself with both hands on the dash as the car skidded around the corner. "We don't want to kill ourselves, do we?"

Chapter 24
Blow Them Out Of the Hilton

Two nights later, at 1:30 a.m. Richard, Brad, and Butch ran along the Minnesota River Bottoms. Their pawed feet sank through the deep snow. On the bluff to the north, Butch caught a glimpse of the outline of old Fort Snelling still guarding the Minnesota River. Below the limestone cliffs, streams of cars moved on Highway 5 toward St. Paul or the International Airport.

Butch's fur-covered legs carried him through stomach-high grasses sticking up through the snow. His thick, padded feet kept him from sinking in too far. He moved his head back and forth, dodging branches that tried to pluck his eyes out.

Butch trembled with the joy of being in werewolf form. His excitement grew when he thought about their assignment tonight. He was proud that Grandfather Jerrold had picked him as a member of the attack team. He threw his head back, relishing the ecstasy of it.

His eyes caught a bit of light streaming through the overhead branches, and he knew right away what was pushing his excitement to such a high level. A quarter-moon hung in the sky like a beacon, bright and golden. Butch growled and lowered his head to let a branch scrape the top of his head.

Uncle Richard led the attack team toward the hotel strip along I-494. It had been Richard and Dean who had located where the Morsching werewolves were staying. Most of the pack couldn't believe the Morschings were so stupid as to stay at such an obvious place. Butch didn't agree, when he considered how long it took to find the invaders.

As they approached the hotel area, Richard surged out ahead of Butch and Brad. Richard carried an ATW (Anti-Tank Weapon) strapped to his back. He claimed it was more comfortable to carry it in that position while running on all fours. Brad carried three high-explosive missiles in pockets of a special vest made for guide dogs to carry objects. Butch carried binoculars strapped tightly against his body to prevent them from flopping around.

A rabbit scurried in front of Butch and then froze, statue-like, to avoid the strange animals running through his woods. The rabbit's fear sent a flash of exhilaration shooting through Butch's brain. He ran on, savoring the moment. There would be another time to chase rabbits.

The werewolves were shadowy blurs, almost invisible because of the darkness and the speed at which they traveled. Butch stopped at the top of a small snow-free knoll and looked at lights flashing from the top of buildings ahead. This had to be the hotel area.

Butch followed Richard and Brad up a steep bank, which brought them out of the bottoms. They crested a small, snow-covered hill, which overlooked the Hilton Hotel parking lot and then stopped. The three werewolves dropped to their bellies in the snow and studied the parking lot for signs of humans.

Brad's body convulsed as he gulped in large volumes of air. He looked back and forth between his father and Butch, who suspected Brad was afraid. Brad seemed very nervous and Butch wondered why Richard had selected Brad for this team when everyone knew he was a young and inexperienced werewolf. But then, he was Richard's son.

Earlier that afternoon, Brad had admitted to Butch that he was scared. Butch had caught Brad's nervous glance but had merely winked.

Brad's mouth now gaped open. "Butch, how can you be so cool? Aren't you afraid?"

Butch shook his head no, turned to Richard and said, "What now?"

Richard nodded his muzzle in the direction of the utility building. "Let's head for that shed in the middle of the parking lot and get on its roof."

Butch looked at Brad and noticed his eyes were closed, "Are you all right?"

"Yeah, I guess so," Brad said, blinking his eyes.

Richard started to sneak forward. He signaled with his paw for them to follow. "Okay, let's go. Once on top of the building, we should be safe. No one will see us up there."

Brad ran across the parking lot behind his father. Their footpads scraped the tar and thin patches of frozen ice. Richard cut behind some cars and zigzagged between several more before reaching the building. As he neared the side of the building, Richard increased his speed, and launched himself eight feet to the rooftop.

Butch passed Brad and leaped to the top of the building.

Brad jumped. His front paws hit the edge of the flat roof, and his body slammed the side of the building.

Butch heard Brad yelp and turned to see his front legs slipping back over the icy edge.

"Help me, I'm falling!" Brad screamed. His front paws were hooked over the edge of the roof, while his back ones scratched against the side of the building in an effort to lift his body up.

Butch reached down and hooked a big paw under Brad's foreleg. With his teeth, he grabbed the nape of Brad's neck and pulled.

Brad tumbled to the rooftop with a yelp and jumped up, "Christ Butch you damn near broke my neck."

The sides of Butch's mouth pulled back in a threatening snarl. "You're welcome," he said, and turned away.

Richard bumped both of them with his shoulder. "Keep quiet. Someone might hear you. Remember, we won't have to change to our human forms. We should be able to shoot by changing our front paws to hands, just like we practiced."

"Good, I don't want to freeze to death," Brad said.

Butch lay in the dark next to Richard. He scanned the parking lot to see if anyone had come outside and seen them jump to the rooftop. The surrounding area remained quiet except for the sound of hard rock music coming from a side entrance to the hotel and traffic noises from the freeway.

After a few minutes, Richard said, "Okay, you two locate their rooms."

Yesterday, Eleanor and Sharrie had visited the Hilton and discovered that the Morsching's occupied three corner rooms on the tenth floor.

With concentration, Butch changed his paws into fur-covered hands. He removed the binoculars from the case strapped to his chest and located the windows on the tenth floor.

Butch lowered the binoculars. "All the rooms are dark."

"Maybe they're sleeping," Richard said, and then added, "What should we do?"

Butch shrugged. This was his first attack against other werewolves. What did he know? He looked to Richard for leadership, but doubts flashed through his mind over Richard's indecisiveness. "Richard you're in charge—whatever."

"They could be up there, smelling us right now," Brad said with a nervous catch in his voice, "Let's blow up the rooms and get out of here."

Butch turned to Brad and saw him shaking—probably from fear.

Richard sat up and positioned the Anti-Tank Weapon on his shoulder. Brad jumped up and pulled one of the missiles from the pouch on his back. The shell slipped from his modified paws. Brad let out a squeak. He caught the shell with his hooked fingers and pinned it against his leg. He grabbed the missile with hairy hands, lifted it up, and shoved it into the ATW tube.

Butch shook his head in disbelief. *They were going to shoot.* "Hold it," Butch said. "We don't even know if they're in the rooms."

Richard looked at Butch with a bewildered frown.

Butch thought, *At least he didn't shoot.* Then he said, "We can't afford to waste this opportunity to just blow up some empty rooms. We won't get another chance to kill them this easily again."

"Yeah, but we can't stay here all night," Brad exclaimed. "It's cold."

He didn't even hear what I said, Butch said. He knew Brad was ready to panic. He was expressing hs fear of being exposed, and of being attacked by the other werewolves.

"Don't worry, Brad," Butch said. "We're safe. No one knows we're here."

Brad gathered courage from Butch's assurance.

"Butch is right," Richard said, lowering the ATW. "We'll wait, but not too long."

Butch changed his hands back into paws and appreciated the warmth of the fur covering. They all settled down on the roof to wait for a sign the enemy was in the rooms.

Butch rolled to his side and brushed at some pebbles that stuck to his fur. He lay down behind the edge of the roof, which sheltered his body from the cold wind. With awkward motions, Brad picked up the binoculars in his modified hands and scanned the rooms looking for some sign of life.

A half hour later, Brad stuttered. "Hey, the lights just went on in two of the rooms."

Richard and Butch jumped to a crouch.

"Shh," Richard cautioned. "Do you see anyone?"

"Yeah, I see four people in the middle room," Brad said.

"Here," Butch said, "Let me see."

Brad watched as Butch's paws altered to elongated hairy fingers, and then handed him the binoculars.

Butch saw a dignified-looking man walk to the balcony door and push it open.

Even without binoculars, Brad could see the man moving onto the balcony.

Butch focused on the man and said, "Shit, that guy looks dangerous." He watched Ralph, the leader of the Morsching pack, lean over the railing. Through the binoculars, Ralph's image was clear. Butch's eyes widened. "He's sniffing."

Brad hissed, "Christ, he—he must smell us. Shoot, Shoot."

Richard brought the ATW to rest on his shoulder and froze, waiting for Brad to double-check the missile.

"What are you waiting for?" Brad cried, "You're still loaded."

Brad's fear was intoxicating.

"Okay, Uncle. Shoot," Butch said.

Butch watched the laser beam come to rest on the second group of windows.

Richard squeezed the trigger.

WHOOSH.

The missile left the tube trailing a red tail of light.

Butch yanked a second missile from Brad's vest and slammed it into the ATW.

Richard sighted on the other lighted room and squeezed the trigger.

WHOOSH.

The side of the hotel lit up with a bright, white flash of fire, as the exploding missiles demolished the entire corner of the building. The roof crashed down on the three rooms. Bricks and chunks of cement dropped through the air to the tarmac below, smashing several cars.

"Come on," Richard said, "let's get the hell out of here."

Butch strapped the ATW to Richard's hairy back, gathered up the spent shells, and shoved them back into the pockets of Brad's pouch. He put the binoculars back in its case and tightened the straps holding it in place.

Richard leaped over the edge of the roof to the parking lot and streaked across the exposed tarmac, dodging between cars.

Butch waited a moment while his hands changed to paws and then raced towards Richard. They both stood on the grassy knoll at the edge of the parking lot and looked back for Brad.

Brad was still on the roof of the utility building.

Butch shouted, "C'mon Brad, we got to get out of here!"

Brad jumped from the roof and flashed between the cars. He slipped on a patch of ice, fell on his side, and skidded until he hit the black tarmac. He got to his feet and scurried up the hill like the devil was after him. When he hit the top, he didn't slow down. Fear drove all three to the safety of the bushes at the bottom of the slope.

Butch didn't stop there. He kept running, throwing up a snow-cloud behind him until he was in the protective shelter of the Minnesota River Bottoms a half-mile from the hotel. He slowed down to wait for the other two to catch up.

Richard and Brad flew by Butch without slowing.

"Hey guys," Butch yelled as they raced by, "slow down." Neither of them paid any attention.

Butch ran after them and drew alongside Brad. "Hey, slow down. We're safe now." He jumped to the right to dodge a tree.

THWACK!

A noise like a watermelon hitting cement sounded next to Butch's head. Frightened, he shied away. He stopped and glanced back to see what had made the noise. Brad was lying in the snow.

"Oh shit," Butch said, letting out a bark that sounded like a laugh. "He ran head on into that oak tree."

Butch swung around and loped back toward Brad's prone body.

Richard skidded to a stop and trotted over to crouch beside his unconscious son. "Brad, wake up," he said. His eyes darted around, as though he expected someone to charge them from the trees. He turned to Butch. "Come on, we will have to carry him."

"He's too heavy," Butch said, trying to hold back his laughter. Caught up in the humor of what had happened, he'd forgotten the fear that had sent him scurrying away from the explosions. "We'll have to wait for him to wake up."

"Uh, okay," was all Richard could say, "but not too long."

Butch could not hold back his laughter any longer. A series of barks came from deep in his chest. He laughed until weakness overcame him, and he plopped over on his side and lay on the snow shaking.

Richard failed to see the humor of the situation. "Damn it, Butch, this isn't funny."

Butch laughed all the harder.

A few minutes later, Brad stirred. Butch stifled his laughter and nudged Brad to his feet. Richard needed to assist him all the way back to the car.

CHAPTER 25
HOW CLOSE TO FAILURE

The next morning, the entire Guhl pack gathered in the basement of Jerrold's mansion in Wedgewood. A twenty-four foot conference table occupied the center of the room. On the wall hung a plaque dedicated to Fred, who had died in a 'motorcycle accident', the day after the Longville massacre.

Jerrold stood at the head of the table with a big smile. He was talking with Richard and Bruce, his two eldest sons.

Butch knew they were waiting for William and Barbara Buchannan and their children to arrive before starting the family meeting. Five minutes later, they arrived,

Irritated at the delay, Jerrold said. "If everyone will sit down we'll get started."

The family members hurried to find a place to sit. The adults occupied the chairs around the table, while younger members filled the second row and spilled over onto the floor.

"I will call on Elliot to share the first piece of good news." Jerrold waved him to his feet.

Elliot, his grandson, stood up and glued his eyes on the paper he was holding. "The credit for finding that the enemy werewolves were staying at the Hilton Hotel off 494 near the airport goes to Uncle Richard and cousin Dean. Later, grandpa sent Sharrie and Eleanor, two of our non-werewolf members, to the hotel to get some more information. They talked to a waitress and one of the janitors at the Hilton yesterday and got the license number of the car the other werewolves came in." He blushed. "Well, they did not go in werewolf form—ah,you know what I mean. Anyway, we now know they came from Madison, Wisconsin."

Everyone applauded.

Jerrold beamed and said, "Thanks Elliot, and now the second bit of good news deals with our raid last night on the Hilton Hotel, where the Madison werewolves were staying." He swung with an exaggerated bow toward Richard. "And now, I give you my son, Richard, one of the heroes of last night's action. C'mon, stand and give your report of the raid."

Richard stood up smugly. "Father assigned Brad, Butch, and me as the team to attack and kill the foreign werewolves. Last night, we left the Fort Snelling parking lot at midnight and followed the Minnesota River bottoms until we arrived at the Hotel Strip across from the airport maintenance area. We waited on top of a utility building in the middle of the hotel's parking lot for them to return to their rooms. When they showed up, we blew up the rooms with our Anti-Tank Weapon.

"According to the news this morning, we accomplished part of our goal. The explosion killed three of the six, two women and a young man. Three others survived. Two of the survivors were in the elevator on their way up to their rooms at the time of the explosions. The third survivor is the one Father believes is the pack leader."

Bruce asked, "Why didn't you wait until they were all in the room?"

Brad answered from the second row of chairs, "Because their Alpha came out on the balcony. He was sniffing the air. I knew he smelled us, and I told Dad to shoot."

"That's right," Richard said, "Brad said one of them was sniffing the wind. I shot before he could warn the others to get out of the room."

Jerrold interrupted, "Richard, tell them what Butch did."

"Well," Richard hesitated before speaking, "if it hadn't been for Butch..." He didn't want to talk of Butch's part in the attack because it wouldn't shed a positive light on his leadership. "We would have destroyed the rooms as soon as we got there and missed our chance to kill the werewolves."

"Explain," Jerrold said.

Richard cringed. "When we first got there, the rooms were dark. Brad and I assumed they were sleeping, but Butch disagreed and convinced us to wait. It turns out Butch was right, they weren't in the rooms. They showed up later and we killed three of the bastards." Richard sat down.

Jerrold clapped. "Good job, guys," he said, looking at each of them. "Next time, don't waste such an opportunity. Be sure to kill them all."

Brad spoke up, "But Grandpa, they smelled us."

Butch listened to Brad and Richard's bungling of the story. He jumped up—red faced and said, "Sure he was sniffing, but I don't agree that he detected us. Next time we'll kill all of them, Grandfather."

The tone and emotion of Butch's words surprised several members of the pack, who leaned forward and stared at him. Butch's voice carried as much authority and promise as if it had come from the Alpha. A few of the pack flinched from the power of his words and nodded their heads.

* * *

After the meeting broke up, most of the family members went home. Butch stayed and helped Jerrold in the office. Butch loaded information on the computer, while Jerrold sat at his desk working on new assignments for the pack.

Jerrold put the tip of his ballpoint pen in his lips and concentrated on finishing one of the assignments. The hair at the base of his neck sprang erect. He shrugged his shoulders, feeling eyes staring at his back. He swiveled his head, looked over the top of the desk lamp and saw Butch staring off into space. Jerrold swung back to his work with a worried look.

A few moments later, Butch said, "You know, Grandfather, if I would have been in charge last night, six enemy werewolves would be dead right now, instead of just three."

Jerrold turned and looked at Butch. He knew by the tone of his voice that Butch was not bragging, simply stating what he believed would have happened if he'd been in charge.

"Why do you say that?" Jerrold demanded.

"For one thing, Uncle Richard and Brad were too impatient. They would have blown up empty rooms until I convinced them to wait."

"You didn't think the man on the balcony smelled you?"

"No, he didn't. I was watching with the binoculars. I did see him sniffing, but that doesn't mean he smelled us," Butch said, shaking his head. "Everything happened so fast. We were downwind from the hotel and I couldn't smell him. So I'm positive he couldn't smell us."

Jerrold's head shot up. "Well, Richard neglected to tell me that."

"Unless that other Alpha has better powers than we do, I don't think he knew we were there. But just before Richard's first shot, I felt someone trying to probe my mind." Butch hesitated. "Even then I would've waited for all of them to show up. If any of those in the room had tried to leave, then I would have blown the rooms up."

Jerrold stared at the portrait of his father, James, on the wall over Butch's head. "You know, I never noticed before how much you look like my father." He studied Butch. "I want you to forget what happened last night. I don't want any internal trouble coming from this. Richard did the best job he could. I know Brad gets too excited and acts before he thinks. I should have replaced him with someone else. With more experience, I think Brad will do better. The important thing is, you did a fine job. I have a feeling it will be just a matter of time until we get the rest of the Madison group. I promise you, we will get them,"

CHAPTER 26
THE CONFLICT WIDENS

A dark-blue Chevy Suburban was parked in the third row of cars in the Woodbury Mall parking lot just off Valley Creek Road. The Suburban had occupied the same spot for the last three days.

Today was Pete and Will's turn on surveillance. They sat huddled in the Suburban, watching the activities going on in the dry cleaning store in front of them—watching and waiting. They tracked the coming and going of the people inside.

Will Franzen sat up, snapping the reclining seat erect, and said, "Uncle Pete, how much longer are we going to sit here? I want to kill them for murdering Gretchen, Joseph, and Alice."

"So do I—they killed my daughter—but we'll wait until we learn all we can." Pete yawned, covering up his own sorrow.

Will turned in his seat and looked at his uncle. "I've learned all I need to know. I know that four of the Guhl pack work here. That's all we've seen inside the shop for the last three days. I'm tired of waiting. Let's just walk in and kill 'em."

Pete rotated his head toward Will. He smiled when he noticed Will's jaw muscles expand and contract, betraying anger and impatience. "No-o-o, we will not do that until the Alpha tells us to," Pete said. The words came out slow and easy, in a fake southern drawl. "Ralph said not to do anything until we checked everything out. We'll make them pay for killing my daughter and the others. For now, though, we'll just sit back, relax, and keep our eyes open."

Will released his seat and it banged into a reclining position.

* * *

The snow started around 6 o'clock, with big, slow-falling flakes sticking to the Suburban windows. Pete thought it was time it snowed. They had had plenty of snow towards the end of November, but nothing since, and here it was December 12. Maybe there was something to this global warming crap after all.

A movement inside the dry cleaning store caught Pete's eye. He saw the woman, who they had identified as Diana, walk to the front door and flip the open sign around. It now read CLOSED. Then he saw Diana's husband, Charles appear from the back room carrying several packages. Two teenagers followed him. Pete recognized the kids as the ones who were in and out of the shop all day making deliveries.

In a few minutes, the lights went out and the store grew dark. Four people came out the front door and waited while Charles locked the door. They walked two rows into the parking lot and got into a gray Dodge Caravan.

Pete nudged Will. "Okay, action man," he drawled, "time to go to work. Tonight we're going to follow them home."

"It's time we did something besides just watch."

Will grabbed the steering wheel and pulled himself to a sitting position. He straightened the seat and started the Suburban. He was relieved to be doing something. Anything was better than sitting around. He recognized Charles and Diana Groschen sitting in the front seat as the Dodge Caravan passed in front of them. He waited until two more cars got between them before he pulled out to follow. The Dodge Caravan turned right on Valley Creek Road and swung over to the left lane. At Woodlane Drive, the van made the tail end of the green arrow, as it turned left.

Will skidded to a stop and said, "Shit!" He hit the steering wheel. "Now we've got to wait for a green arrow. We're gonna lose 'em."

Pete laid his hand on Will's arm. "Take it easy. They don't have any reason to lose us. They don't know we're following them."

When Will got a green arrow, he accelerated onto Woodlane Drive and sped south faster than the posted limit, feeling the need to catch up. At the intersection with Lake Street, the light was red.

"There they are," Will said, as he noticed the gray van stopped in the left turn lane.

He pulled behind the van. When the light changed, Will dropped back and stayed in the left lane as the gray van moved over to the right. In a couple of blocks, the van signaled for a right turn. Will moved to the right, put his signals on and followed the van around the corner.

When Will finished the turn, he saw the van ahead. Will hit Pete on the arm and said, "Hey, they're turning in to that driveway."

"I can see," Pete said, rubbing his arm.

"Take it easy. Just drive by."

Pete turned as they drove by and watched the gray van pull into the garage. "Ah—8—5—46," he said, repeating the numbers he read from the side of the door, "8546-Stratford Road. Let me write it down."

* * *

At 8:30 in the Woodbury Mall lot, Ralph opened the door of the Suburban and stepped out on the snow-packed parking lot. "Okay," he said, "We're just going in to have a look around. We don't want to cause a scene or draw attention to ourselves, but if an opportunity comes up we'll take advantage of it." He looked in the back seat. "Pete, take the timer and the C4 with you, just in case."

Pete reached under the front seat and grabbed a small black box with two wires dangling from it. "Got it."

Will led the way toward the mall entrance. The three men walked through the main doors and turned right down the first hallway. Two-thirds of the way down the hall, Ralph saw a sign: Groschen's Dry Cleaners.

Ralph stopped at a maintenance door twenty-five feet beyond the dry cleaner's entrance. He backed against the door and leaned back. Pete stopped next to him and Will stood in front of them. Ralph glanced self-consciously up and down the hall.

An old couple was moving up the hall towards them. The old man stopped in front of one of the display windows. He put out an arm and stopped his wife. They both stared at the display. A kid screamed and Ralph swiveled his head in the opposite direction to see a woman pushing a grocery cart with a howling kid in it.

When the hallway cleared, Ralph nudged Pete and said, "Open the door."

Pete glanced at Ralph for a second, and then understood. He reached behind his back, as hair threaded out from the follicles of his hands. He grabbed the doorknob and twisted. The tearing of metal echoed down the hall.

Pete smiled and looked at Ralph, "Piece of cake."

Ralph pushed the door inward and backed into the storage room. Pete and Will scurried in behind him. Will closed the door, remembering not to slam it.

A nightlight dimly illuminated the storeroom. Ralph walked over to three rows of boxes stacked against the wall. His eyes swept to the rear corner where five metal barrels sat huddled in the dark.

"Pete," Ralph said, pointing to the barrels. "We found a way to annihilate some more of the crazy bastards."

The barrels were marked:

CAUTION DRY CLEANING FLUID EXTREMLY FLAMMABLE.

"Excellent," Ralph said, "Attach the C4 and timer on the back of the middle barrel."

Pete walked over and grabbed the rim of the center barrel. He tried to move it, but he couldn't budge it. He grunted, "Will, give me a hand."

Together, the two wrestled the barrel forward a foot. Pete reached over the top of the barrel. Halfway down, he attached the explosives to the backside with a piece of duct tape. Five minutes later, the three 'shoppers' walked out of the mall.

They met light traffic as Will drove toward their new hideout in downtown St. Paul. He looked at Ralph. "Grandpa, when are we going to set off the bomb?"

"We'll wait and see if they discover the broken doorknob tomorrow. If they find the bomb, we'll know—the police will be all over the place. At any rate, we'll keep the store staked out and try to kill as many of them as we can. It would be nice to catch more than four of them in there—*and then boom.*"

"BOOM," Pete echoed.

Will jumped and then threw an angry look at Pete through the rear view mirror.

Pete's face took on a crazed expression. "We'll send their asses to hell." A gurgle escaped from his mouth.

* * *

The next evening, Will and Pete sat in the Suburban outside Groschen Dry Cleaners. Will shivered as the minus twenty degree cold seeped into the Suburban through the metal doors. He reached for the ignition and started the engine. In a few minutes, the heater was putting out warm air.

They took turns watching customers enter and leave the store. By last count, Pete figured there were four members of the Guhl pack inside. There were never more than four targets in the store at any given time, and most of the time just two.

Will looked at Pete and asked, "When should we blow the bastards up? I'm getting tired of sitting out here doing nothing. If we wait too long, they might discover the explosives. We're never gonna get more than four in the store."

It was as dark as it was going to get. Will knew they would be closing the store soon.

"I suppose you're right, kid," Pete said, nodding his head toward the storefront.

"Here's what we're gonna do. We'll wait until the two customers leave and then do it. How does that grab you?"

Surprised, Will said, "Do you mean it?"

"Yeah," Pete said.

* * *

Inside the store, Francis Guhl's two daughters, Judy, sixteen years old, and Carol, fourteen, were busy waiting on the last two customers. Charles and Diana Groschen were busy turning off equipment and cleaning up.

After a few minutes, the two customers walked out of the store carrying several hangers of clothing draped in plastic.

Will waited. His hands held the detonator on his lap. He turned to Pete, who stared into the storefront. Pete nodded, and Will pushed the silver lever up on the side of the small black box. A red light blinked on.

Will placed his thumb on the blinking button and pushed down. A tremendous muffled explosion erupted within the store. The glass windows ballooned outward and shattered into a million pieces. A fiery ball crashed through two adjacent shop walls, sending merchandise into the parking lot.

Will watched the top of the building explode into the air. The cement slab roof lifted like chunks of Styrofoam. Pieces of concrete and twisted steel girders rained down on the parking lot.

Will jumped when the car next to him disappeared under a large piece of concrete. Small chunks fell on the Suburban, causing three dents on the hood. Will's eyes and mouth opened wide as he put the Suburban in gear and drove slowly out of the parking lot.

Chapter 27
Wild Challenge

Francis pleaded, "Father, we have to do a better job of finding them." Tears of anger and helplessness coursed down his cheeks. Francis was Jerrold's fourth child. He had lost his daughters, Judy and Carol, in the dry cleaning store explosion.

Jerrold and Francis faced each other from opposite sides of the living room in Jerrold's mansion. Family members returning from the funeral home entered through the front door. They froze when they heard Jerrold and Francis arguing.

"We're looking everywhere for them Francis," Jerrold said. As leader of the pack, and father and grandfather to those killed, Jerrold felt the loss of his his family members as much, if not more, than anyone else did. He knew he needed to remain strong for everyone.

"That's not good enough," Francis said.

An angry look spread across Jerrold's face. Francis was becoming hysterical. Jerrold thought he might lose control if he didn't do something.

Francis screamed, "Everyone including you should be out looking for those bastards." He shook his fist at his father. "Sitting in your office hiding, while our pack is being destroyed, is not good leadership. You should be out there leading us."

Shocked by the intensity of his son's anger, Jerrold staggered back a step, releasing a mournful growl.

Francis lost his usual steel grip on his emotions. His body rushed into his change.

A pack leader could not tolerate any challenge to his authority. Jerrold froze for a moment when he felt Francis tumble over the edge. He watched speechlessly as hair sprouted from Francis's hands and face, his skull bones began to melt and reshape, his face expanded into an elongated muzzle.

Jerrold shook himself out of his inactivity. Why had he hesitated? He telepathically shouted to Francis, "Francis, stop the change—NOW—or I will be forced to hurt you!"

Francis ignored the warning. Jerrold could not postpone his change any longer. If Francis became a werewolf before Jerrold, he would attack Jerrold and kill him.

The veins on Jerrold's temple popped out and squirmed like night crawlers. Jerrold enjoyed the familiar feeling washing over him, as the change flooded his mind and body. Jerrold made the complete transition in forty-five seconds, catching Francis just reaching the end of his change.

During the challenge between Jerrold and his son, Butch was sitting in the basement office staring at the phone. He had hurried back from the funeral home, not wanting to talk with anyone. Like many of the pack, he was upset with his grandfather for the passive way in which he was dealing with the Morsching Pack.

They knew where this pack came from, and should be attacking them in their home territory. But Jerrold wouldn't let them do it. Ever since the explosion, Butch wanted revenge for the deaths of Uncle Charles, Diana, and his two cousins, but for some reason Jerrold was reluctant to initiate any action against them.

Butch became alert when he heard someone run by outside the office. With a loud crash, Brad burst into the room and plopped down on a chair opposite Butch. "How did you get home so fast?" Brad asked.

Butch said, "Can't you ever walk into a room?"

Butch leaned forward. "I left early." He twisted the phone cord in his fingers. "I was getting too angry. I didn't feel like talking to anyone."

An uncomfortable stillness fell over the room. Butch coiled the phone cord around his wrist, looked at Brad, and said, "Is everyone back?"

"Yeah, most of them are upstairs, but two teams decided to take the long way home, if you understand what I'm saying."

Butch fidgeted and bit the inside of his cheek, drawing blood. "You mean they went off hunting on their own? Grandpa is going to be mad they didn't clear it with him."

Brad said, "You know what his answer would have been."

Butch threw the phone cord on the desk. "The pack is falling apart. We're starting to get on each other's nerves." A tight knot grew in his stomach. Everyone was upset over the deaths of four more pack members. Butch knew that if the family didn't work together as a unit, they would be easy pickings for the Morsching werewolves.

He stared at the phone. Maybe one of the teams would call and tell him they had found the enemy's new hideout. Butch slapped the table. This inactivity was upsetting everyone. If they didn't find the Morsching pack soon…

Brad turned and looked at Butch. "Maybe the other werewolves went back to Madison!"

"No, I don't think so. With their recent success, they'll want to finish the job, just like we would."

A loud crash shook the ceiling. Butch froze and then his face paled. A scream tore through his mind. He 'heard' the forceful mind-message that Jerrold had sent to Francis. Frightened, he leaped to his feet and rushed upstairs.

A bewildered Brad followed behind.

Butch rushed into the living room and skidded to a stop. Several members of the pack were in the room with their backs against the wall.

Butch saw Jerrold and Francis facing each other in werewolf form. They stood fang to fang. Blood dripped in a steady stream from cuts on Francis's shoulder and neck.

Francis shook, like a dog shaking water off his fur after a swim. His lips curled back and he sent out a mental scream, "Kill—Kill." Frothy strings of saliva hung from his fangs and splattered to the floor.

Butch turned to those standing wide-eyed against the walls and said, "What happened? Somebody do something."

No one answered or moved.

With no forewarning, Francis leaped at Jerrold and sank his fangs into his father's shoulder. Francis shook his head back and forth, ripping out a chunk of flesh. Jerrold stumbled back with a howl of pain as blood spurted from the wound.

Jerrold feinted to the left. When Francis moved to meet his thrust, Jerrold changed directions, flipped over in mid-air and dove under him.

Jerrold reached up with his muzzle and clamped down on Francis's throat. The two bounced and rolled on the floor. Francis struggled, trying to throw Jerrold off, but he didn't have the strength to break the hold on his neck. Francis's trachea collapsed, shutting off his air supply. He thrashed for a moment, and then went limp.

Jerrold maintained a firm grip until Francis was unconscious, then released his hold.

Jerrold staggered back against the desk. He was dizzy from loss of blood, which covered the floor, desk, and a number of books on the shelves. Jerrold wobbled on his four legs, and then sagged to his knees. He tottered there before toppling to his side and banging his head on the floor. His mouth opened and closed, like a fish out of water. His jaws moved, but no words came out.

Butch glanced at Brad, whose face was white as chalk. Butch was disturbed by what he had witnessed, but still felt excitement and pride in the way Grandfather had handled Francis. He was awed by Jerrold's strength and power. Butch watched the unconscious body of Francis transform back into his human form.

Xianth walked over to Francis and tended his wounds.

Butch asked, "How bad is he?"

Xianth probed one of the bloodier wounds. "He'll be okay. Not life threatening. The self-healing process will take care of it in a couple of hours."

Jerrold was unconscious from loss of blood. With each breath, his chest quivered. In a minute, his body transformed back to its human form.

Butch walked over to Jerrold and knelt over his body. He stuck his thumb against an artery that was squirting blood. Using his other hand, he applied pressure on another bleeder in Jerrold's groin area. Butch knew the missing chunk of flesh from his shoulder would replace itself if Grandfather did not die from all the blood he lost. Butch saw more blood squirting from a wound on Grandfather's side.

Eleanor was standing against the wall with a dazed look.

"Eleanor, I could use your help," Butch said.

Eleanor shook her head as if she was coming out of shock. "Yah, coming." She walked forward and dropped to her knees next to Grandfather and Butch.

"Here, hold your hand on this wound," Butch said, as he released the pressure on the groin. Eleanor pushed down with both hands. "Not so hard," Butch said, pulling up on Eleanor's arm. Butch then shifted his hand to the side wound and applied pressure. The flow of blood stopped.

Fifteen minutes later, Jerrold rolled his head from side to side, regaining consciousness. He moved his good arm up and probed his wounded shoulder. The wound was already beginning to heal, but it would take a couple of weeks before new flesh replaced the jagged hole. Scabs covered the other wounds, but fluid still seeped from the damaged flesh.

"Just lay still and rest, Grandfather," Butch said.

Butch turned and walked over to Francis, who was still lying on the floor, eyes staring up at the ceiling. Butch knelt down next to his uncle and their eyes locked. Butch stared deep into Francis's eyes, his nostrils flared as he whispered, "You stupid jerk. Your lack of control could have killed Grandfather. If you ever do something like that again, I'll kill you myself."

Francis turned white. Something in Butch's eyes terrified him. He whimpered, and with difficulty tore his eyes away from Butch's hard cold stare. He knew that if he responded in the wrong way, Butch would kill him where he lay.

Francis turned and looked at his father. Sane once again, he knew that what he'd done was wrong. "Father, forgive me," he cried. "I was overcome with grief over the death of my girls. I just lost control. Will you forgive me?"

Jerrold looked at Francis with contempt, but his eyes softened. "I'll forgive you this time." A menacing growl escaped from his throat.

Francis knew the next time he challenged his father he would die.

"Remember, you are not the only one who has suffered a loss," Jerrold said.

CHAPTER 28
BUTCH GETS HIS CHANCE

A few days later, Jerrold sat at his desk, rotating his shoulder and wincing from the pain. New flesh had restored the deep wound to its original form, but the pain reminded him it still needed time to heal.

Jerrold turned his focus on the conflict with the Morsching pack. He wracked his brain for a way to end the war. He knew he was getting too old to lead the Guhl Pack. Maybe it was time to give up his Alpha position and let someone else lead.

In the basement, Butch sat in front of the phones logging reports from the teams in the field. Four teams were scouring the suburbs for the Morsching hideout.

Butch had been in the basement since six o'clock in the morning, although he would rather be in the field searching for the intruders. He propped his feet on top of the desk and popped the top of a Sprite taking a big swallow.

One of the phones rang. Startled, Butch jerked his feet off the desk and the front legs of the chair slammed to the floor. His hand shook as he picked up the receiver. He knew even before anyone spoke that it was not one of the teams reporting in.

"Yeah," he said, then listened. His eyes grew round and glassy. He laid the receiver on the desk and ran upstairs.

"Grandfather!" Butch slammed into the office door. The door banged against the doorstop and bounced halfway closed. "Aunt Barbara is on line two."

Jerrold stared at Butch, his face suddenly ashen and his left eye twitching. He knew the news would not be good.

"She's at United Hospital," Butch blurted out.

"What's wrong now?"

"She told me Sue and Amy were killed in a hit and run accident. Elliot was injured, but is still alive."

"Oh, God! When did it happen?" A vacant look crept across Jerrold's face.

Butch glanced at his watch. "One o'clock, just an hour ago."

Jerrold didn't move.

Pointing at the telephone, Butch said, "Grandfather, pick up the phone. Barbara's waiting."

Jerrold still did not move. He stared at the telephone for a few more seconds. Butch guessed he didn't want to hear the bad news from Barbara.

"Grandfather," Butch said again, "she's on the phone."

Jerrold picked up the receiver. "Hello, Barbara. Butch told me what happened. I'm sorry. Give me the details."

"This was no accident," Barbara cried, then was unable to continue.

Butch could hear her on the phone.

Jerrold interrupted the sobbing. "Their deaths will be avenged by the pack."

Barbara started to babble between sobs.

"Easy now, don't cry," Jerrold pleaded.

For a moment, Butch thought Jerrold was going to break down, but instead his grandfather sat up straighter in his chair. Color rushed into his face. He appeared angry, but in control of himself again. "Barbara, stay at the hospital, I'll be there in half an hour."

Jerrold hung up the phone, then his shoulders slumped and he dropped a tear-stained face into his hands. His shoulders shook.

Butch didn't know what to do. It embarrassed him to see his grandfather like this. In a hushed voice, Butch said, "Grandfather, this is such a senseless loss."

Jerrold looked up. "I don't understand how this could have happened. I thought I was protecting everybody by keeping them close to home. Yet they still find ways of whittling the pack down no matter what I do. He didn't have the heart to ask Barbara why she didn't attack the killers. Butch, do you know what happened? How the girls were killed?"

Butch frowned, "Just that a semi rear-ended them on purpose. It happened on I-94 a block east of Snelling Avenue. The car flipped over and both girls were thrown from it. The bastard stopped the truck and backed up over them, making sure they were dead."

As Butch repeated the details, coarse hair started to sprout on his face and hands. He noticed and stopped the change.

"Oh, God," Jerrold said. "Why are they killing us? This must end before any more of my pack is lost."

"Grandfather, you have to be strong. We started out aggressively, but then after our attack on the hotel we withdrew into a cocoon and let them choose when to come after us. We should have stayed on the offensive right from the beginning. To win, we have to take the fight to them. We've got to throw a scare into them so they'll back off."

"What would you do Butch?"

"It's not my place to tell you what to do, but I have a couple of suggestions. It might be a good idea to have the more vulnerable members of the pack stay together in a secure area. No one should go out without an escort of two or three pack members." Butch picked up a pencil from the desk and clicked it against his fingers.

Jerrold shook his head and said, "I'm too tired to decide what to do right now. Stay on the phone. I have to get to the hospital."

Butch jumped in front of Jerrold. He felt now was the time to tell Grandfather his plan. "I've got one other suggestion," he persisted. "I know this isn't the best time, Grandfather, but I'm going to ask it anyway."

Jerrold looked surprised, but stopped and nodded approval.

"I want you to let me frm my own team, one that works separate from the rest of the pack. I promise you I'll find the rest of the werewolves and kill them."

Jerrold's face broke into a sad smile. "You're too young and inexperienced, Butch. I'm touched by your sincerity and determination, but if anyone is going to lead a team as you suggest, it should be someone like Richard."

Butch's face contorted in anger. "Richard can't get it done. I will not fail. Please, you have to trust me. I know I can do it. No one else in our pack has been able to track them down—but I will."

Jerrold hesitated. He thought of the ramifications of allowing Butch to strike out on his own. It was crazy, but then he remembered Butch was no ordinary werewolf. The family members who had already died flashed through his mind. He needed to do something different. He weighed the pros and cons. Butch had handled the hotel attack well, and he had shown the kind of abilities needed for leadership. Maybe he could do it.

"Okay Butch," Jerrold said, "I'll let you set up your own strike force under three conditions. First, you have to see if anyone will follow you. Second, the team must be limited to five members. The third requirement is that you must clear any action you take with me before you carry it out. Do you agree to these rules?"

"I sure do," Butch said, not believing his ears. "You won't be sorry."

Jerrold's lips cracked a half smile and he gave Butch a shove on the shoulder. "Now get out of here." Sadness suddenly washed over his face. "I have to get to the hospital."

Butch hurried out of the office before his grandfather changed his mind.

Chapter 29
Butch Shows What He Can Do

George stood next to the kitchen sink flexing his biceps. George's parents, Charles and Diana Groschen, had died in the dry cleaning explosion. At fifteen, he was big for his age, husky and athletic. He stared out the window, losing his gaze in the clouds as he pondered the death of his parents.

George was angry. He didn't know how to grieve—anger always got in the way. Feelings of guilt plagued him. He should have been in the store with them when it had exploded. He survived and they had not. It was not fair. He seethed with hatred for the Morsching werewolves. They had killed his parents. If his grandfather would let him hunt on his own, he could satisfy his wicked desires. But Grandfather had forbidden that.

George's two sisters, Coreen, thirteen, and Cheryl, twelve, sat at the kitchen table, staring at a bunch of puzzle pieces. The three were going through the motions of working on the puzzle. Their parents had spoiled the girls and George had been trying unsuccessfully to get them to help with housework. When Dad's Cousin Freda arrived to take care of them, maybe things would get better.

Coreen was tall for her age and well developed. George tried to protect her from older boys, who were hitting on her all the time. Her golden hair was held in place by a red banana clip, which allowed several strands to swing free over her left eye. She wore a yellow t-shirt, which overlapped tight-fitting blue jeans that showed off her cute, petite body.

Cheryl was very different. She was a skinny, black-haired tomboy, interested in climbing trees, playing soccer and wrestling with the neighbor boys.

George turned from the sink and walked back to the kitchen table. He looked down at the pile of puzzle pieces and pushed some of them back from the edge of the table. He sat down on a kitchen chair and rested his elbows on the table, hands holding up his chin. He picked up a piece and tried to find where it fit.

Coreen wiped tears from her face and stared at the puzzle. "I don't want to do this anymore."

Cheryl patted her on the arm and said, "It'll be okay. Don't cry."

George heard a noise at the kitchen door. It sounded like a growl. He dropped the piece he was holding and froze. "Shh, girls! It might be the were-wolves coming for us."

Since the explosion that killed their parents, warnings in the back of his mind kept surfacing, telling him that the Morsching werewolf pack would be coming to finish the job. He growled and jumped up, putting his arms around the girls.

Coreen screamed, more at George's quick movement than the apparent threat. Cheryl shrugged George's arm from around her and began her change.

George was amazed at the spunk of his younger sister, and also began his change. "Coreen, stop it and change."

There was a knock on the kitchen door. George put his hairy hand over Coreen's mouth and stood with his eyes wide open, afraid to answer.

A voice called from the porch. "George, are you in there? Come on, I know you are there. Open up. I need to talk to you. George, this is Butch, open up."

"Butch!" Relief flooded George's tense body. His hand dropped from Coreen's mouth and slid down to grab her by the elbow. Coreen and George were both halfway through their changes. Cheryl stood in her werewolf form ready for action.

"George, open up." Butch banged on the door again.

George hurried to the kitchen door. He pulled back the deadbolt. When the door swung open, he was relieved to see that it was really Butch. He shoved the storm door open, grabbed Butch by the arm, and pulled him into the kitchen. "Boy, I'm glad it's you."

Butch just stared when he saw his cousins in different stages of change, their shredded clothing hanging from their bodies. He realized why George was happy to see him. "I'm sorry, George. I didn't think I might frighten you. I should have called." He banged his fist on the kitchen cabinet. "I told Grandfather he should bring all of us together for our own protection. He's so paralyzed by fear that nothing is getting done to protect us."

As he spoke, George and his sisters returned to their human forms.

The two girls stood in tattered clothing staring at Butch.

Butch looked at them and his face grew red. He turned and looked out the window over the sink. He said, "Maybe you guys should get dressed."

The girls screamed and raced for the stairs.

George chuckled and said, "Now you know how scared we were. I better put some clothes on too."

Butch sat down at the kitchen table and waited. When Coreen walked down the stairs, she was embarrassed, but came over and sat on Butch's lap for the safety he offered. She put her arm around his neck and laid her head on his shoulder.

A minute later, both Cheryl and George came bouncing down the stairs. Cheryl's face was beet red.

Butch lied, "Hey, Cheryl, don't worry. I didn't see anything."

"Oh good I just about died."

"We have to get the Alpha to take more precautions." Butch said, "He should have seen that you were better protected." He put his arms around Coreen and gave her a hug. "You're safe now," he said with a smile.

Butch watched George fight back tears. He looked away to avoid embarrassing him. Butch felt the sadness George was experiencing and his eyes became moist.

George wiped his eyes and said, "I'm mad at Grandfather for not letting me hunt those bastards. They killed my mom and dad, and he thinks I'm supposed to do nothing? I feel so helpless."

Butch nodded. He knew how George felt. In fact, he sensed the hate within him. He thought, *If I were in George's shoes, I'd be out hunting the other werewolves, no matter what Grandfather said.*

"George, that's why I'm here, I know you want revenge for your parents' death." He shifted Coreen to his right knee and leaned forward. "Let me get right to the point. Grandfather has given me permission to put together an independent team to hunt the Morsching werewolves. I want you on my team. Are you interested?"

"You bet I am," George said.

"Great." Butch was relieved. One team member was a start. "You have to follow my orders, without question. If you can do that, you're in."

George sat up straight. "Butch, I promise to follow your orders as long as we track them down and kill them."

"Good, that's what I plan to do," Butch said. "Welcome to the team."

Cheryl looked alarmed, "What's going to happen to us when you're out hunting?"

"Don't worry, we'll take you girls over to my parents' house," Butch said. "You'll be safe there."

George nodded agreement.

Butch pushed Coreen forward, to see her face. "Coreen, is that okay with you?"

Coreen's lips grew into a pout, but then spread into a smile. "Yes, I'll be happy to get out of this house. All we do is sit around and cry. It's so hard to believe Mom and Dad are never coming back." She sniffled, and looked into Butch's blue-gray eyes. "But I'd really like to go with you and help kill those werewolves," she said, her face brightening at the thought. "I don't suppose you'd let me do that, would you?"

"No, I'm afraid not," Butch said. "You'll have to let George do the killing for you. Grandfather limited me to five team members." He put his arm around Coreen's shoulder and gave her a hug.

"Yeah, Sis, I'll get them for you," George promised.

* * *

Butch dropped Coreen and Cheryl at his parents' home and then drove to United Hospital, where Elliot Buchannan was still a patient. He had made a miraculous recovery from the hit-and-run accident in which his two sisters had been killed. The doctors thought it was because of their own efforts that Elliot had recovered, but the Guhl family knew it was from the family blood he carried within his veins.

Elliot was twenty-five years old and stood over six feet tall. He weighed two hundred eighty-five pounds, all solid muscle.

When Butch and George walked into Elliot's hospital room, Elliot appeared to be sleeping. A book lay open on his stomach. Elliot was not sleeping; he was thinking of his dead sisters. A low rumbling growl slipped out of his chest, probably motivated by the frustration of doing nothing to avenge their deaths. In the hospital, he struggled to maintain control and not let his anger push him into a change.

Butch saw that Elliot was wearing one of those asinine hospital gowns, split in the back and just covering his boxer shorts. A picture of Elliot walking down the hallway with his butt hanging out flashed through Butch's mind and he smiled

Elliot blurted out, "Who-o-o, hey guys, you startled me. I'm glad it was you and not . . . well you know." He sat up and swung his legs over the side of the bed. Self-conscious, he pulled the front of his gown down to cover his shorts. "What are you guys doing here?"

George wrinkled his nose. He did not like the smell of hospitals. "Visiting an injured cousin. How are you feeling?" He plopped down in a stuffed chair near the window.

"I'm okay. Ready to get out of here."

Butch smiled. "Elliot, how would you like to get revenge for the death of your sisters?"

Elliot cocked his head and stared at Butch before answering. "I'm willing to do anything the Alpha asks," Elliot said, not quite sure what Butch meant by the question.

Butch put his hands on the back of a chair and made direct eye contact with Elliot. "Grandfather has given me permission to form my own hunting team and I want you to be part of it. If you decide to join my team, you will have to follow my orders. Can you do that?"

"I won't have any trouble with that, but you have to promise that I get to kill at least one of those bastards with my bare hands."

"If that is all you want, you have my permission," Butch said and then added, "You will get your wish."

Butch walked around the chair and sat down on the bed next to Elliot, touching his arm. "Now, we have to pick two more for the team. Do you have any ideas who should be included?"

"Maybe Brad?" George said.

"I don't know," Butch said. "I've worked with him a couple of times and he tends to get too excited." Butch smiled, remembering Brad running into a tree. "But he is a good fighter."

"He can change faster than any pack member, except for Grandfather. And maybe you," Elliot said.

"I think Brad would be a good addition to the group," George said.

Butch shrugged his shoulders, "Okay, if you guys say he's okay, he's in. Who else?"

George thought a moment, "Maybe we should include Jake."

Elliot's eyebrow rose as he looked at George. "Isn't he too young? He's only fourteen."

"I know, but he's shown some talent in reading people's minds, and he's big for his age," George countered.

Butch looked surprised. "He can do that? It might be a good trait to have on our team." He looked at the other two.

They both nodded their heads.

CHAPTER 30
BUTCH MAKES A POINT

The next day, Butch reported the composition of his team to Jerrold for approval. "Congratulations," Jerrold said. "It surprises me a little that you were able to get four members to follow you."

"I had no problem. They were eager to join."

Butch's goal was simple. His team would locate the Morsching pack's hideout and kill them. He knew from the hotel registration there were six members in the original group of werewolves. Two women and a man had died in the ATW bombing of the Hilton Hotel, which meant three were still alive, and probably still in the Twin Cities.

Of course, more of their pack could have joined them by now. Butch cringed at the thought. If the whole Morsching pack were here, that would spell big trouble for the Guhl pack.

Five days later, an unknown assailant robbed and clubbed to death Richard's daughter, Sharrie. The police said it was a homicide committed when she resisted the robber.

The Guhl pack knew it was more than that. Many of the members wanted to forgo the Alpha's decision to take out the Morsching's in human form. Jerrold was able to maintain control by making one concession: Butch's team could kill in werewolf form.

* * *

One o'clock in the morning found Butch and his strike team starting another search for the Morsching werewolves. There was a hint of cedar in the air from a pile of wood chips beneath the wood lathe in Jerrold's garage.

Butch said, "Remember to carry your cell phones with you at all times. If you locate them, call me. When the whole team is together, I will decide how best to carry out the attack. Does everyone understand?" He scowled, waiting for everyone to acknowledge his order.

George turned away angrily.

"George, there'll be no attack on the other werewolves until the whole team is present. Do you understand?"

"Okay, but remember, you said I could get revenge."

"I remember, but if you can't follow orders you'll be off the team," Butch threatened.

"No problem," George said.

Butch looked at the others. They all nodded their agreement.

The team drove into downtown St. Paul to begin their search. If the surrounding suburbs did not hold the Morsching Pack, maybe they were in one of the downtown areas. Tonight they would search around the state capitol.

Elliot drove north on Wabasha. The city was quiet. Streetlights showed a scattering of people still out at two o'clock in the morning. He turned left down a narrow, dark alley and emerged in the loading area behind a retail building.

Butch looked around. He noticed a dim light from a clear glass globe, over a steel-jacketed door.

Elliot pulled in behind a parked delivery truck and stopped. The van would be hard to see in the shadow of the truck.

Butch stepped out of the van, his feet crunching on a crusty layer of snow. He glanced up at the overcast night sky. It felt like it was going to snow. He leaned over the hood of the van and opened up a map of St. Paul. "Does everyone remember their assignments?" Butch illuminated the map with a small flashlight.

The others gathered around.

"Jake and Elliot, are you okay with your assignment?" Butch asked.

"Yeah, we know where we're going," Elliot said.

"We do too," Brad said.

"Okay," Butch said, "Make sure you cover your areas carefully. I'll be cruising around in the van. Call me if you catch their stench."

The team members shed their clothes. Jake and Elliot were the first to complete their change. They twirled around and loped along the side of the building toward Wabasha Street. Moments later, Brad and George followed. The werewolf pairs raced north at speeds over fifty miles per hour, stopping in shadowy areas whenever a car passed by.

Three people came around a corner and caught Brad and George out in the open. Surprised, the two werewolves accelerated. The humans felt the breeze of their passing, but did not see them.

Butch waited a half hour before leaving the safety of the loading dock. It was 3:00 a.m. when he passed the capitol building. He found a secluded side street and parked between two cars waiting for a call from the teams.

He stared at his cell phone, willing it to ring, hoping someone would report finding the other werewolves. But no call came.

Then, just after 4:00 a. m., his cell phone rang.

"Butch," Elliot said in a harsh whisper. "We found them."

Butch swallowed, choking on his saliva, but managed to ask, "Where?"

"We're at the corner of Lexington and St. Clair. There is an open garage in the back of a blue house on the corner. Meet me and Jake there."

"Okay, give me fifteen minutes. I'll call Brad and George. Depending on where they are, they might reach you before I do. Make sure you wait for me."

"Park down the block," Elliot said. "The bastards are in an old two-story white house on St. Clair Street, 7699. Hurry, Butch, and remember your promise."

Fifteen minutes later, halfway between the corner streetlights, Butch coasted to a stop on St. Clair. He looked around. A dark, rusted Buick was parked two car-lengths in front of his van. Across the street, a light from the peak of the garage reflected on the snow, creating a glistening field.

In the van, Butch removed his clothes and changed into his werewolf form. He jumped out of the van, cursing when the dome light illuminated him. He quickly closed the door and crouched beside the van, shaking.

With a silent growl, he ran through the snow, dragging his feet so he would not leave clear paw prints. He stopped in a dark shadow near the side of a house and surveyed his surroundings. The neighborhood was quiet. He loped across two yards and followed the side of a stucco house toward the alley.

Spotting the blue house Elliot had mentioned, he ran to the side of the open garage and peeked in. Four members of his team huddled together at the far end. Butch made his way along the side of a car to join the others.

"Okay," Butch said. "What's the set up?" He leaned back against the two by four walls to steady himself, and appear calmer than he felt. The others stood around the front of an old rusted Ford Taurus.

Elliot hunched his back forward. With eyes sparkling in the dark, and his muzzle showing his large canine teeth, he removed a sheet of paper and a small flashlight from a fur-covered pouch. He laid the paper on the hood of the Ford and cupped his furry paw around the end of a small flashlight. A narrow beam of light illuminated the paper. Butch moved closer and looked at the hand-drawn map.

Elliot explained the situation. "The house they're in is just two doors west of here. It has a front and a back door, four windows on the east side, and four on the west," He pointed at the drawing with his other front paw. "Two upstairs windows are open a crack."

George shrugged, bumping Jake's shoulder on one side and Butch on the other as he said, "I suppose they like fresh air."

Elliot snarled at him and said, "We need to stay downwind as we make our approach or they might smell us."

"How many do you figure are in there?" Brad asked.

"I don't know."

Butch watched the fur along Elliot's arm ripple as his friend flexed his muscles.

Jake said, "Ah—there are two Morsching men upstairs in separate bedrooms."

Butch glanced at Jake and noticed his red eyes were staring at the side of the garage, as though fixed on the white house.

"How do you know?" Brad asked.

"I can see them," Jake said.

"Ah, bullshit," Brad cursed. "Nobody can see through buildings."

"If Jake says there are two, that's what we will find," George insisted.

Butch moved away from the hood of the Ford. "Okay—Elliot and Brad, I want you to cover the outside in case they try to escape."

Elliot looked disappointed, but nodded.

"The rest of us will go in the front door and decide what to do once we get inside. Any questions?" Hearing none, Butch said, "Let's go."

Brad and Elliot scampered out of the garage and loped to the back porch of the white house. The others followed Butch across the back yard toward the front of the house. Butch stopped at the corner of the house and then crept to the front door. He pointed to George and then to the doorknob. George nodded and twisted the doorknob until the mechanism broke and the door popped open.

The three werewolves froze for a moment, wondering if anyone had heard. Then they crept in, closing the door behind them.

An archway led into the living room .A short hall continued into the kitchen at the back of the house. Next to the archway, stairs led to the second floor.

Butch took the stairs two at a time, his claws clicking on the wooden steps. A stair squeaked when Jake put his weight on it. Butch froze and waited a few seconds before continuing up the steps.

At the top of the landing, light from the street entered through a small circular window and reflected off the hallway light fixture. There were three doors along the hall and a bathroom at the end. Butch shrugged, not knowing which door separated him from the two Morschings.

Jake tapped Butch on the shoulder. When Butch turned, Jake pointed to the closest door, held up one finger, and then pointed to the third door down the hall and held up one finger.

Butch sent a mind-message. "I will take the third door. George—you and Jake take care of whoever is behind the first door."

Butch tiptoed past the first two doors, unable to keep his claws from clicking on the hardwood floor. He heard George let out a low gasp when Butch brushed loudly against a strip of peeling wallpaper. Butch pushed the strip back in place, but it just curled away from the wall again.

Butch glanced at George and Jake. He was surprised at the massive shadows they cast on the wall. Jake's eyes glowed bright red.

"Ready? Here I go," Butch messaged telepathically. With a snarl, Butch hurled his bulk against the door. The door ripped from its frame and crashed into the room, bouncing off the dresser and falling to the floor.

Butch's werewolf vision allowed him to see a pale image of a young man's face sitting up in the bed. The sudden attack had caught him off guard and he was still in human form. Butch leaped on the bed, driving the man to the mattress.

"If you try to change," Butch said, "I will tear your throat out."

Will Franzen cried out, "I won't, just don't hurt me." He ceased his struggles under Butch's weight.

Butch sensed how terrified the young man was and restrained his urge to kill him. Will struggled to sit up. Butch grabbed him by an arm, just as he heard scuffling sounds coming from the first bedroom. *Oh, shit,* he said to himself. *They're in trouble.*

A window shattered in the bathroom at the end of the hall. Glass rained down on the roof of the back porch. Someone jumped through the broken window and landed on the porch roof with a loud crunch. Whoever it was ran a few steps and then jumped. Butch heard a grunt as the person hit the ground. Then someone else hit the porch roof and jumped to the ground.

Shit, Butch thought, *the other Morsching werewolf is escaping.* He wanted to give chase, but knew he could not leave his own prisoner. He growled in frustration.

Butch thrust a paw at Will's arm, pushing him toward the door. From outside, Butch heard a loud, cracking sound followed by a muffled scream. The cry came from the backyard, where Elliot and Brad were on guard.

Jake burst into Butch's room with a frightened look. "He got away. George went after him."

Butch shoved Will toward Jake. "Bring him," he said, and then ran from the room, Butch smashing through the back door and landing on the snow in the backyard. He was afraid he'd find Elliot or Brad dead and the Morsching werewolf gone.

A movement on the porch caught Butch by surprise and he swung his clawed fist toward the outline of a werewolf.

Just millimeters from slashing the werewolf's neck, Butch recognized George.

"God, Butch," George squealed, "You could have killed me."

"Sorry, Buddy."

Elliot and Brad were standing over the limp form of a heavy-set man who had begun his conversion to his werewolf form. From the contorted angle at which the body lay, Butch could see that the man's back was broken.

"I stopped him," Elliot said matter-of-factly. "He came through the window, trying to change. As soon as he hit the ground, I grabbed him. He was no match for me. I broke his back, twice." Elliot pantomimed how he bent the body over his leg and moved his two arms down.

"You've avenged your sisters," Butch said.

Elliot said. "I've avenged one of them, but I'm still not satisfied. I won't be until all of them are dead." He turned toward Will.

Will looked with fear at the big werewolf. Will took a step back and looked at the dead body of his uncle, "You killed Uncle Pete!"

"Just like I am gonna kill you." Elliot stepped toward Will. "Your uncle's death doesn't make up for my two sisters and the others," Elliot said, spewing saliva. "I will take pleasure in tearing you apart."

Will shuffled backwards under Elliot's glare. He tripped over Brad's extended leg and fell. Elliot moved towards him.

Butch said, "Wait. Take him with us," Butch said. "We need to learn as much as we can about that other pack." Then he turned back to Elliot. "Drag the other body next to the house and cover it with snow."

Elliot lunged at Will, who let cut a scream.

"Come on, let's get to the van and change," Butch said, "We need to get out of here before someone wakes up and sees us."

CHAPTER 31
BUTCH ISSUES A CHALLENGE

Drops of condensed moisture ran to the corner of the basement window in Jerrold's mansion. In the droplets, Butch imagined an outline of a wolf crouching on the top of a hill, staring down at a deer. Butch stared, not seeing beyond the glass. New beads of moisture slipped down the glass, washing away the wolf and deer.

Brad cleared his throat. Butch turned back to the prisoner sitting on the sofa sandwiched between Brad and George.

Jake leaned against the wall with his feet crossed as he studied the prisoner. Suddenly he shoved off the wall, "Oh my God!" He shook his head in disbelief. "These guys have a chemical called al—aldopamine. It eliminates the killing urge for a long time."

Startled Will looked up at Jake. "How do you know that?"

Jake ignored the interruption, "When they hunt, they just have to kill one human for the entire pack."

Butch smiled and moved away from the window. "Good work, Jake. I'm going upstairs and tell Grandfather. This is gonna make him happy."

* * *

Jerrold was coming out of the kitchen. He motioned for Butch to follow him and they walked in his office.

"Grandfather," Butch said. "Jake has extracted some interesting information from our prisoner."

Jerrold turned and threw Butch a chunk of bologna he had taken from the refrigerator. "Wonderful! I could use some good news." Jerrold sat down in his swivel chair.

"This other pack has a chemical that represses the need to kill humans."

Jerrold rocked forward, placing his elbows on the desk and stared back. "How does it work?"

"Jake says it's called aldopamine. It blocks the urge to kill humans. He says the Morsching pack only has to kill one human to satisfy the whole pack's craving."

Jerrold swiveled and poured himself a drink. "My God, that's something we could use."

"We'll see if we can get the formula."

Jerrold rubbed his hands together. "This could eliminate our need to kill so many humans every five years. What else?"

"And—we know where all of the Morsching werewolves live."

The bushy brow over Jerrold's left eye rose, producing wrinkles on his forehead.

Butch stared at Jerrold. "If it's okay with you, my team will be paying a visit to Madison, Wisconsin. We'll give them some of their own medicine, but this time in their own territory."

Jerrold slammed his glass down. It exploded, spilling the contents. He jumped up and said. "Aren't you forgetting something? I am the Alpha. I make all the decisions that pertain to my pack, and you need my permission for such a venture."

Caught off guard, Butch's eyes flashed with anger. What had he done to deserve such a violent reaction? "I did ask. I said if it's okay with you."

"Our agreement pertained to local hunts," Jerrold said. "You should have enough glory to last you for a while." Jerrold punctuated each word by stabbing his forefinger on the desktop. His face was beet red and his eyes bulged. He leaned back in his chair. "We're not going to do anything more to provoke them for a while. Time to wait and see what they will do. Maybe we scared them off."

Butch could not believe what he was hearing. He was hurt and angry. He sat up and stared at Grandfather. "Alpha," he said in a low, controlled whisper. Each word echoed with crispness and challenge. "I did ask your permission to carry the fight to them. Why do you bring *glory* into the conversation? I haven't done any of this for glory or recognition. My team has carried the fight to them because you haven't. I've done everything I promised. My team has done a good job, and now you want us to sit back and do nothing! That is not the way to protect our pack. We can't win this war waiting for them to attack. We need to act now, while we have the initiative."

Vessels pulsed in Butch's neck. "That has been the problem with your leadership all along. You want to wait for them to take the offensive." Butch's voice grew loud and raspy. His jaw muscles bulged and his face flushed. "You're out of touch with what's going on. You no longer deserve to be the Alpha."

Jerrold's chest puffed out, "I am the Alpha! As pack leader, I will decide what we do, and I've made up my mind."

Butch jumped to his feet and slammed his fists down on the desk.

Jerrold thought Butch was attacking him and threw his hands up to protect his face.

Butch pounded the desk again and said, "No, I will not accept that. I don't agree with you, and the pack doesn't agree either. From now on I'll decide what is best for the pack."

He couldn't believe what he'd just said. He stood up straight and pointed at Jerrold, realizing there was no turning back. He had just challenged his Alpha. He screamed, "No more!"

Jerrold jumped to his feet, sending the swivel chair crashing against the table behind him. Bottles crashed to the floor. "You upstart! You're forgetting your place!"

Butch shoved the desk into Jerrold's legs and hunched his back, beginning his transformation into his werewolf form. "No, I'm not forgetting myself. You are no longer fit to lead us."

Jerrold hunched his back, rushing into his change.

Butch completed his change first and leaped across the desk. He grabbed Jerrold by the shoulder and bit down hard. His muscular jaws brought canine teeth together. Butch felt Grandfather's humerus separate from the socket with a pop. He released his hold and jumped back.

Jerrold howled in pain as he completed his change, "You have attacked the Alpha. For that you will pay with your life." Jerrold limped around the desk on three legs and faced Butch. Blood poured from the wound in his shoulder, matting his shaggy fur. Saliva leaked from his jaws, leaving white streaks on his chest. His anger was so great he did not feel the pain radiating from his dislocated shoulder.

"Grandfather," Butch said. "Back down or I'll make you."

"You—you are nothing but a mere pup," Jerrold screamed. "How dare you challenge me? I will kill you!" Jerrold launched himself through the air.

Butch knew what was coming and rolled to his side. Even though anticipating the move, he was barely able to get out of the way. He felt the scrape of Jerrold's teeth as they just missed his throat. He scrambled to his feet and wheeled to face his snarling grandfather.

Jerrold looked puzzled. He couldn't understand how that move had failed him. It had always worked for him in the past.

A few feet separated the two contestants.

Butch feinted to the left and then sprang towards Jerrold, turning over in mid-air. On his back, he slid under Jerrold and used his front paws to force Grandfather's head into the air. He shoved his muzzle up between his paws and clamped down on Jerrold's throat. He held on while his rear end swung around, taking Jerrold's feet out from under him.

The vice-like grip on Jerrold's throat cut off the flow of air to his lungs. Butch increased the pressure, stopping just before the cartilage rings in Jerrold's trachea snapped.

With each jerk and twitch, Jerrold's windpipe closed even tighter. In a last attempt to escape, Jerrold brought his hind legs up and raked fur and flesh from Butch's stomach. Even though the pain was unbearable, Butch did not relinquish his hold on Jerrold's throat.

Jerrold's hind legs ceased their clawing.

Butch relaxed his grip on Jerrold's throat, but did not release his hold. He was afraid Jerrold might be faking. After a few seconds, Butch opened his jaws and rose on shaky legs. He stumbled back toward the desk. He shook his head. He could not believe he had defeated the Alpha. He raised his muzzle and howled. He was the victor!

Butch jumped to the top of the desk, sat back on his haunches and released another blood-curdling howl.

Telepathically, he broadcast, "I have defeated Grandfather. I am the new pack leader. I now rule the Guhl pack. From this day on, I will take care of mine."

The others received the message in the basement. The strength of the message drove them to their knees. Elliot howled in pain and covered his ears. Brad and Jake dropped to their knees. George just stood with his mouth open, not believing what he had heard.

Elliot fought his way to his feet, hands still covering his ears. "Jake, guard the prisoner. Brad and George, follow me."

The three raced for the stairs and bounded up three at a time. They burst into the office and saw Butch in werewolf form crouched on the desk, strips of clothes hanging from his body, blood seeping from gashes on his stomach. Grandfather Jerrold was lying behind the desk on the floor. A slowly growing red pool of blood seeped out beneath him.

In disbelief, Elliot said, "Butch—what have you done?"

George ran to Grandfather's side and knelt next to him. He watched Grandfather change back to his human form. George checked him over and said, "He's still breathing. He'll live. His shoulder is dislocated." He rotated the arm and the humerus popped back into the socket.

Elliot stared menacingly at Butch.

Butch looked at his team members and knew that this was a crucial moment. Either they would kill him for attacking the Alpha, or they would accept him as the new leader of the Guhl pack. "I challenged Grandfather for pack leadership. From now on, we'll be more aggressive in searching out and destroying our enemy."

Grandfather blinked his eyes and sat up slowly.

Brad asked, "Are you okay, Grandfather?"

"I'll live," Jerrold said. He moved his injured shoulder and moaned.

Butch rose onto his four legs and said, "Grandfather, I've defeated you in combat. Do you submit?"

Jerrold made his way to his feet, holding his injured arm. He looked at Butch and then lowered his head. "I don't have any other choice. You are the new Alpha of the Guhl pack."

George and Brad stepped forward and assisted Jerrold to the couch. They lowered him to a reclining position.

Now would come the true test, Butch thought.

He said, "Elliot, George, and Brad, I need your help. Will you recognize me as your new pack leader?" He stared at them, waiting for their response. Elliot looked at his grandfather and noticed his closed eyes. He looked like he was dead. Jerrold looked weak, vulnerable, and beaten.

Butch was shell-shocked. He knew that each pack member would decide to either accept his leadership or fight him on behalf of the Alpha.

Elliot looked at Butch and said, "I'll follow you, Butch. Grandfather submitted."

"I will too," George said, nodding toward Butch. "You'll make a good pack leader."

Brad hesitated and then stepped forward. "You were not afraid to take the fight to the Morsching Pack. We did some good work. I will follow you."

* * *

That evening, the entire pack gathered in Jerrold's basement. Each family member had learned what happened between Jerrold and Butch. They also knew that Butch's team supported him. Anyone who might have wanted to challenge Butch needed to consider his team's sworn allegiance. In the end, they all renewed their promise to lay down their lives for the pack and the new Alpha.

The last one to step forward was Jerrold. They watched him, wondering if he would challenge Butch.

In a deep voice, Jerrold said. "Butch, this was my pack. You defeated me and now the pack is yours." He turned to face everyone. "I want all of you to understand that this family cannot afford dissension, and for that reason I will follow Butch." He looked at Butch. "I pledge my total allegiance." Jerrold removed the ring from his right ring finger and handed it to Butch. "As pack leader, this is yours."

Butch looked at the ring, covered with ancient symbols and other mysterious inscriptions. In the center of the ring, a large, green Emerald caused Butch to swoon for a moment.

Jerrold said, "This ring belonged to my grandfather, the first Alpha."

Butch took the ring and slipped it on his finger. "Grandfather, thank you." A broad smile crossed his face.

Jerrold looked puzzled.

Butch noted the raised eyebrows on Jerrold's face and said, "Grandfather, the ring doesn't fit me . . . yet." He handed it back to Jerrold. "Will you hold it for me until I grow into it?"

Everyone laughed and the tension melted.

Chapter 32
One Invasion Deserves Another

The middle of March should have meant warmer weather was on the way, but Tuesday morning dawned cold and blustery with a hint of snow in the air. A blood-red sun rose over the edge of the eastern horizon, casting frigid, yellow-red rays through the kitchen window of Jerrold's home. A single dark cloud floated across the face of the sun. Jerrold's mansion still served as headquarters for the pack, and Butch stood at the kitchen window watching the sunrise.

Jerrold walked in and glanced out the window. He said, "My father used to say a dark cloud over the sun was a sign of impending death."

Butch glanced at his grandfather and thought, *a sign of death for whom.* He looked at the sun again before turning from the window.

He thought of the dangers that lay ahead. "Grandfather, as you know, I'm not one to sit back and wait for the Morsching pack to attack. I've decided to take the battle to their territory."

Jerrold's neck grew red. "It sounds like you have made up your mind. I don't have to agree, but I will do whatever you ask."

* * *

For over an hour, Butch's team hurried between the house and garage, packing, and joking with each other. Butch's mind raced, trying to think of anything he might have overlooked. He was anxious to leave. "Okay guys, finish up. I want to reach Madison before dark."

Fifteen minutes later, George walked into the kitchen. "The van is loaded," he told Butch. "But Brad isn't here."

"He went home for the Anti-Tank Weapon," Butch said. "He'll be here in a few minutes."

George shrugged, and sat down at the kitchen table.

Elliot came in from outside rubbing his hands together. "Boy, this cold seeps into my bones. When is it going to warm up?" He detoured to the counter and grabbed three cups, filling them with coffee. The others nodded their thanks.

George and Elliot stared into their cups with blank expressions. Butch got up, walked to the window, and stared into the red sun, wondering what would be the outcome of this expedition.

At last, Brad pulled into the driveway, honking the horn. Jake opened the garage door grabbing the camouflaged ATW from the back seat and putting it into the van.

Excitement ran through the whole team as they piled into the van. They were nervous. It was a big step and their first major attack under the new Alpha.

CHAPTER 33
WE TOO CAN INVADE

Five hours later, they arrived in Madison. Because Jake had accessed Will's thoughts, the Guhl team knew where all of the Morsching homes and warehouses were located. Butch was surprised to learn that one of their principle businesses was dealing in weapons on a worldwide scale. Butch knew the Morschings would station extra guards around their properties.

Butch decided to attack their warehouses first to disrupt their business. He hoped his pack might kill a few enemy werewolves in the process.

They drove around Madison to get a feel for the city and possibly pick up the telltale werewolf scent. At six o'clock, Butch checked the GPS for directions to a Morsching warehouse, their first target.

"There's a warehouse a couple of miles from here, he told Brad. "Let's burn it down and let them know we're in town."

Five minutes later, they picked up the distinct smell of werewolf on an easterly wind.

Elliot grabbed the front seat and said, "Let's kill the bastards."

"Everyone stay calm," Butch said. "If we get a chance we'll take them out. But we have to be careful. We're in their territory. The warehouse we're heading for is just a couple of blocks from here. Maybe that's where these guys are headed. Brad, let's stop here and follow them on foot."

Everyone piled out of the van and stood with noses sniffing into the wind and smiling at their good fortune. They had expected to spend several days checking the Morsching buildings, trying to locate a few werewolves in a vulnerable situation.

The sun had dropped behind the surrounding buildings. The sky was gray with dark cumulus clouds floating from the northwest toward the southeast. At ground level, a flurry of snowflakes had begun to fall.

Brad raised his head and cast around. "I can smell them. Three of them are just ahead of us." He pointed up the street.

The others drew air into their nostrils, trying but failing to pick up the distinctive scent.

Butch kept sniffing. For just a moment, he thought he detected the familiar wet hair of a dog, tinged with a taste of rusting iron, but he was not sure.

"Are you sure you smelled three of them?" Elliot asked, showing his frustration.

Brad glanced at him. "Yes, they're a block ahead, crossing the street." He pointed at the deep shadows alongside a tall building ahead.

Butch squinted, probing the area Brad was pointing at. "Let's go, but be quiet and stay alert."

"Aw, you're shitting me," George scoffed. "You can't smell that much better than the rest of us."

Butch turned to George. "If he says they're there you better believe it. Come on." Butch started across the street. He jogged to close the gap between the three enemy werewolves and his team.

"I still can't smell them," George said.

The street was not a good place to attack. They were on one of Madison's downtown streets, six blocks off Main Street. A car with its lights on came towards them. The snowfall made it difficult to see more that twenty feet in front of them.

Jake hushed George and Brad, who were arguing. "I'm reading one of them. They're going to turn right at the end of the next block, heading for their warehouse. It's filled with high tech supplies and weapons."

George whined, "Jake are you sure?"

Butch grabbed George by the arm and said, "That's enough! Don't be a dumb ass, you know Jake read Will's mind and learned that stuff about aldopamine and where the Morschings live. If he says he is reading the thoughts of one of those guys up ahead, believe him. Now shut up!"

Elliot put his arm around Jake's neck and gave him a squeeze. "Nice going, kid. I don't know how you do it, but I'm glad you can."

Brad put his arms out to stop the group. "Wait!" he said. "They're entering the warehouse."

Chapter 34
Death in a Warehouse

Butch watched Ralph Morsching unlock the heavy metal door and step into the warehouse, followed by two other men. He waited with the team for five minutes, then said, "Okay let's go get them."

They cautiously approached the warehouse, undressed, and began their transformation into werewolves. It was still a mystery to Butch how the change from human to werewolf and back was possible. It was scientifically impossible to explain. Nevertheless, he marveled at the efficiency of the process. In less than two minutes, he grew a foot taller, added four inches of hair, and redistributed muscle and bone into a new body pattern.

Butch gathered up his clothes and headed for the door. The others followed. The large footprints left behind in the snow betrayed their presence.

Butch leaned his weight against the door. Locked, he nodded to Elliot, who grasped the doorknob and twisted. The inner mechanism screeched. Elliot leaned his weight on the door and it swung open.

Butch led the four Guhl werewolves into the warehouse. They laid their clothes in a neat row next to the door, then sniffed, trying to locate their enemies.

Brad said, "They're on the far end of the warehouse."

Wooden crates were stacked in rows, with aisles wide enough for a forklift to pass between them. Cross aisles intersected the long rows, allowing access to adjacent rows.

Butch telepathically messaged to the others. "Spread out and head toward them."

Following one of the aisles, Butch approached the far end. He heard voices. At the end of the row, Butch peeked around a stack of crates and saw the three men seated around a table.

A single bulb hung from the ceiling on a long cord, casting a circle of light over the table. A long workbench stacked with tools and boxes stood against the wall. A lighted Coke machine illuminated one end of the workbench, pushing back the dark. There were several rifles and shotguns propped against the wall next to it.

Butch listened to the conversation. Ralph Morsching stood up, put his foot on the chair and braced his upper body on his knee. "I'm worried we haven't heard from Will or Pete. We'll have to assume they're either dead or captured. Tomorrow I'm taking a team to the Twin Cities to find out what happened to them. We need to knock a few more of those bastards off anyway."

"That's just great," Roger said sarcastically. "You were wrong to take such a small group to the Twin Cities the first time."

Ralph leaned toward the men and said, "Is that a challenge?"

"No, but I still say it was a mistake."

Ralph leaned back and crossed his arms. "Maybe you're right. I'll take a bigger group this time."

"What are we going to do now?" the third man asked.

"If my instincts are right," Ralph said, "I have a feeling they will be coming for us. It wouldn't surprise me if they were already in Madison." He slapped his fist down on the table. "As soon as Tom arrives, we'll figure out a way for you to ambush them when I am gone."

Ralph stood and dug his knuckles into his tense back muscles. "Brandon, get three beers from the pop machine." He added, "While you do that, I'm gonna walk down and get a couple of those machine guns that just came in. We need to take a look at them before we ship them out."

Ralph left the table and walked toward the far aisle, where he disappeared into the blackness. Brandon walked to the pop machine, grabbed three bottles of beer, and circled back to the table.

Roger was jotting down some notes. He jumped when Brandon banged the beer bottles on the table.

Brandon smiled, "Hey, Dad, why are so jumpy?" He sat down.

"You heard Ralph. Those Guhl werewolves might be in town."

The Guhl werewolves waited for Butch's signal to attack. Butch was primed, his breathing deep and rapid.

Brad stood in the next dark aisle. His heart fluttered, damn near on the verge of fibrillation.

In Elliot, the killing madness mounted until it was unbearable to wait. He fought to maintain control.

George quivered with anticipation.

Butch started to second-guess his impromptu plan. Should they take the two of them sitting at the table or wait for the other one to return? He hesitated, realizing that command had its problems.

Carrying two machine guns wrapped in plastic, Ralph haded back toward the other Morschings. He stopped and swiveled his head. A puzzled expression grew on his face. He telepathically sent, *Hey, guys, are you screwing around?*

Roger looked up from his writing. "What do you mean?"

"Are you guys mumbling? Trying to scare me?" Ralph projected via his mental link.

"No, we are sitting here having a beer," Roger said.

"Okay." Ralph shook his head dismissing the problem for now. He started walking back to the table, but stopped again. "Roger—Brandon, the Guhl werewolves are in the warehouse. Run for it!"

"Oh, shit!" Butch screamed over his mind-link. "They know we're here! Elliot you and Jake go after the single guy. The rest of us will attack the two at the table."

Roger and Brandon did not bother to change into werewolves. They jumped from their chairs and raced toward the back door.

George and Brad flew from the aisles in pursuit. In werewolf form, they were on Roger and Brandon before they reached the door. Roger attempted to change, but George leaped onto his back and grabbed him by the throat, tearing through carotid arteries and pulling cartilage from his trachea.

Butch flew past Brad and pounced on the back of Brandon, whose scream was cut off when his neck vertebrae snapped. Two Morsching werewolves had died in less than thirty seconds.

"Thanks a lot," Brad said to Butch, as he looked down at the two dead men. "You could have let me kill him."

A cry from Jake burst into Butch's mind, sending him to his knees. Jake was injured. Butch jumped to his feet and ran for the far aisle, followed by George and Brad.

* * *

Elliot found Jake on the floor of a dark aisle, bleeding from a wolf bite to his arm and leg. He looked around, but too late. Ralph—monstrous and furry—was on him.

The size and strength of the Morsching werewolf surprised Elliot. He grew frightened when he was not able to overpower him. For the first time in his life he wondered if he had met his match. He knew that if he kept his opponent occupied, the others would arrive to help. If he did not kill or disable this foe quickly, he would be the next to die.

He was stronger than Ralph was, but not as fast. As Butch approached, Elliot kicked out with his hind feet and bulled Ralph onto his back. Ralph's head bent to the side, briefly exposing his neck, Elliot went for the vulnerable spot, but Ralph recovered and raked his hind legs across Elliot's exposed stomach.

Wicked, long claws ripped strips of flesh from Elliot's stomach. Elliot ignored the pain, and fastened his teeth on Ralph's head. He bit down hard trying to crush the skull, but his teeth slid down the bone stopping at the cheek and ear. Elliot yanked his head back, tearing pieces of flesh from the side of Ralph's face. Ralph lashed out in pain and sent Elliot skidding across the floor. Elliot slammed against a crate and lay stunned. He was growing weak and exhausted from the prolonged battle.

Ralph leaped to his feet and ran toward the front door.

Butch telepathically told George and Brad to chase after the Morsching. The two whooped and howled when they caught sight of the enemy werewolf.

Butch skidded to a stop next to Jake's thrashing body. Jake was still conscious but in a lot of pain. He was gasping for air and groaning with every inhalation. Butch ran his paw down Jake's crooked arm and felt the jagged end of broken bones sticking through the fur.

Butch took Jake's uninjured paw and placed it over the spurting blood coming from his leg. The blood stopped flowing. He grabbed Jake's broken arm and pulled. Jake screamed. Butch realigned the bones and marveled at the fact that Jake was still conscious.

Then Butch slid over to Elliot and checked the deep claw marks on his chest and abdomen and the bite on his leg. Elliot was holding strips of flesh in place. Blood oozed from around the edges of his paws. Butch looked for any large streams of blood, but didn't see any.

"I'm sorry," Elliot said. "I'm to blame for letting him get away."

"Don't worry Elliot. You did your best." Butch pawed Elliot's good shoulder, "Can you change back to your human form?"

"Yes, in a couple of minutes," Elliot moaned.

George and Brad trotted up the aisle.

"He got away," Brad said.

"Don't worry," Butch said. "We have other problems that need our attention. Brad, we need the van—Jake is in too much pain to change back right now. We need to get out of here before reinforcements show up."

Brad raced for the door, made his change, dressed, and ran through the snow for the van.

George asked, "What do you want me to do?"

"Change form and then help me get Jake and Elliot to the front door."

The van pulled up to the steel front door and Brad honked.

"Elliot, you have to change, it will be easier to get you in the van. You're too damn heavy for us to carry."

Elliot struggled to change. It took him longer than normal. When he finished, wicked red welts remained on his stomach and chest. He stood up on his own, shoulders hunched to lessen the strain on torn stomach muscles.

George dressed and helped Elliot put on his clothes. When he tried to tie Elliot's shoes, the large man said, "Quit fussing, I'm okay."

George ignored him.

Elliot walked over to Jake. "Here, Butch," he said, "let me carry him."

George laid a hand on Elliot's arm and said, "Are you sure you should do that?"

"Yeah," Elliot sighed.

Elliot lifted Jake, who was still in werewolf form and put him on the floor of the van.

Butch changed back to human form and yelled, "George, give me a hand."

George jumped out of the van and ran back into the warehouse. "Yeah, what do you want?"

"Let's set this place on fire."

Butch found a forklift, unscrewed the gas cap, lit a book of matches and tossed the flame into the tank. A mushroom of flames and gas blew out into the air setting a stack of boxes on fire. George ran down the next aisle and set fire to a large stack of cardboard boxes, and then ran for the van.

Brad accelerated as a loud explosion lit up the sky behind them.

Butch turned from the front seat with a big smile on his face. "Good job everyone. Even though we took a few licks, we did well for our first battle in Madison. Two down and a couple dozen to go."

* * *

All night, the Morsching pack hunted for the Guhl werewolves. Ralph was frantic. He pushed his pack hard. They scoured the black and Asian districts at night as werewolves.

Traveling at high speed, they spread out to cover half of the city. With dawn, they reverted to their human forms and used vehicles to crisscross the city. They found no evidence of the foreign werewolves in Madison—not a single scent.

"Either the bastards are stashed away in one of the outer suburbs or they went back to the Twin Cities," Ralph howled in frustration. "But they'll pay for what they did."

CHAPTER 35
VOTE FOR TRUCE

Butch's team fled Madison and raced back to Minnesota. They had completed the first step of their mission. If they stayed in Madison, there was a chance the Morschings would find them. What they had done would put the Morschings on notice that they were just as vulnerable as the Guhl Pack had been. Butch figured to let them stew over their whereabouts for a week and then return to Madison for another attack.

Two days later Jake was sitting in Jerrold's basement in front of the fireplace. His arm was still in a sling, but the rest of his injuries had healed.

The rest of the pack was sitting around the room waiting for the meeting to start. Finally, Butch walked in and patted Jake on the shoulder as he passed by. A few latecomers hurried in behind Butch, who waited until everyone settled down before calling the meeting to order.

A few pack members had already heard of the team's success in Madison. Butch figured the rest of the pack needed some positive news to lift their spirits. He took his time describing what happened in Madison and why he considered the attack a success. Not only had Butch's team killed two werewolves and destroyed one of their warehouses, but it had also sent a strong message that the Guhl Pack could do them a lot of harm. He expected the whole pack to be elated.

When finished, he stepped back and waited for praise, but most of the pack did not appear very excited. Only a half dozen members showed enthusiasm.

Butch sensed an undercurrent of dissatisfaction. He scrutinized those in the room, wondering why anyone would be unhappy with the team's accomplishments.

Butch telepathically sent a note to Elliot: *C'mon, Elliot, I need some help.*

Elliot stood up to address the group. He waited until everyone had settled down and then said, "In spite of injuries to Jake and me, we were successful in our first raid. We should start planning our next raid before they recover and attack us again."

A few members nodded agreement. The majority sat in silence. Elliot was confused by the reaction. He shook his head and sat down.

Richard unhappily had been singled out as spokesperson for the opposition. He rose, put his hands in his pockets, and then took them out. He saw an angry scowl flash across Butch's face. He spoke with a tremor. "Butch, some of us are not happy with the direction you've taken the pack. A few have even considered your behavior irresponsible."

The corners of Butch's mouth curled upward releasing a growl in Richard's direction.

"Easy, Butch," Richard said. "I'm not challenging you. Please, listen to what I have to say without getting angry. We want you to know how we feel and what concerns us. I'm sorry to be the one to tell you, but they made me the spokesperson."

Butch's face turned crimson. "What do you mean? How have I been irresponsible?" His fists clenched and unclenched as he tried to rein in his anger. "Haven't I carried the battle to them?"

Richard looked at the others for support, "That's the problem. When you took your team to Madison, you left the rest of the pack without your leadership."

"Yeah, that's right," Richard's wife chimed in.

Butch noticed the determined expression on her face.

Eleanor, Bruce's wife, sat farther down the table. She said, "Just to carry out revenge against the Madison werewolf pack was no reason for you to leave us so vulnerable."

Butch released his pent-up anger with a sigh. He knew what they were saying was true, and yet he was frustrated by their accusations.

Butch said, "I left you with enough protection. I took just a small team with me. I left behind enough werewolves to fend off any attack the Madison pack might have launched.

"Maybe some of you do not understand what we accomplished by attacking the Morsching werewolves in their own territory. Christ, most of them will have to stay in Madison, because they don't know if we're still there, or when we'll attack again. We've put them on the defensive for the first time—just as I promised you I would. Don't you realize that they'll not be able to launch a concerted attack on us for fear we'll be doing the same to them?"

He was feeling betrayed by his own pack. "If you don't like what I've been trying to do for you, then someone needs to challenge me."

"Butch, no one wants to challenge you. We just want you to listen to our concerns," Jerrold said from across the table. "Attacking the Morsching pack in their territory did put them on notice, but Richard is right. You should have stayed behind. We can't afford to lose our Alpha."

Bruce cleared his throat and with a shaky voice added, "As leader of the pack, you were irresponsible by taking such a risk."

Thomas pushed his chair back and stood. He glared at Butch. "Your major duty is to give the pack the leadership it requires. You should have put someone else in charge of the mission and stayed behind with your pack."

Others mumbled agreement. Jerrold studied Butch, to see how he was taking the criticism.

Butch slid his chair back and stood up. He looked around the great hall, stopping at the face of each family member. He raised his right hand and then dropped it to his side. He did not know how to express what he was feeling. He started to speak and then stopped, then started again and stopped once more. After a lengthy pause, he cleared his throat. "I understand that being pack leader requires more learning on my part. My greatest goal has been to protect my pack. You need to understand that I can best protect my pack by destroying those responsible for attacking it."

He brought his shoulders back and stood taller. "I can see that maybe I should have stayed with the pack. I am the Alpha. But, I didn't want to send someone else to do a job I felt I should do. I didn't realize my presence was so critical to the survival of the pack. Now that you've told me how you feel—I apologize for leaving you. It won't happen again."

"Well put, Butch," Jerrold said. He was growing more content without all the responsibilities of leadership.

Butch nodded towards Jerrold, then smiled. "As long as everyone is speaking their mind, let me have my turn." He wondered how best to propose his idea. "Before the Madison attack, I began thinking about the future of our pack. I'd like you to think about something. This is not an order, decree, or anything like that. This is just an idea I want you to think about."

"What has plagued me ever since the Morsching Pack first attacked us and killed Marsha is the senselessness of it all. All of the deaths have been such a waste. What good does it do for werewolf to kill werewolf? What are we accomplishing? If we keep on as we have soon we'll all be dead. Will the killing stop when one werewolf is left standing?"

He noticed that many were nodding their heads in agreement. He found the courage to continue, "Here is what I'd like to do—offer the Morsching pack a truce."

Both agreement and opposition erupted in the room.

Butch spoke louder. "Hey, listen, I know some of you agree with me and some of you don't. Here's your chance to express your opinions, but do it one at a time." He sat down.

George jumped up, furious. "You never told me you were going to do this! How can you suggest we beg for peace? Those bastards killed my parents," he sobbed. "I haven't received my pound of flesh, yet. My body cries for their blood. We need to kill them until they're all dead."

Shouts of agreement and growls of vengeance accompanied George's stirring speech.

Jennifer, the wife of Francis, stood up, holding on to the edge of the table. Tears welled in her eyes. "Listen to me," she pleaded.

Butch was surprised. This was the first time Jennifer had spoken at any meeting.

Members of the group started yelling at each other. The situation was getting out of hand.

"SILENCE," Butch's voice boomed.

Everyone froze. Fear permeated the room.

Butch stood and scowled at everyone, "You will show courtesy to those wanting to speak. Wait your turn."

The pack studied Butch. No one was willing to challenge him. Those standing quietly sat down, and were quiet.

Jennifer looked embarrassed but spoke up. "As you know, I lost my daughters, Judy and Carol, to the Morsching pack when they died in the store explosion. They died at the same time George's parents did. Our pack has also killed some of the Morsching werewolves."

Jennifer stopped and took a couple of deep breaths before continuing. "In spite of what has happened between our packs, the Morsching werewolves are like us. They are werewolf. Would it hurt us to try what Butch suggests? Can talking to them hurt? If we tried to understand them, maybe we could live in peace. I don't know…"

Jennifer grew even more embarrassed and sat down. She leaned her head against her husband's shoulder, and he put his arm around her.

William Buchannan pushed his chair back and rose.

Butch was surprised. William was another quiet, dependable member of the family, who had attended meetings but seldom said anything in front of the group. He was the husband of Barbara, Jerrold's oldest daughter.

Smiling, William waited until everyone was quiet. "The butchers backed a truck over my two daughters, killing them, and for that we have killed some of them, but vengeance will not bring back my girls. If we must continue to fight—if we've no other choice, then that is what we will do. I agree with Jennifer, it wouldn't weaken us to talk with the other wolf pack. At least, try to find out why they attacked us. If they won't listen, then we've lost nothing. We can always continue the killing."

The room grew very quiet. No one else indicated a desire to speak.

Butch played with a pen, twirling it through his fingers. He waited for another minute and then stood. "Does anyone else wish to speak?"

When no one responded, Butch said, "I see two options. One, we continue to fight and kill the Morsching werewolves, and I'm sure, some of us in turn will die. Or two, we can contact them and ask if they're willing to sit down and discuss the situation. If they don't want to talk, our path is obvious. Let's vote."

Jerrold's head turned. He jumped to his feet with a stunned look. "Butch, the pack does not vote." He was shocked at the thought of letting everyone have a say in a decision reserved for the Alpha. "The Alpha always makes the final decision. We have never voted on anything. Starting with my Grandfa…"

Butch slapped his hand on the table, "Grandfather," Butch interrupted, "I agree there are some things that should not change, but I am the new leader and this is one change I will make. We will vote. Now please sit down."

Jerrold's face flushed and he sputtered, "Yes—yes."

Butch raised a hand. "Now, all those who want to continue the fight against the Morsching werewolves, raise your hand."

George Groschen, Elliot, Thomas, Arial and two others raised their hands.

"Okay, all those willing to contact the Morsching pack and find out if they are interested in sitting down and voicing our differences, raise your hands."

All the rest, except for Jerrold and Richard raised their hands.

"Okay, that's settled Butch said. "I'll contact the Morsching werewolf pack."

Several asked at the same time, "How?"

"I'm going to release our captive, Will Franzen. He'll take the offer back to Madison."

George jumped to his feet and wailed. "We can't let our prisoner go."

"GEORGE!" Butch screamed.

The blast caused George to wilt.

Butch stared at George and said, "George, listen to me. We will not always vote. I will still make decisions when I feel they are in the best interest of the pack. Let me explain why I'm going to release Will. I hope the Morsching Pack will take our act as a sign of good faith. Anyway, we've learned everything we can from him. I say it will be done."

George raised his head defiantly.

Butch glared back. "George, do you agree with my decision, or do you wish to challenge me?"

George blanched "No—no—I agree." George had seen Butch in action. There was no way he wanted to fight him.

"Okay," Butch said. "If that is settled, as soon I get an answer, you'll be informed. In the meantime, stay alert. They may already be in the Twin Cities looking for revenge."

CHAPTER 36
PARLEY

Butch was not surprised when Ralph Morsching agreed to attend a meeting. But he was surprised that Ralph agreed to come to Woodbury rather than insist on a neutral site.

Butch asked Richard to arrange the rental of a conference room at United Realty in Woodbury. He figured it was the most neutral spot, and it did offer a degree of privacy. The meeting was scheduled for the following Tuesday. Five members were to represent each pack at the table. Each pack would provide one guard for the doors.

* * *

Tuesday arrived. Butch was nervous when he walked into the meeting room with Jerrold, Richard, Elliot Buchannan, and Jake representing the Guhl Pack. The Morsching Pack had not arrived.

A hideous shag carpet covered the floor. Sterile, white walls set the atmosphere. An oak conference table dominated the middle of the room. Five captain's chairs lined each side of the table. Double glass doors allowed access from either end of the room. The west doors gave access to the outside, while the east doors opened into another meeting room and the stairs to the first floor.

Brad poked his head through the double doors between the two meeting rooms. "Here they come."

The Morsching representatives walked into the room with an air of confidence. They seated themselves on the open side of the table. The Morsching team consisted of Ralph, Ralph's brother-in-law, Tom, Henry and Joan Franzen, and their son Will.

The two teams stared at each other across the table.

Ralph turned to Jerrold and said, "You called the meeting. Why don't you explain what you have in mind?"

Butch smiled. The Morsching leader had made his first mistake by assuming the oldest Guhl member was the pack leader.

"Thank you, Mr. Morsching, I will," Butch said, holding back a smile. Ralph turned with a shocked look.

Henry Franzen angrily hit the table with his fist. "We have killed six of your pack members."

Ralph growled and shot a withering stare at Henry. Henry blanched and sat back in his chair.

Butch turned toward Henry and said, "I need to set the record straight. Your pack has killed eight of our members." Butch turned back to Ralph. "I didn't suggest this meeting for the purpose of flaunting our kills. We thought it might benefit both packs if we met before any more killings occurred. Seeing that we both have 'the trait', it might be in our mutual interest to put an end to any more killings. Of course, you might prefer to continue the war until only one of us is left standing."

Butch poured himself a cup of coffee and gazed across the table at Ralph, waiting for a response.

Ralph let his gaze settle on Butch before he said, "You don't know why we attacked you, do you?"

"Now that you mention it, we don't." Butch said.

"Your pack attacked the city of Longville and killed fifty-four of its residents, then left incriminating evidence behind, such as footprints, bodies, and witnesses. Didn't you realize your carelessness put your pack at risk . . . *as well as ours*?"

Butch was shocked. "Is that why you attacked us?" He pointed a finger at Ralph. "Is that why you came into our territory and killed members of my pack?"

Jerrold opened his hands and slapped them down on the table. "Please, we need to remain calm. With your permission, Butch, let me explain why we acted as we did. We learned from Will that your pack has a chemical to curtail your madness. But we don't, so we have to satisfy our needs in the traditional way. Each individual has to kill a human every five years. I can't believe it was any different for your pack before you discovered the chemical. Without human flesh, we lose our sanity and become wild beasts. For well over five hundred years, eating human flesh has been the only way to hold the wild side from overpowering us. Certainly you understand this."

Ralph only showed disgust. "We understand the need as well as you, but we've learned to control ours. We limit our entire kill for the pack to one human." He frowned, and then with an accusing glare said, "You were responsible for the Longville massacre, for the killing of fifty-four humans. To us, that was excessive and put us all at risk."

Butch answered, "Yes, we ended up killing more humans than required, but they killed one and wounded another of ours. We let things get out of hand, but I can assure you that will never happen again. Even so, what gave you the right to come into our territory and attack us?"

Ralph leaned forward, "We thought you were already on the wild side."

"I think it is a stretch thinking our attack on Longville would have exposed your pack," Butch said. "Even if they found out werewolves were responsible for the killing, why would they have any reason to suspect more than one pack existed in the U. S.?"

"The need to kill, to gather human flesh can't be ignored," Elliot said. "You're a werewolf—you must understand that."

Ralph started to interrupt, but Butch sat up with a threatening growl. "We learned from our captive—Will—that your pack has a drug that reduces the need to kill so many humans. Without your drug, we took action to retain our sanity. Our pack tried to control the hunt, in order to escape detection, but things got out of hand in Longville."

"As I well know," Ralph said. "I was the person in charge of the investigation in Longville, and was able to divert the blame to the wild wolves in the area."

"For that we thank you," Butch said.

"We didn't know there were other werewolves on the face of the earth," Richard said. "We lived as our ancestors taught us and we'll make no excuses for our behavior."

Butch stared threateningly at Richard.

Richard closed his mouth, sat back and remained quiet.

Ralph bowed his head. He understood.

Butch folded his hands. "Now that you know we haven't gone over to the wild side, does that affect your perception of us?"

"I admit we miscalculated, perhaps." Ralph's shoulders slumped. "There are so few of us left in the world, we would be wise to call off this war and pool our resources." Ralph breathed out an audible sigh, shocked by his own admission.

"I agree," Butch said. He looked across the table into the eyes of his former adversary. He stood up and extended his hand. "We have more to gain through cooperation than from killing each other. With your help and the drug, my pack will be less conspicuous in the future. We have no wish to be discovered by the humans."

* * *

After several hours of discussion, both sides accepted the peace terms, understanding that members from both sides would continue to harbor grudges. Enforcing the truce and stopping further killing would be up to the leaders. Butch and Ralph agreed to meet once a month to discuss mutual problems.

Butch left the meeting feeling a sense of accomplishment. The future looked brighter for his pack and the continuation of both packs. He could now concentrate on other problems, such as expanding the size of his small pack to fifty werewolves. One way to gain new pack members was to infect selected humans with the 'blood'. Another way was to push for a selective breeding program within the family. Butch expected a great deal of opposition to the second idea. He knew it would take time to convince his members, but now he had the time to work on them.

CHAPTER 37
EXPOSED AT LAST

As a rookie cop, Fredrick Brucker was handsome and dashing in his dress blues. Now fifteen years later, he was not so appealing, but appearance was not his major problem. He was a detective working out of the St. Paul Homicide Division. With his intelligence and police shrewdness, he should have been a top detective, but he wasn't. He was a brown-nosing, backstabbing sneak. He had climbed the ladder by doing or saying anything that pleased his superiors. He wanted respect, but no one liked him or wanted to work with him.

It was not that he didn't work hard or put in as much time as anyone else, it was just that his methods were too obvious. In a rugged sort of way, he was still handsome, with receding dark, wavy hair, a prominent, chiseled nose and a hard athletic body.

Lieutenant Brucker had been following up on the murder of Marsha Guhl at the University of Minnesota, when he had learned that a meeting of the Guhl and Morsching families was going to take place. Suspicious over the deaths that had occurred in both families, he decided to bug the United Realty meeting room in Woodbury.

He was shocked with the damning information he obtained. He decided he had to bring it to the attention of his superior—even if he didn't like the bastard.

Bill Kollecki was shocked when Lieutenant Brucker walked into his office and closed the door. He wondered what Brucker was doing there. He had no time for the prick.

"Captain, I have something you need to listen to," Brucker said. "But if I share this with you, you have to promise to let me be part of the team that investigates."

"What makes you think I want to work with you?"

"After you listen to this tape you will."

With regrets, Captain Kollecki agreed. He listened to the tape, and an hour later sat in his office with elbows propped on his desk, fingers tugging at his lower lip. He was a large man, a former college athlete, but at fifty-two, he now carried a respectable potbelly. He possessed a brilliant analytical mind, which had helped him solve some of the toughest cases in St. Paul over the past several years. But he had never heard anything like this.

"Well Captain, what do you think?" Brucker said.

A cup of coffee sat on Bill Kollecki's desk, untouched. "Unbelievable—weird," was all Kollecki said.

Werewolves, he had always believed, were pretend creatures, found in fantasies and science fiction stories. But the tape proved they were real... and killing humans.

* * *

The next day Captain Bill Kollecki played the tape before the metropolitan area Police Commissioners in a closed meeting. After the expected stunned reactions, he was directed to set up a task force to investigate the unusual number of homicides involving the well-known Guhl family from Woodbury, and the Morsching family from Madison, and the existence of werewolves in their area. It was Kollecki's job to gather evidence and prevent them from continuing to carry out attacks on humans.

Chief Dan Robertson instructed Captain Kollecki to handle the investigation with delicacy because both families had a lot of influence with powerful politicians and law enforcement officials.

Kollecki met with Lieutenant Brucker to begin setting up the investigative team.

"Well, Lieutenant, it looks like we'll be working together," Bill said. "I'm going to call our group the 'Fur Bearer Task Force'. What do you think of the name?"

"Okay, I guess."

Bill frowned. "We will use the title internally. We need to involve the FBI. This problem is too big for us to handle alone. Besides the FBI, we need to include the Minneapolis Police Force, the Woodbury Police, the Washington County Sheriff's Department, and the Madison City Police Force. Let's set up a meeting with those groups as soon as possible."

"I'll get right on it," Brucker said.

After the Lieutenant left, Bill sat alone thinking for a long time. Where did the werewolves come from? If they exist in the Twin Cities and Madison, how many more packs were there in the United States, or for that matter throughout the world? It was still hard for him to accept the fact that werewolves were real, yet he had heard them on the tape. What more proof did he need?

My God, they had admitted to killing all those people in Longville. How many more disappearances and deaths had they been responsible for over the years?

He shook his head, unable to fully comprehend the horror of it.

* * *

The first meeting of the Metropolitan Fur Bearer Task Force started out on a dreary note. A dark cloudbank had rolled in from the west, threatening rain.

As FBI agent, Jim Fillispie hurried across the street rain began to fall. A white Ford van bore down on him and he jumped for the curb. He gave the driver a dirty look, but the driver didn't even notice him.

Ahead, wet gray steps led up to the doors of the St. Paul Police Station. Stepping through the door, Jim glanced around the interior of the station and smiled. How many similar stations had he been inside during his career?

As Fillispie stepped off the elevator on the second floor, he noticed a police officer standing outside the meeting room. He angled across the hallway toward the officer.

"I need to see some identification," the officer said, placing his right hand on the handle of his revolver and taking a step forward.

Fillispie showed his badge and ID.

The officer checked a list, and opened the door. Fillispie walked into the room and looked at the large group of officers. They were talking and drinking coffee. Four men stood toward the far end of the room, in front of a wooden table that held a projector.

Fillispie recognized Captain Kollecki talking with the three men. He knew two of these men. One was Captain Grant Richards from the Minneapolis Police Force; the other was Bob Franklin, Sheriff of Washington County. The third man he didn't know.

There were twenty-five police officers present from various Minnesota local, county, and state agencies, plus three police officers from Madison and Fillispie. Most were not prepared for what they were going to learn today.

Captain Kollecki moved to the small wooden podium, as everyone found a seat. He raised his hands and waved for everyone's attention. "A few of you know why we are here today, but for the new Task Force members, I would like to bring you up to date."

The first power point image flashed on the screen. The picture showed the body of a man with his arms and head detached and lying next to his body. Beneath the picture, the caption read, THE WORST OF THE LONGVILLE KILLINGS. The next few slides showed more humans ripped apart. Additional images showed close-ups of bodies with limbs missing large chunks of flesh. Shredded clothing and bloody flesh showed deep teeth and claw marks.

To a stunned silent group, Kollecki said, "We have proof the Longville killings, together with a number of recent deaths throughout the Twin Cities and Madison, are linked to the Guhl and Morsching families. These two families have been killing each other. At first we thought the deaths were gang related, maybe involving drugs, but that isn't the case, at all."

"Just a minute," FBI agent Jim Fillispie interrupted. "Is this Morsching any relation to Federal Marshal Ralph Morsching, out of Madison?"

"The same," Kollecki said. "Neither group has any affiliation with organized crime. Until Lieutenant Brucker stumbled across a meeting between the two families, we had no knowledge that there were any ties between them. Brucker taped a recent meeting between the two families in Woodbury. I'd like to play the tape at this time."

Agent Fillispie asked, "Did you have a court order for the taping?"

"Just a bench warrant based on a lie," Bill said.

"Then you know the tape is not admissible in court," Fillispie reminded the others.

"We don't intend to ever use the tape in court," Kollecki confessed. "Agent Fillispie, you will understand why after you lhear what is going on."

Bill turned to the others. "We have edited out nonessential material and digitally enhanced some parts. The original tape is available for anyone wish-ing to listen to the unedited version. Go ahead Lieutenant."

The tape played for forty-five minutes. After it was finished, no one moved. Most of them were shocked.

Agent Fillispie stood up. "Captain," he said. "Other than this tape, do you have any other concrete evidence linking any of these individuals to the kill-ings in Longville, the Twin Cities, or Madison?"

"No."

"Are there any witnesses who have seen either a Guhl or a Morsching as a werewolf?"

"No."

"You are basing your belief that they are solely werewolves on this tape?"

"Yes."

"We obviously need more evidence than just this tape—evidence we can use in court."

"Evidence, yes. Court, no."

Grant Johnson, a Minneapolis police officer, interrupted. His pupils dilated to the size of dimes and his arms moved in jerking motions. "Bullshit," he said. "Werewolves don't exist. They're just fairy tales—you know, in movies and comic books. You people are nuts. I don't believe any of this crap. I will not . . . ."

Grant suddenly calmed down and his face broke into a weird smile He stared at Bill. "I get it. This is just an elaborate joke."

Kollecki did not smile.

Grant paled and said, "You're not kidding, are you? What are you guys trying to do?"

"Sit down, Grant," Kollecki said. "No one is trying to freak you out. This is on the level and we need your help."

Grant took a deep breath.

"Are you okay?" Captain Bill Kollecki asked.

"What's our next step?" Fillispie asked.

"Like you said, we need more evidence."

Sheriff Franklin stood up and walked to the front. "The Fur Bearer Steering Committee has decided to conduct a raid on one of the families. It looks like that may be the only way we can get direct evidence. If we can get one of them to change into a werewolf and get it on video tape, we should have all the evidence we need."

Deputy Alan Baker shook his head. "You can't do that without a search warrant."

"Chances are whatever we learn will never appear in court," Sheriff Franklin said.

"You realize we'll be acting outside of the law if we do things that way? We'll be nothing more than a bunch of vigilantes," Fillispie said.

Kollecki asked, "Do you have any doubt about what we're facing after hearing the tape?"

Fillispie shook his head. "No, not really." He hesitated. "Maybe a raid is the one way to find out for sure."

Lieutenant Brucker smacked his lips and said, "We've tried putting these guys under surveillance, but they're cautious. We've had no luck catching them in werewolf form—or for that matter, doing anything illegal."

"Okay," Kollecki said. "We'll be working outside the law, but that is the way we have to handle this situation. There is no way we can convince a judge to issue a search warrant. He'd laugh us out of his chambers. And you're right, Agent Fillispie. Eliminating the werewolves will make us nothing more than a vigilante committee." He stopped and grimaced, then said, "How many of you are with me?"

Everyone present nodded.

CHAPTER 38
REPORT TO THE FBI DIRECTOR

Agent Fillispie took the next flight to Washington D. C. and reported to Fenton Cooper, Director of the FBI, what he had learned in Minnesota. Cooper was flabbergasted.

Cooper was also paranoid. He didn't want the knowledge that werewolves existed to get out. If this information became public, he could imagine how many innocent people would die for acting strange or walking on the streets at night.

The Director asked, "How sure are you that this task force will not leak this to the press?"

"I believe every member of the group is on board. Tell me how you want it handled."

"The way I see this is—the Fur Bearer task force will have to act as an independent group outside the usual channels. I'll use my authority to get you whatever you need. What your Task Force does to rid our country of werewolves is up to them. Just don't get too far outside the law. The FBI will give you all the resources and help we can. Remember this—if you're caught breaking the law, the FBI will try to cover for you, but if what you have done becomes public knowledge, we'll disclaim any knowledge of your actions."

CHAPTER 39
THE BEGINNING OF THE END

It took several weeks for the Fur Bearer Task Force to get all of their special-ized teams organized and ready to carry out their missions. On the first day of summer, three unmarked cars sat in the darkness waiting for Captain Kollecki to arrive. One of the cars contained three men, the other two vehicles held two men each. A few drops of rain splattered on the windshields.

Shortly before one a.m., a single car with its lights off coasted to a stop behind the others. Captain Kollecki glanced at his watch before exiting the car. Seven task force members poured out of the other vehicles.

Lieutenant Brucker leaned into his unmarked vehicle, pulled out a shotgun, and walked back to the Captain's car. Kollecki pulled on his Kevlar vest and a black jacket.

Brucker said, "I've had the house under surveillance since 2 o'clock this afternoon. There are three people inside, Richard Guhl, his wife, Mary, and their son, Brad. Their daughter Sherrie was the one killed by a robber a while back."

"Yeah, maybe it wasn't a robber that killed her after all," Kollecki said.

This raid was critical. Kollecki knew that the attacks by the other teams depended on what they found during this raid. If they found proof that any of Richard Guhl's family were werewolves, the other teams would raid the homes of Jerrold Guhl's other children.

Also awaiting the outcome of the raid were teams in Madison, Wisconsin. The homes of Ralph Morsching, Tom and Francie Jarvis and Herbert and Collette Morsching were under surveillance. All the other teams were waiting for the signal from Captain Kollecki to attack and destroy the occupants.

Jim Fillispie stood next to him. He leaned over and whispered, "It still bothers me, what if we're wrong? If they aren't werewolves, we're in deep shit."

"You're right," the Captain said. "But, we have been over this many times. If you can't give the team your support, stay out of it."

"No, I'm in. We don't really have any other choice."

Two officers used the metal door buster to break open the front door. Eight masked, black-clothed men rushed into the living room. No warning was given that it was the police. The lamps on the officer's heads cast bright circles of light on the walls. Some of the light beams collided, as heads swung around the room searching for the occupants.

As a group, the eight officers rushed upstairs and started kicking open doors. Kollecki, leading the charge entered the first bedroom and found Richard standing next to his bed, partially through his change into a werewolf. Red glowing eyes stared at Kollecki, whose helmet cam captured everything.

Richard growled, "You bastards! I thought there was a peace agreement."

Bill was shocked at the size of the werewolf before him and frightened at what it could do to him. He stared at the red-coated monster, a few feet away His headlamp illuminated the upper body of the beast. Richard's mouth was wide-open, showing fangs and glistening red eyes.

Richard turned his elongated muzzle toward Bill and howled. Bill froze. Richard snapped his fangs together and the clacking of teeth brought Bill out of his frozen state.

Kollecki screamed, "Kill everyone." He brought his 9 mm up and emptied the clip into Richard's chest.

Kollecki was surprised to see red blood gush from the chest wounds. For reasons he couldn't explain, he expected werewolves to be a different from humans. He watched, mesmerized, as Richard fell across the bed, critically wounded.

Sheriff Franklin stepped into the room. His lamp illuminated the werewolf. "God, help us," he cried out.

Mary leaped at Sheriff Franklin from the corner of the room. He heard the click of her claws on the wooden floor. He wheeled around and shot the black-haired beast three times, killing her. Mary's momentum carried her forward. She threw her paws around the Sheriff and they tumbled to the floor.

Kollecki directed his beam onto the Sheriff and the beast. He was stunned when the werewolf changed before his eyes into a naked human female.

Directing his attention back at the male werewolf on the bed, he watched as it also transformed into the body of a man. All werewolf features disappeared. He gasped when the flesh around the bullet holes began to close.

Lieutenant Brucker knelt on the bed next to Richard and drew a hunting knife across Richard's throat. He sawed away until the head rolled free. "I read this in a book. It's one way of making sure they stay dead." He threw Richard's head on the floor. "Now let's see the bastard get up,"

He walked over to the naked body of the woman and decapitated her.

In the next room, Brad was fighting for his life. He had completed his change to a werewolf before the team had broken into his bedroom. As the masked men entered, he'd attacked them from behind the door.

Brad grabbed the nearest agent and raked claws down the front of his body, tearing clothes and flesh away. Blood gushed from a torn artery. Brad threw the body into the legs of a man raising his rifle, knocking him backwards. The third agent leaned into the room and shot Brad three times with a magnum 45.

Though wounded, Brad still jumped forward, biting down on the agent's arm. Bones cracked. The agent screamed and dropped his gun. Brad grabbed the man by his head and threw him against the wall. The agent on the floor pulled his revolver and emptied it into Brad.

"That was an expensive raid in terms of people," agent Fillispie said to Kollecki as they hurried out of Richard's house. But he was grinning with satisfaction. He felt like he had just scored the winning touchdown in his high school's championship game.

"Did you okay the other raids?" he asked Kollecki.

"Yeah, just now."

Chapter 40
Werewolves at a Premium

The Fur Bearer teams killed Jerrold Guhl, Thomas Guhl, his wife LuAnn, and their children, Jake and Nicole. No agents were injured.

Back at headquarters, Kollecki picked up the phone on his desk and hit the button for line two, expecting a team report. "Who is this?"

"Captain Perkins, code 15 Charlie Zulu."

"What have you got, John?"

"Two agents killed and three injured. But our first three missions were a success, considering how ferocious those bastards are. We processed Ralph Morsching and his wife, their son Joe, his wife, Marian, and their three children. Pete's wife, Mary was at Franzen's home and died along with their children. Will and Ann escaped. I've got a squad out looking for them. How'd you guys do?"

"We lost one man and another wounded, but we were successful in knocking out our first three targets. We'll be leaving on our second excursion as soon as the other two teams get back to the station."

"Good Luck, Bill, I'll call you when we finish up here."

The three task force teams split up to attack the last three Guhl families.

If someone warned the Guhls of the first attacks, there would be hell to pay.

The raid on Bruce Guhl's home killed everyone inside except for Bruce's daughter, Cherrie. She jumped out of a second story window and escaped into the night.

* * *

Butch woke out of a sound sleep. The clock said it was 3:10 a.m. He sat up. His t-shirt, saturated with perspiration, stuck to his body. He squinted, trying to recall the nightmare that woke him. He remembered giant bears surrounding his pack and killing them one at a time.

He watched as werewolf heads—plucked like grapes from their bodies— tumbled through the air. The pictures in his mind blurred before he was able to identify the bears.

Butch felt a lingering apprehension, as though something from his nightmare was waiting to come to life. He grabbed his pillow and smacked his fist into it, trying to force himself to concentrate.

He focused his hearing on other rooms in the house. His parents, Rod and Elizabeth, were tossing and turning in the next room. Ann was sleeping. He got out of bed and walked to the window.

He pushed the curtain aside and looked down on the ghostly-gray sidewalk. His red Mazda sat in the driveway.

No one was up at this ungodly hour. He relaxed, dismissing the sense of doom. As he turned back toward the bed, he caught a flash of car lights coming down the street from the north. The car was two blocks away. Probably someone coming home from work or from a late party.

Then he saw two more cars following the first one. He jumped back from the window. The car sent shivers down his spine.

The first car glided to the curb three houses down the street. Butch's apprehension grew. He watched four men get out of the first car. No lights went on when the doors opened.

He started his change.

More men piled out of the other two cars and gathered in a group. The men started down the sidewalk toward Butch's house. Butch ran into the hall and burst into his parent's bedroom. "Dad, Mom, wake up."

Rod rolled to an upright position, rubbing his eyes. "What's the matter?"

His mother sat up fearfully.

"A bunch of men are coming for us."

Rod asked, "Who, the Morschings?"

"I don't know who…"

Just then, the front door smashed in and Butch heard running footsteps downstairs. He finished his change. "Mom, Dad, you hide. I'll protect you," He ran out to meet the gang rushing up the stairs.

The first man up the stairs reached the top. Butch reached over the railing and raked his claws across the man's throat. Blood spurted from his neck in two pencil-sized streams, followed by a hissing of air. The agent toppled down the steps, and like a bowling ball, took down the agents below him.

The agents started shouting. Butch ran down the hall toward Ann's room just as Rod came out of the bedroom and ran to the head of the stairs.

Butch watched bullets rip across his father's chest. He howled with anger as his father died.

Like a nightmare in slow motion, he watched his mother run down the hall and drop to her knees over her husband's body. A hail of gunfire slammed into her and she slumped to the floor, dead.

Several agents rushed up the stairs swinging automatic weapons over their heads. Running, Butch vaulted over the railing and landed in the middle of them. He screamed. Butch moved fast. He ripped, bit, tore and crushed any flesh he could touch. More shots and a great deal of shouting warned him of additional men entering the house.

Butch left the dying remains of those around him and vaulted up over the railing. He raced down the hallway and into his room. He looked for a place to hide, but knew they would search the whole house until they found him. Footsteps raced down the hallway. Butch heard his sister scream, followed by several gunshots and then silence. He knew she was dead.

Butch turned to meet his death, but vowed to take more of them with him.

He stopped as a thought tore through his mind: "Who will lead the pack?" He slumped in anguish and howled. "AARRRRRooooooooooooo". He turned and ran for the window, putting his arms up just as he smashed through the glass. Glass fragments followed him to the lawn below. On the ground, he raced away, across yards and down alleys, until his house was far behind. But the visions of his dying family haunted him.

* * *

The second team annihilated Barbara and William Buchannan and their son Elliot without any losses.

* * *

At the Groschen house, a cousin who had come to care for the children was sleeping in the master bedroom. Coreen and Cheryl were asleep just down the hall from George. A bad dream had woke George at five a.m. In the dream, people were hunting and killing werewolves. The nightmare was so realistic that he rolled out of bed and tried to call Butch, but no one answered.

Alarmed, he dialed Grandfather's number and got a busy signal. He thought of waking the girls and driving over to Jerrold's house, but the front door blew off its hinges. He heard running feet coming up the stairs and started his transformation.

The first agent to enter his bedroom lost his head.

"Coreen—Cheryl," he mind-screamed, "We're being attacked. Get out—run."

Two agents rushed into George's room. The first agent through the door shot George in the shoulder. George pounced on the man, ripping open his chest. The second agent screamed when he saw the fate of his partner. He turned and tried to escape, but George launched himself through the air and landed on his back, driving him to the hall floor.

George bit down on the man's neck, crushing the cervical vertebrae. His legs felt like they weighed a ton. He shook his head, trying to clear his vision. Blood leaked from his shoulder, bringing on overwhelming weakness. He struggled to breathe. He saw a man standing down the hall with a twelve-gauge shotgun pointed at him. With his mouth, he managed to pull up the dead man's body.

The corpse absorbed the full blast of the shotgun and slammed back into George, knocking both of them to the floor. Lead pellets from the second blast tore through his back, breaking his right shoulder and puncturing his lung. George coughed and wobbled, but managed to stand on three legs. In a mighty effort, he lunged at the man. As he fell, he caught the man by the upper thigh. Frothy blood streamed out of George's mouth as he snapped his head to the side.

The agent screamed in agony as his leg muscles tore loose.

George ripped up through the man's stomach, sending intestinal coils flying through the room.

Another man raced up the stairs and pointed a pistol. George released a weak growl. His limbs trembled as he tried to respond. A stream of 9 mm bullets slammed his head into the floor.

* * *

During George's stand, thirteen-year-old Coreen Groschen transformed herself into a werewolf and climbed out the second story window. She dropped to the ground and looked up, waiting for Cheryl to join her. A series of shots rang out and Cheryl flew out the window and dropped to the ground, dead. With a keening cry, Coreen fled into the dark. George had saved her life, but not Cheryl's.

* * *

Out of the entire Guhl family, only three members had escaped, Butch, Coreen Groschen, and Cherrie Guhl, Bruce's daughter.

In Madison, the surviving werewolves were Will and his sister, Ann Franzen. They had been at a late night party and arrived home after the police had killed their parents.

Captain Kollecki felt like his task force had failed. Five werewolves had escaped. As long as they were alive, he considered his mission unfulfilled. If the Metropolitan Fur Bearer Task Force got their way, the last five werewolves would soon be dead.

CHAPTER 41
LAYING LOW

Butch threw back the flap of the green Eureka tent. For a half mile around, the prairie grasses gleamed golden in the morning sun. His campsite was perched on the top of a plateau overlooking the St. Croix River. Everything was so quiet. It created a false impression of peace.

Butch tried not to think about what had happened the previous night, but he could not blot out the killing of his family.

Last night, after escaping from the raid he had run through the ditches along Bailey Road until he'd reached County Road 19. From there, he cut across field and forest until he reached Afton State Park. He filled out a registration form to camp for five nights and ran up to the campgrounds on the plateau.

At the edge of the prairie grass, Butch dug up the camping supplies and money the pack had buried months ago, just in case someone needed to seek shelter.

He needed time to think, to figure out what his next move should be. He figured he would be safe in the campground high above the St. Croix River for at least a few days.

He didn't know how many, if any, of his pack had survived. Chances were they all were dead.

The bastards, he thought. *Some of my pack were not even werewolves, but they probably killed them anyway.*

* * *

The second morning, sadness over the loss of his family still disrupted his thoughts. At 9:00 a.m., he heard a truck approaching. It bumped down the grassy trail headed for his tent. His heart thumped in his chest as fear paralyzed him. He shook himself free of the fear and began to change.

The truck stopped, casting a shadow over half the tent. They had found him! He would not give up without a fight.

The truck door slammed and Butch jumped. Halfway through his change he rose up on four legs, poised to tear through the tent and fight for his life.

A voice outside called, "Hello, is anyone in the tent? I'm the park ranger. I just stopped by to see if everything is okay."

A growl escaped from the tent. Butch relaxed, reversing his change. After a long silence, he was able to say, "Everything is fine. I was just sleeping."

"Oh, sorry, I didn't mean to wake you," the ranger said. "Say, be sure to keep your dog on a leash in the park."

"Okay," Butch said.

Butch heard the truck door open and then slam. The starter turned over and the shadow on the tent moved away. Butch fell back on his sleeping bag, trembling.

That afternoon, Butch walked down to the visitor's center to use a pay phone outside the bathrooms to call the other Guhl homes. No one answered. He decided to try the Morschings in Madison. Maybe they could give him some answers...

Butch dialed Ralph Morsching's home and let the phone ring. No one answered. Next, he tried Will Franzen's cell phone. Butch let the phone ring ten times and was ready to hang up, when the phone stopped ringing. He heard someone breathing on the other end. "Hello, Hello, is anybody there?" Butch said. "This is Butch Guhl. Don't hang up."

Will cried into the mouthpiece, "You bastards."

Butch felt the frustration, pain, and anger pour out in those two words.

"I thought there was a peace agreement between our packs," Will said. "I'm going to get even with you. We will…"

"Listen to me, Will," Butch pleaded, "We were not responsible for the attacks. My entire pack is dead. Some governmental group must have found out we were werewolves. I'm not lying."

Sobs came from the other end of the line. Butch heard Will talking to a girl.

After a few moments, Will said. "Okay, we believe you. What are we going to do?"

Butch said, "Our family has a safe hideout located on Little Sand Lake just north and west of the little town of Remer. Join me there as soon as you can.

When you get close enough, you will be able to find me by scent. Whatever you do, make sure you're not followed."

"They wiped everyone out, Butch. As far as I know, my sister and I are the only ones alive. None of your pack survived?" Will asked.

"Not as far as I know. Nobody has answered any of my mental calls and all their phones are dead," Butch said.

"What will we do when we get there?"

"I don't know," Butch said. "I haven't had a chance to think that far ahead. I just know I have to get out of the Twin Cities."

There was a long silence, but the line was still open. After a moment Butch asked, "Are you coming?"

After more silence he heard, "Yeah, Ann and I will be there as soon as we can."

CHAPTER 42
BUTCH HEADS FOR REMER

Ten days ago, Butch had arrived at the cabin on the east shore of Little Sand Lake. He spent most of his time swimming and hiking through the surrounding forest. Twice he drove to Remer for groceries and newspapers.

There was one small paragraph in the St. Paul Pioneer Press regarding a burglary of the Jerrold Guhl home in Woodbury, which resulted in the death of the occupants. The perpetrator was unknown. There was no mention of the deaths of his other relatives. How could they keep all of their deaths out of the press? Some very powerful forces must be at work in ridding the country of the werewolves. Butch was nervous waiting for Will and his sister to show up. Many things could have happened to them as they journeyed to Remer, but Butch could not leave without giving them ample time to join him. Anyway, he still did not have any idea where he would go.

Before leaving Woodbury, Butch had withdrawn eighty thousand dollars from the bank, then contacted a man at a pawnshop Grandfather had taken him to once and then arranged for forged identification papers to help him change his identity.

The station wagon Butch had driven to Remer sat in the driveway. The car had belonged to a senile old woman, now a resident in the Woodbury Nursing Home. The car registration was still in her name. Butch was sure no one remembered the transaction. Jerrold had purchased the vehicle from the old woman's nephew two months ago and the car had remained hidden in a rented garage until Butch had taken it.

When he'd left Afton State Park, he had made his way to the garage where the car was stored. From there he drove to Grand Rapids, where he slept in the front seat until morning and then purchased enough groceries to last a couple of weeks. He drove around the countryside all day to see if anyone was following him. As darkness turned the sky gray, he had made a dash for the cabin on Little Sand Lake. Other than Will, no one knew he was here.

Butch decided to give Will seven more days to show up. If he did not turn up by then, he would leave. One of the options he was considering was to head for Montana and lose himself in the mountains for a few years.

He had given up hope any of his own pack was still alive. They all knew of this safe house. If anyone survived, they would have shown up by now.

CHAPTER 43
UNANTICIPATED COMPANY

Butch bolted upright in bed. It was two o'clock in the morning. Sweat covered his body and wet pajamas stuck to his chest and arms.

"Oh, shit, another dream," he moaned. He swung his legs over the edge of the bed and sat up holding his head. The dream was bad, but he couldn't remember any details.

He sat for a few minutes until the terror subsided. He started to lay back down when he heard a calling in his head.

A pleading female voice cried out, "I can smell you. Who's in the cabin? Please answer me."

A second female voice blended with the other. "Grandfather, are you there?"

Butch was shocked to hear a mental attempt to communicate with him. He could not answer for a few moments, then projected: *This is Butch, who is out there?*

When there was not an immediate answer, he sent with greater force, *Who are you?*

"Butch, thank God. This is Cherrie and I have Coreen with me."

Butch heard muffled sobs.

"Oh Butch, can we come in?" She sounded exhausted.

"Yes, you're safe here. Change to your human forms. I'm coming out to get you."

Butch ran for the front door. Cherrie was already running up the steps in her naked human form. Butch draped a blanket around her. She threw herself into his arms and sobbed. Butch hugged her, as tears bunched in the corners of his eyes.

He looked up and saw Coreen appear out of the darkness, trying to cover her naked body. Her eyes were large, reminding him of a fawn. She looked as though she would melt back into the bushes at the slightest movement from him. She needed the assurance of the pack leader, and the safety he was supposed to provide.

"Come here, Coreen," Butch whispered.

Butch held out his arm and Coreen raced to him, hugging his waist. She began to sob. A lump grew in Butch's throat as he fought back his own tears. Now was the time to show his strength. He was still the pack leader. He wrapped her in a blanket.

"Come on, let's go in," Butch said, leading the two girls into the cabin. They would not let go of him.

"You look like you had a tough time getting here," he said.

"Oh Butch, it was bad," Coreen said, holding on to his arm with no intention of letting him go. She didn't want to take a chance of losing him like she had lost the rest of her family.

"We are so tired," Cherrie said.

"How did you get here?" Butch said.

Coreen said, "We ran the whole way."

"We traveled in the woods as werewolves," Cherrie said. "We thought it would be dangerous to take one of our cars. We thought whoever killed our parents would still be looking for us."

"You're right," Butch nodded, pulling them toward the kitchen. Sit down and I'll make you something to eat."

The two girls wolfed down everything Butch set on the table. After eating for half an hour, the girls slowed down and pushed their chairs back from the table.

Cherrie looked up sadly. "Is anyone else alive?"

"If anyone from our pack was alive they would've been here by now," Butch said. "I'd given up on the idea that anyone else had survived."

Cherrie carried her dishes to the sink and then turned, asking, "What are we going to do, Butch? Everyone else is dead, and I'm afraid whoever killed them is still looking for us."

Coreen started to cry. "What if they find us?"

"Hey, they're not going to find us. Everything is going to be all right."

Butch got up and took Coreen's hand. "Come on, let's sit by the fireplace," he said, leading them into the living room.

Butch sat on the sofa with Coreen, holding her close. Cherrie threw a pillow in front of the fireplace and curled up in the blanket Butch had given her.

The girls explained how they made the hundred and seventy mile trek to Remer by hiding in the forest and eating squirrels and rabbits.

"Yuk, I don't like squirrel meat, but I got so hungry I ate it," Coreen said.

Butch shared some of his thoughts for their future. He was concerned about how they would survive the search that was taking place for them.

Cherrie's eyes were half-closed as a big yawn spread across her face. Butch looked down at Coreen and smiled protectively. She was asleep on the sofa. Butch whispered to Cherrie, "You two need to get some sleep. We'll talk more in the morning."

Butch carried Coreen into a bedroom and tucked her in. He showed Cherrie to her room. He gave Cherrie a hug and closed the door as he left. The clock on his nightstand said it was 4:10 a.m. The sky outside his bedroom window was already starting to brighten.

* * *

Butch woke with a start. It was eight o'clock. Scraping noises were coming from the kitchen. With a pounding heart, he jumped out of bed and raced toward the kitchen. He skidded to a stop when he remembered the girls were here. Cherrie was up and cleaning his messy kitchen.

He returned to his bedroom and put on an old striped robe someone had left in the cabin. The smell of toast, eggs, and bacon started his stomach rumbling. He followed his nose toward the kitchen and blinked in disbelief. The table was set and Cherrie was standing over the stove.

"I couldn't sleep," she said, looking embarrassed.

* * *

Butch finished his breakfast just as Coreen stumbled into the kitchen, rubbing sleep from her eyes. "Hey, I'm hungry too."

Cherrie said, "Too late, Butch ate everything."

"Hey," Coreen said. "I can smell the food."

After breakfast, everyone got dressed and sat on the porch swing. The girls needed to talk about what had happened to them and the rest of the family. Butch listened and seethed, feeling hatred growing. He knew nothing would ever be the same again.

About an hour later, he spotted a red Ford Escort coming up the driveway.

He grew alarmed, grabbing Cherrie by the elbow and taking Coreen's hand, ready to run. He squinted and sniffed the air, chest pounding.

"Oh, God, they've found us already," Coreen cried.

There were two people in the front seat of the car, but they were still too far down the driveway for Butch to recognize. Light reflecting from the windshield further hampered his vision. Butch pushed the girls into the cabin and waited in the doorway. The car pulled to a stop next to his station wagon.

Then his shoulders relaxed. It was Will Franzen and his sister. Both stepped out of the car and looked toward the cabin.

Butch turned to Cherrie and Coreen. "It's okay," he said.

He ran out and threw his arms around Will, saying, "Boy, I'm glad you made it."

A couple of months ago they had been mortal enemies, plotting to kill each other. But the truce and the recent annihilation of their packs somehow had made Butch consider Will a brother. The blond female walked over to Will and slipped her arm through his.

Will said, "Butch, this is my sister, Ann."

"Hi, Ann." Butch gave her a hug and she returned it with a big sigh. "I was worried you ran into trouble."

Ann looked into Butch's eyes. "No, we got out of Madison okay. I hope we've left all the killing behind us."

"They're still looking for us," Butch said, convinced of the truth of it. He grabbed Will and Ann by an arm and led them toward the cabin. "Come on, I want you to meet my two cousins."

Will pulled his arm free and said, "Just a minute." He walked back to his car, leaned in the open window and grabbed two bags from the back seat. He jogged to catch up to Butch and Ann.

As they mounted the porch steps, Cherrie and Coreen inched out of the cabin. Butch introduced Will and Ann to his cousins.

The five surviving werewolves sat in the living room well into the afternoon, sharing their stories.

CHAPTER 44
A QUIET INTERLUDE

In St. Paul, Captain Kollecki, Task Force leader of the Fur Bearer Squad was mounting an intensive manhunt. The Task Force knew five werewolf members were still alive. But they had no idea where to look for them.

The Fur Bearer team from Madison convinced Kollecki that the two Morsching survivors were no longer in that city. He suspected they might have joined forces and were now somewhere in Minnesota.

When they first came up with the name of their squad, the Captain thought the name 'Fur Bearer' was appropriate. Now, he was not so sure. If someone outside of the team saw the Task Force's title, he would have a difficult time explaining what it meant.

Kollecki knew the media was investigating the killings of the Guhl families and would soon start to come up with embarrassing questions. The press accepted the initial report that the killings were drug related, but couldn't find one shred of evidence linking the Guhl's to drugs.

Kollecki had already sidetracked two reporters who questioned the drug story. Jerrold Guhl had been a pillar of Woodbury society and leader of many charities. Something fishy was going on and reporters loved nothing as much as exposing a good story.

Reporters were linking the explosion of the dry cleanings store owned by Charles & Diana Groschen, in which four people had died, to the death of Jerrold Guhl. The St. Paul Pioneer Press was calling for a more intensive investigation into the death of the extended Guhl family.

The mayor of Woodbury expressed his concern over the deaths of the Guhl family members. The Guhl families were solid members of his community and for all of them to die violent deaths deserved a much deeper investigation.

So far, the Task Force had been able to cover up any suggestion that the law enforcement community was involved in any of the deaths, but the media was beginning to ask very specific questions and uncover damaging evidence. All it would take is for one small piece of evidence to point to a police officer being involved in the killings and the public would learn the secret Captain Bill Kollecki was trying to keep hidden.

From this point, the task force's efforts would be devoted to finding the five werewolves. Once they had disposed of them, things would quiet down. In a few months, any reference to the Guhl and Morsching families would be old news. Bill could not use the normal law enforcement channels to track the fugitives down. He knew if he asked for help from other agencies, someone might learn they were after werewolves.

* * *

Members of the task force began to visit town after town in Minnesota, showing a few pictures around and asking if anyone had seen the fugitives. They knew who was still alive.

Bill's search teams were frustrated. It was as though the five remaining werewolves had just vanished, at least from Minnesota and Wisconsin. In spite of the difficulties, Kollecki was a patient man. He knew the five werewolves were out there, somewhere. In time, a break would come his way. When it did, he would gather the Task Force and end the chapter on werewolves in the United States.

* * *

I'm getting tired of sitting around this stupid cabin," Coreen grumbled. She threw the remains of a glass of water back into the sink. Some of the water splashed up the side and on the counter top.

"Well," Butch said, "What do you want to do?" He was tired of listening to a spoiled thirteen-year-old girl pout. She had complained for the last three days.

"I wanna go home," Coreen cried. "I want to hang out with my friends and do fun things again." She sprawled on the sofa.

"So go ahead—go home," Butch said, throwing his hands into the air. He was tired of explaining why she could not go back to the Twin Cities.

"Can I really?" Coreen said.

"Sure, why not? If that's what you want to do. I'll even give the police a call and let them know you're coming. That way it won't take them as long to find you and do to you what they did to your family."

Coreen started to cry. "You don't care what happens to me!" Tears rolled down her round cheeks.

Cherrie glared at Butch, "That's cruel!" She put her arms around Coreen.

Butch relented. "Coreen, I'm sorry. I do care what happens to you, really. But, I'm tired of listening to the whining. You know darn well we can't ever go back."

"Ah, Butch," Cherrie said, patting Coreen on the back. "She knows we can't go home, but that doesn't stop her from missing her friends and all the things she used to do."

Cherrie sat on the edge of the couch holding Coreen in her arms. She rubbed Coreen's back and rocked her back and forth like a baby. "Coreen," Cherrie said. "You need to stop talking about things that can never be. You need to work with Butch and the rest of us. That way we can all stay alive. Remember, those government people killed our parents and relatives. And you know they're still out there searching for us."

Butch grinned and walked over to the couch. "I'm sorry, Coreen." He gave her a pat on the back and then walked out on the porch.

He felt the outdoors tugging at him and decided to take a walk. With hands in his pockets and head down, watching the ground in front of his feet, he followed the worn trail down to the edge of the lake.

Stepping onto the weathered dock, he walked to the end of an L-shaped section and gazed across the water at the row of brown cabins on the west shore—Little Sand Resort. People were swimming and splashing around, without a care in the world. His eyes telescoped on two attractive women throwing a beach ball back and forth.

Under different circumstances, he would have gone over to check them out. Knowing he couldn't do that, he turned and looked down the lake. On the far north end, he spotted two fishing boats. From this distance, the people looked like mannequins perched on the edge of their boats holding matchsticks over the water.

Butch wondered if he would ever be able to live a normal life again. Where would he and his pack end up? For all that, would he even survive to see next summer?

* * *

Captain Kollecki was sitting at his desk waiting for a call from the officers that were out canvassing the whole state. It had been two weeks, and other than the calls to tell him where the werewolves weren't, he had received no encouraging information.

His secretary's voice sounded on the intercom. "Captain. Lieutenant Brucker is on line two."

Bill picked up, "Hi Fredrick, what have you got?"

Lieutenant Brucker hoarsely announced, "I found them."

"Oh my God, where are you?"

"I'm in Remer…"

With excitement coursing through him, Kollecki interjected, "Yeah, I know where it is. Stay put, I'll round up the crew. We'll be there early tomorrow morning."

* * *

The next morning, Ann and Butch were sitting together on the porch swing while Will and Cherrie finished the dishes. Coreen decided to take a walk.

Butch watched her skip down the steps singing a song she had sung when she was a kid—a million years ago. She skipped down the driveway and headed toward the old abandoned cabin near the county road. The old cabin kept people from seeing Butch's cabin behind it. Driving in off the county road, the driveway appeared to end at the old cabin, but did not. A grassy track continued around the old cabin and ended at Butch's cabin.

Butch glanced at Ann, who was staring peacefully at the lake. Over the last few days, he had been thinking about her, a lot. She was beautiful, mature for her age, and when she walked by, Butch could not help but watch. But he didn't know how to tell her he was interested.

He shook his head. Maybe this was not the time to start a romance. Next year, Ann would have been a high school junior. Now she would never get that chance. Could be though, that she might appreciate having something else on her mind besides death and fear.

Butch wanted to ask Ann to go out to dinner. He squirmed on the porch swing, trying to screw up enough courage to ask. In the end he just blurted it out. "Ann... uh... would you like to go out with me to, uh... dinner or a movie?"

Ann looked at Butch with a shy smile and a faint blush. "Yes, I'd like that very much." She stood saying, "I'll tell the others we are going out to eat."

"No, don't do that. I—I meant, just the two of us—to go," Butch blushed and could not look at her. *Boy,* he thought, *I'm a pack leader. I shouldn't be afraid to talk to her.*

"Oh, I thought. . ." was all Ann could say.

In a split second, Butch's face switched from a smile to a look of sheer agony. He slapped his hands over his ears and jumped up from the swing.

Chapter 45
The Showdown

Coreen's mental scream tore through Butch's mind, "BUTCH, BUTCH, a big car just turned into our driveway and it's going around the old cabin. There are five men in the car, they smell angry and afraid."

"Where are you?" Butch thought, frightened for her welfare.

"I'm okay. I'm hiding in the bushes at the side of the road. They didn't see me. But they smell bad, Butch. Watch out."

"Good job, Coreen," Butch said, proud of how calm she sounded.

Ann grabbed Butch's arm when he jumped up. The frightened look on his face alarmed her. "Butch, what's the matter?"

Cherrie heard Coreen's mind-message and came running out of the cabin, followed by a bewildered Will.

"Butch, what are we going to do?" Cherrie asked.

Butch raised a hand. He realized by the look on their faces that Will and Ann had not heard Coreen's warning.

He said to them. "A car full of men just turned into our driveway. Coreen spotted them and sent me a message,"

"Who are they?" Will asked. Then his expression changed as he realized who the men were.

Butch looked at Will with a weird smile. "Killers are coming, but they don't realize they're about to become the victims." His face turned serious.

"Will and Cherrie, I want you to change and go into the woods east of the garage. Ann and I will change and head through the woods toward the lake."

Butch sprinted into the bushes, followed by Ann. They both disrobed and changed themselves. Butch felt a pleasurable ripple pass through his body. In a matter of minutes, the two werewolves stood behind a clump of hazel bushes. Their mouths hung open, exposing long upper and lower canine teeth.

Ann growled, freeing herself of any last restraints. Butch answered. The killing urge was strong in both of them.

Butch was angry. How did these men dare invade his territory? Along with his anger, though, he felt relief, because he no longer had to deal with the unknown. They were here and he was glad.

Ann watched Butch become agitated and said, "Butch you need to maintain self-control."

It took Butch a moment to bring the animal side under control. He crouched down and waited. Through a screen of trees and bushes, he watched a large black van stop fifty feet from the garage. He watched the men study the cabin. The van doors opened and the five men piled out. They hurried to the back of the van. One of the men threw open the rear door and began passing out shotguns and belts of ammo.

"They're well-armed, Cherrie," Butch broadcast. "Coreen, I want you to change into your werewolf form after we leave. Then move into the cedar grove east of the cabin. Hide in the bushes. If any of them return to the cabin, kill them. Can you do that?"

"You bet I can, after what they did to my parents and the rest of the pack."

"Watch out, Cherrie," Butch broadcast. "They're coming around the garage toward you and Will."

"We see them," Cherrie said. "How do you want to handle this?"

"Our best chance is to lure them deeper into the woods," Butch messaged. "You and Will, make some noise, let them see you. Then head north through the woods. They'll follow you. Ann and I will be right behind them. Coreen, are you still there?"

"Yes, but I'm scared."

Butch knew by the quivering in her mental message that she was fright-ened. "Don't take any chances," he told her. "Keep a close lookout and let me know if anyone else shows up. Will you be okay?"

"Yes, but will you hurt them bad for me? Hurt them for killing my parents."

"Yeah, we'll hurt them," Butch promised. A growl low in his throat rein-forced his words. "We will hurt them real bad."

* * *

Captain Kollecki, Agent Fillispie, and Grant Richard circled the garage and moved toward the back of the cabin. They made enough noise to put a pack of elephants to shame. Grant stepped on a brittle oak branch, which cracked with a resounding snap.

Lieutenant Brucker and Sheriff Franklin pushed through a clump of hazel brush on the lakeside of the cabin, rattling leaves. They also did a good job of announcing their presence.

Butch and Ann were between the lake and Brucker and Franklin. They waited until the two men passed thirty yards from them before tagging along behind.

Will and Cherrie watched the three men come around the garage in their direction. When they were forty yards away, Will ran through a clump of hazel brush, making as much noise as he could. Cherrie swung to Will's left and ran parallel to him.

The three men saw the two werewolves streaking through the bushes. Grant raised his shotgun, pointed in the general direction of Will and pulled the trigger. The buckshot whistled five feet behind Will, mowing a path through the brush.

Kollecki yelled into his radio. "Hey, Sheriff and Fredrick, get your asses up here. We just spotted two of the werewolves. They are heading north. We're fifty yards north of the cabin."

Brucker ran at an angle away from the lake. He saw a flash of a werewolf at the same time Kollecki was calling for the two of them to come toward him. Brucker flicked the button on his walkie-talkie. "Christ Captain, I just saw one of the bastards in front of me and it's running on its hind legs. My God, he's big," Frightened, he stopped and looked around.

He panicked when he didn't see or hear any of his team. "Where are you guys?" he screamed into his mike. "I'm not moving until I know where you are."

Sheriff Franklin saw Brucker thirty yards ahead and crashed through the brush toward him. He shouted, "Don't be such a coward, Lieutenant."

Brucker swore and said, "You wouldn't be so brave if you'd seen one of them running toward you."

The sheriff jogged by Brucker, "Come on, let's get them."

Kollecki held his walkie-talkie to his flushed lips. "Hurry up, you guys. There's a couple of them just ahead of me."

"Kollecki, this is Fillispie. Where the hell are you?"

"I'm a hundred and fifty yards from the lake and maybe a half mile north of the cabin. Hurry up, we need to stick together."

Richards shrugged his shoulders. "Kollecki, I'm not very good at this Boy Scout stuff. I don't know if I am ahead of you or behind you and I don't think we should be separated. Yell a few times so I can follow your voice."

Bill Kollecki sputtered and swore to himself, then realized it wasn't such a bad idea. "Over here. I'm over here!" he yelled.

It took a minute before Fillispie, followed by Richards and the sheriff, to come crashing through the brush. After a minute, Brucker stumbled in and dropped to his knees, blowing like a floundering horse. Sheriff Franklin lifted Brucker to his feet.

Kollecki shook his head. "We have to stay in sight of each other or someone's going to get lost or worse," he said. "I want you guys to fan out on each side of me, forty yards apart. Stay even with me and we'll push them along the lake. If you see them, yell out."

Brucker and the sheriff took the lakeside. Fillispie and Richards took off deeper into the woods. Kollecki stayed in the middle.

Brucker walked within thirty yards of the lake. He spotted Sheriff Franklin bending and dodging through the brush. A minute later, he caught a glimpse of Kollecki. Brucker thought he was doing a good job of staying in a straight line. He picked up his pace when he noticed the sheriff was getting ahead of him.

* * *

O kay, Butch," Cherrie messaged telepathically. "Will and I have them spread out and following us. Where are you?"

"About fifty yards behind them,"

Butch said. "If I remember right, you should be coming to a bunch of evergreen trees soon. When you see them, veer off to the northeast. Let them get a glimpse of you. That should entice them to keep following."

The woods around Butch was a mix of dark-green spruce, birch, and trembling aspen. Butch inhaled, smelling the resinous pitch from the evergreens mixed with the smell of dying algae from the lake. He ran on all four legs, followed by Ann. They increased their speed until they closed to thirty yards behind the men. Then Butch slowed down.

The agents made a lot of noise. It was easy for Butch and Ann to know where they were. Butch weaved back and forth to keep track of each of the men.

"Cherrie, are you close to the open field?"

"Yes, the opening is just ahead," she communicated.

"Good, this is it," Butch said. "Cross to the other side of the field. Make sure they get a glimpse of you before you disappear into the spruces. Then I want you to double back and get ready to ambush them. When they get halfway across the field, Ann and I will attack from their backside. When they turn back toward us, that's your signal to attack."

"Message understood," Cherrie said. "I'll tell Will. We'll wait for them to turn toward you."

Will and Cherrie loped across the short grassy field. Under different circumstances, Cherrie would have stopped to enjoy the yellow coneflowers with their dark brown buttons and yellow petals. They grew in bunches among the tall stalks of grass.

She cut around a jack pine standing alone in the center of the field.

Just as Will and Cherrie reached the far side, Kollecki stumbled into the clearing. "Hey, there they are," Bill yelled. He raised the shotgun to his shoulder and squeezed off two rounds at the shaggy beasts. They disappeared into the trees on the far side of the clearing.

Fillispie and Richards burst out of the bushes behind Kollecki and caught a glimpse of the werewolves.

Brucker and the sheriff crashed into the field, puffing like a couple of locomotives. The sheriff bent over with his shotgun across his knees, trying to catch his breath. Brucker dropped to his knees and raised his head to catch as much air as possible.

Brucker shouted at Kollecki, "Where are they?"

The Captain gave him a disgusted look before replying. "They disappeared on the other side of the field. Come on, let's go."

Brucker lifted his head and wheezed.

Kollecki took off across the field, yelling back, "We're gaining on them."

The other agents followed Kollecki, except for Brucker. He hadn't caught his breath yet. It didn't take him long to notice that no one had waited for him. Suddenly he was scared. He jumped up and raced after the others, jogging across the open field holding his left side.

As soon as Will and Cherrie made it through the evergreens, they cut to the left, dropped to all fours, and crept back toward the edge of the open field. They lay down under a spruce tree and crawled on their stomachs behind a thin shield of tall grass overlooking the field. They watched the agents run across the field toward them and waited.

The five agents spread out as they jogged across the field.

Cherrie grew nervous with anticipation. The front two agents, followed by Brucker, were fifty feet from the spruce tree where they were hiding. "Butch they're getting kind of close."

"We've reached the field. We see them. Get them, now!" Butch screamed these last words aloud.

The agents heard Butch yell. They skidded to a stop and swung around.

Will's muscles bunched, as he leaped forward following Cherrie, who had charged out ahead of him. Will surged to catch up and they flashed across the timothy grass, eating up the distance to the two closest agents in a matter of seconds.

From the other side of the opening Butch took the lead, bursting into the open field. Ann, sleek and graceful, pulled up alongside him. They approached the two closest agents. Butch launched his body through the air with a blood-curdling howl.

At the same time, Will and Cherrie hit the agents from the other side. All of the men were facing Butch when he entered the open field. At the last second, Kollecki and Fillispie heard a noise behind them and whirled, aware too late. They had walked into an ambush.

Still, they brought their shotguns up and fired. They didn't have time to aim or adjust for the speed that the werewolves were traveling at. The buckshot went over the heads of the werewolves.

Butch's front legs slammed into Richard's chest, driving him backwards. He landed on the ground with Butch on top of him. Butch reached down with his fangs and surgically ripped out Richard's carotid arteries and windpipe. Richard tried to scream, but he no longer had a voice box. His eyes glazed over.

To Butch's right, Ann slammed into sheriff Franklin, sending him flying. He hit the ground on his back, losing his grip on the shotgun, which tumbled through the grass. Ann jumped on his stomach and shoved her muzzle toward his throat. The sheriff used his arms like swords as he tried to fend off her sharp fangs.

She was in such a killing frenzy, moving with super speed and strength. She pushed his arms out of the way and clamped her jaws down on his exposed throat.

The flesh in the sheriff's neck ripped with the sound of tearing fabric. The tender flesh pulled loose in one chunk. Blood spurted, shooting several feet through the air. Drops of blood splashed onto Ann's face. She stood over his convulsing body and licked the fresh blood from her muzzle.

Will reached agent Fillispie and rose up on his hind legs. He grabbed the agent by his shoulder and yanked. The shoulder joint separated with a bone crunching pop. Their bodies intertwined. They landed with a thud on the field. Will raked his hind feet along Fillispie's stomach, shredding clothes and flesh with each kick.

The agent's eyes rolled up as he brought his .45 automatic up. Even with the spasmodic jerking of his body, he was able to place the barrel against Will's back and pull the trigger several times. The bullets tore through Will's spine and shattered his heart. The two died together.

Cherrie threw her body at the feet of captain Kollecki, causing him to topple. She spun and thrust her muzzle into his groin. She clamped down and jerked her head to the side. Fabric and flesh parted, accompanied by a high-pitched scream. Cherrie ripped open his chest and tore out his heart.

Lieutenant Fredrick Brucker stood in the middle the carnage not knowing where to point his shotgun. He first leveled the gun at Butch, then swung to Ann as she ripped the sheriff to pieces. Before pulling the trigger, he heard Fillispie scream and pivoted to watch him die.

Brucker freaked out. He stopped moving, closed his eyes, and started praying. When the noise stopped, he heard birds chirping. He opened his eyes to find himself surrounded by four very large werewolves. His gun hung at his side. It did not cross his mind to defend himself, for he knew he was already dead.

With a smack of his lips, Brucker pleaded, "Please. Let me go, please."

The fear within him was so great that Butch felt ecstatic.

Brucker lost control of his bladder and a wet flow of urine ran down his leg. Butch said, "Cherrie, kill him for what they did to your parents."

* * *

A week later, chief Dan Robertson received a call from a sheriff's deputy in Cass County telling him that a Black Chevy van registered to the St. Paul Police Department had turned up in Longville, Minnesota.

The Chief knew what that meant—Captain Kollecki and the other agents with him were dead. All he knew was that the team had a lead and had headed north to check it out.

Chief Robertson was not surprised the car showed up in Longville. After all, that was where it had all begun last October. He believed the werewolves were hiding out in the Longville area. As discreetly as possible, he concentrated the rest of Bill's Fur Bearer Task Force agents there. Instructions were to search the surrounding country for the werewolves and not to come back until they found them.

CHAPTER 46
SANCTUARY

Butch, Cherrie, Coreen, and Ann, buried Will and the five dead agents in the field where they died. Butch knew Ann was depressed over her brother's death, even though she tried to hide her sorrow. Butch was very attentive to her, which was not hard to do.

One night, a week after Will's death, the four remaining werewolves sat in the living room around the fireplace. A fire sent yellow-red flames up the chimney and heat into the room. It was quiet. They stared at the flickering flames, each lost in thoughts of their own.

Some thought of those who had died. Others wondered what was going to happen next. They knew they would have to leave this place and find a new sanctuary. If one group of agents had found them, others could do the same. It was just a matter of time.

Butch and Ann moved to the sofa. He looked into her eyes and took her hand. "It's time for us to make plans for our future—and the future of our kind."

"What kind of plans?" Coreen's face lit up with an idea. "Are we going home?"

"No, I'm afraid not Coreen, "We can't ever go home, honey."

"I know, but I still miss everything I used to have."

"We can't stay in the cabin any longer," Butch said. "They'll just keep coming. Next time even more agents will come and they'll be better prepared."

Cherrie's face started to glow. The edges of her eyes crinkled. One of her dreams was to live free in the beautiful Rocky Mountains. "Why don't we go live in the mountains, maybe Wyoming or Montana?" she said.

"We could do that," Butch said. "We have more than enough money hidden away in secret accounts to do anything we want. The only problem I see is that they will still be looking for us. If we go now, we might attract too much attention. If we try to buy land, a house or a car, at our ages, people will question where four teenagers got all that money. I don't want to have to explain anything to anyone. When they start asking questions, they're going to want to know where our parents are. What do we say then? Maybe after things cool down we'll go there."

"Well, then let's just go live in the woods," Coreen suggested angrily, her lips sticking out in a pout. She was still mad at Butch for knocking her idea of going back to the Twin Cities.

"That's a good idea. We found a lot of food in the woods when we ran to Remer," Cherrie said.

Butch smiled, "Funny, I was thinking the same thing. We could live deep in the forest. We would not draw attention to ourselves. Food would not be a problem with all the wildlife that lives there. The place I'm thinking of is so isolated no one would find us. We could lose ourselves for…"

"Butch, I was just kidding. I don't want to live in the woods," Coreen cried. "We won't have any television or ice cream. I don't like my idea at all."

"No, Coreen," Ann said. She moved from the sofa and stood in front of the fireplace. "I think for right now it's the only option we have. We can do it for several months. At least until they get tired of looking for us. Then we can move somewhere else and begin a new life among the humans again."

Cherrie thought for a moment and said. "I guess you guys are right. Where will we go?"

Butch said excitedly, "I know of an isolated spot not far from here where we'd be safe. Four years ago, I canoed up in the Boundary Waters Canoe Area. The place is isolated and has several packs of wolves to cover our tracks. We could blend in. Coreen, you've always wanted me to take you to the Boundary Waters. Well, here is your chance. What do you say?"

"Yippee," Coreen said.

Ann frowned, "We could do the same in Montana, couldn't we?"

"Sure we could, Ann," Butch said, "but the BWCA is much closer."

EPILOGUE

Hard, crusty patches of snow lay on the north-facing slope of a secluded cliff, deep in the Boundary Waters Canoe Area. Rocky crags jutted high over the trees, looking down on Rose Lake far below. Halfway up the inner curve of the cliff, a rocky ledge slanted into the air, blocking the cave entrance from below.

Swirling air currents carried the smell of spring to the cave. It would not be long before the buds on the aspens below would break out of their dormant state and the white of winter would disappear for a brief, warm interlude.

The sun's rays played on patches of ice and water below, sending splashes of light reflecting back against the rocks and into the cave. Behind the curved uplifted rock that blocked the cave entrance, a yelping noise made its way to the opening. Inside, three female werewolves were playfully chasing each other. Dried grass littered the floor of the cave, insulating it from the cold rock beneath.

The blond werewolf nipped the ear of the younger black female, who in turn poked the hazel-colored female with a sharp-pointed claw. Cherrie's reflex action caused her to jump with a yip. After a few minutes, the three females settled down, lying next to each other on the grass.

Two of them rolled over to lie on their sides. The blond female displayed a large extended stomach. Within the week, she would bear a litter of pups.

Butch padded into the cave. He growled to get the attention of the other three werewolves and said, "As soon as the snow is gone, we'll be heading for Montana."

Coreen jumped up and pranced around, yipping to show her happiness.

Butch continued, "We have to give some thought to increasing the size cf our pack."

Cherrie said, "We will as soon as Ann gives birth to her pups."

Ann looked sheepishly away from the others.

Butch's chest puffed out and he sat up taller. "That will be a welcome increase to our pack. But I also mean we need to convert humans into werewolves. That will that give us a larger base and also bring new blood into our pack. We need a couple of older members to act as our parents."

Cherrie asked, "Will we recruit here in Minnesota?"

"No, I think it's best to wait until we get settled in Montana." Butch stocd on all four legs and stretched before adding, "I just wanted you to think about this. I'll let you know when it is safe to leave."

Butch left the cave to sit at the entrance.

A few minutes later, Ann, the blonder of the three female werewolves rose clumsily on four legs and waddled toward Butch. Butch's ears perked up ard his head swiveled toward her as she approached. He turned back to give most of his attention to the forest below. Intrigued by the movement of three deer moving along a trail below, Butch watched them until they disappeared.

Ann used her muzzle to nudge him with affection. Butch's mouth dropped open, showing his canine teeth. He leaned over and licked the silken fur on the side of her face. He whispered to her, "This isn't such a bad life, is it Ann?"

"No, it isn't. But I've had a difficult time keeping myself from going over to the wild side. I'm ready to live as a human again."

"Me too. As soon as our pups are born."